T0245730

Indebted

Charmayne Hafen

Publisher's Cataloging-In-Publication Data
(Prepared by The Donohue Group, Inc.)

Names: Hafen, Charmayne.
Title: Indebted / Charmayne Hafen.
Description: Littleton, Colorado : [Capture Books], [2018] | Interest
    grade level: High school.| Summary: After the mother of 12-
    year-old princess Wren disappears, King Belodawn seems to
    blame his daughter for the disappearance and avoids her. When
    Wren is befriended by the son of the castle cook, she believes
    she will find a way to escape her loneliness. Daring to leave the
    kingdom of Greenham, Wren ventures out to Shaw where she is
    confronted with a task so impossible, she will need something
    beyond her own strength to defy death and destruction.
Identifiers: ISBN 9780999635339 (hardcover) | ISBN
    9780999635391 (paperback) | ISBN 9780999635346 (ebook)
Subjects: LCSH: Princesses--England--Berkshire--Juvenile fiction. |
    Runaway teenagers--England--Berkshire--Juvenile fiction. |
    Dragons--England--Berkshire--Juvenile fiction. | Berkshire
    (England)--History--16th century--Juvenile fiction. | CYAC:
    Princesses--England--Berkshire--Fiction. | Runaway teenagers--
    England--Berkshire--Fiction. | Dragons--England--Berkshire--
    Fiction. | Berkshire (England)--History--16th century--Fiction. |
    LCGFT: Fantasy fiction.
Classification: LCC PZ7.1.H225 In 2018 (print) | LCC PZ7.1.H225
    (ebook) | DDC [Fic]--dc23

Dedication

To my husband, John, who has taught me what it means to

be loved for who I am.

Foreword

Indebted, by Charmayne Hafen is a Masterpiece. Princess Wren could very well be any young woman who has lost her way feeling she does not have the love and guidance she needs from her parents. Childhood abandonment causes Wren to make some life choices that other young women in her station of life would not make. After learning to wield a sword like a champion, the princess is able to go into arenas that would have otherwise been closed off to her. Fortunately, Wren finds her desires are met when she is introduced to a Being who loves her without measure. In a new place, Princess Wren finds herself surrounded by others who care. Unfortunately, she finds that one particular new arena is not as satisfying as she believed it would be.

In our society today, the younger generations need to know that they personally matter whether or not this belief in them is nurtured. At the end of the day, the Heavenly Father is the only One who will provide a place of belonging for us and never leave or forsake us. Charmayne Hafen has provided this generation and the generations to come with a well-constructed cast of characters who will help build an unshakable faith in God, enabling a person to become all they were created, and desire, to be...in spite of life circumstances. I highly recommend *Indebted.* Excellent!

—Beatrice Bruno, Author - Speaker - US Army Veteran
How to Get Over Yourself, Get Out of Your Own Way, and Get What YOU Want Out of Life

iv

Readers' Favorite Reviewers

Describing a time of dragons, witches, and sword fighting, Indebted takes you to a place where a young princess blames herself for her mother's disappearance.

The style and theme of Charmayne Hafen's writing is comparable to works from authors such as Suzanne Collins, J.R.R. Tolkien, and C.S. Lewis. Indebted is centered on a strong female character, Princess Wren, whose loneliness sends her on an adventure that changes her life forever. Without a mother to guide her and with a father that abandoned her, Wren unknowingly seeks companionship and acceptance from others. When faced with imprisonment or death-by-dragon, Princess Wren finds she has another Father on whom she can always rely. She is tied to a vow from which only death can release her and wonders how she could ever have a normal life.

I found Indebted to be an art piece, lovingly penned by an author who took great care in developing her characters. This is an excellent novel, not only for enjoyment but also for the moral ethics outlined through this character.

— Peggy Jo Wipf

The passing of time in the story is handled slightly differently compared to most fantasy novels I've read, where a character's younger years are summarized in flashbacks. Hafen, on the other hand, ages Wren up from 12 to 17, and finally to 18 years old, while telling her story at the same time in clear-cut prose. This suits the character-driven tale, as Wren struggles with the memories of her cynical mother and her estranged father.

The plot has a good twist, and the sketches serve wonderfully as illustrations for Indebted. At its heart, Indebted is about parental issues, forgiveness, love, confidence, inner strength, friendship, greed, and—to a great extent—faith. On the whole, it's a well-written and thought-provoking tale from Hafen.

— Lit Amri

I know a lot of people will find it hard to put Christianity and an epic fantasy together, but Indebted has both of these elements and works very well. In fact, it was this uniqueness that made it stand out from other fantasy novels I've read before.

— Maureen Dangarembizi

Prologue

I don't know how long I've been a slave to the beast.

It feels as if I've always been indebted to it. If I hadn't entered into the contest, I would have never come in contact with the horrible creature. The very thing I am most proud of - my skill with a sword - led me to bondage worse than living in a prison cell.

1

My mother had spoken very little about the changes that would take place in my body. I stumbled upon them without her guidance. She spoke very little about anything except to tell me what I was doing wrong. "You are a princess," she would say at the end of each lecture, through clenched teeth. "You will act like one."

Perhaps if I had been a boy, the king would have wanted to spend time with me. As it was, my father rarely acknowledged that I was alive.

I stood in my sleeping gown in front of the mirror stationed in the corner of my living quarters and wondered if it was my appearance that made my father turn away. Since my twelfth birthday, I no longer looked or acted like myself. My hair was still a morning sun blonde and my eyes a robin's egg blue, but my legs stretched out in front of me when I walked and often got tangled up. My chest, previously as flat as a chopping block, now had form and shape that could not be denied. It was shameful, and I wanted no part of this thing called "becoming a woman." I grabbed a pillow from a nearby chair and hugged it to my chest.

Perhaps I should have missed my mother more since her disappearance three long months ago. I recall with great clarity that day. She had banished me to my room for forgetting her birthday. She was angry with me and told me, in her cool, collected manner, that I was to remain in my room until after dinner so that I could learn to think of someone other than myself.

"But mother, I want to celebrate your birthday with you," I remember crying with honest repentance.

Her light gray eyes were pieces of ice as she remarked, "You should have thought my birthday important enough to remember in the first place. Besides, I want to spend some time alone in the garden." Those were the last words I heard my mother speak. By nightfall, no one could find any trace of her.

King Belodawn came to my room that evening asking me where she was, as if he had only noticed both of our absences himself.

"I don't know, father. She commanded me to stay here all day because I'd forgotten her birthday. The last I saw her was this morning when she told me she was going to remain in the garden."

"I have soldiers looking for her in the garden as we speak," he said, running his hand through his wavy, blond hair. His icy blue eyes flitted over me with nervous, accusatory glances. "Everyone I've spoken with says she was with you in the garden this morning and no one has seen her since that time."

The search went on for days and extended to the forest beyond the garden walls. Still, there was no sign of my mother. Notices were sent out to the surrounding kingdoms offering a grand reward to whoever found her or knew of her whereabouts. That proved to be a waste of time. No one had seen her in Greenham, my father's land, or in the other kingdoms. She was gone.

From that moment on, my father barely acknowledged my existence. It was as though he blamed me for her disappearance. And so, I was on my own.

2 |

Without my mother and father to guide me, I found myself drawn to Mrs. Pendelin, the castle cook. I would rise in the early hours of the morning before the sun was up and head down to the kitchen to knead bread with her. She was the only one who seemed to care that I existed.

Her kind, brown eyes were always warm and cheery when I arrived, and she would greet me with a hug from her plump arms. The cold, dark castle stood in stark contrast to the warmth of Mrs. Pendelin bustling between pantry and table. I received her hug with great enthusiasm and loved the way even her skin smelled of warm bread. She wore her graying hair in a tight knot on top of her head to "keep her hair from falling into the food," as she explained. Her drab gray dress and flour-white apron made it clear that she was a castle servant. She was like a mother to me.

I didn't particularly enjoy kneading bread, it made my hands ache, but I wanted to be close to Mrs. Pendelin. "Now put some muscle into it, Princess," she would say. After helping to make the morning bread, I would sit by the fire in the kitchen and eat my fruit, meat pies, and porridge while Mrs. Pendelin sang to the Heavenly Father, preparing a variety of cuts from deer, fowl, or rabbits for our evening meals. The savory smells spilling from the meat roasting over the open fire of the kitchen hearth would make my stomach growl in spite of the breakfast that filled it. I lingered as long as I could to hear her beautiful voice, so rich and deep. It comforted me in spite of my terrible loneliness.

When Mrs. Pendelin stopped singing and began chopping vegetables, I would often grow restless and wander through the castle. When my mother disappeared, my father began removing art from the walls. He seemed to always hate my mother's extravagant, flamboyant decor. Yet, removing it made the castle feel even colder. What remained on the bones of our royal interior was the gold paint and wood paneling. These covered the walls in most all nine bedrooms as well as the common areas where the king would meet with visitors. There were no fires lit in the hearths, outside of my bedroom and the kitchen, due to the king's command that they only be lit for special occasions. He was afraid we would run out of wood, even though we had more than enough in the surrounding woods to last.

Despite its bare interior, the inside of the castle was much more elegant than the outside. Although my father was forever roaming to distant countries, searching for someone to conquer or for an opportunity to increase his wealth, he had one of the smallest castles in the land. It looked more like a stone mansion than a castle. It was square with three stories, five chimneys, and eight windows that faced the pillared gates signifying the front entrance and many hectares of land surrounding the castle.

The indifference oozing from the mind of our castle usually caused me to return to my room as a recluse. There, I could sit next to my bed in a stiff, blue high-back chair with soft, golden pillows and read or look over the window ledge. The window provided an ideal perch above the southwest garden. I imagined I was still allowed to play and roam through the garden the way I did before my mother disappeared, talking to the birds and other forest creatures that happened along. Even the toadstools had been my friends, their white, puffy tops smiling up at me from the rich, dark soil. I remembered building birdhouses out of twigs and flowers. Long, ornamental grasses proved to make perfect bindings to tie twigs and attach white, yellow and pink roses. Many hours were spent sitting by the beautiful pool in the center of the garden, making one house after another.

I remembered stringing the houses from low hanging branches of the apple and pear trees scattered throughout the garden. I had snuck a knife from the castle kitchen to cut pieces of apples and pears which I would place in the birdhouses. Robins with their orange-red chests and blue jays would enter the houses and enjoy a fruity feast. Hummingbirds, moths, and cardinals came with the monarch butterflies in early spring. This gave me great joy. I didn't miss my mother as much as I missed spending time in the garden. When she disappeared, it was as if things had not changed all that much except for my freedom to enjoy life.

The king forbade me to leave the castle grounds, so I occupied my time with study and embroidery. It didn't take long, however, for me to grow weary of these domestic tasks.

One morning during our breakfast ritual, Mrs. Pendelin looked me in the eye with her plump face only inches from my own and said, "Child, you need to be outside breathing fresh air! It's not good for you to be inside day in and day out. I want you to meet my son. He will teach you to ride a horse. After we've made the bread and you've had your porridge, I will introduce you."

Jealous at the realization that she was a true mother to someone else, I wasn't all that interested in meeting her son, but learning to ride a horse seemed like a good idea. King

Belodawn loved to ride, and I figured this might be a way to spend time with him eventually. It had been at least a month since I had last spoken with my father. He was rarely at home for an evening meal and if he was here, he ate alone in his chambers. Not only had my mother disappeared, but so had my father.

"This is my son Aleric," Mrs. Pendelin said, as we stood in front of a sable-headed boy about the age of thirteen who was busy grooming one of the horses in the castle stable.

"Hello," he said, not even looking at us, but continuing to brush the white and brown speckled horse gleaming in the morning sun, his coat as shiny as a new sword.

"Aleric, this is Princess Wren."

Hearing the impatient tone in his mother's voice, the boy dropped the brush and jerked his head toward us. He looked at me, frowned, looked at his mother and then picked up his brush and went back to grooming his horse.

"Aleric, son, is that any way to greet the princess?"

Sighing, the boy stood and bowed before me. "Your Highness, I apologize. I did not know you were Princess Wren. I thought you would be older than what you appear to be."

"I told you she was the princess...."

Aleric began to cough or at least pretended to be coughing. I could tell it was forced. He turned away and returned to his stool.

"Always putting me to the test aren't you? I told Princess Wren that you would teach her to ride a horse."

"I can't, mother," Aleric said without looking at us. "I have to clean these stables after I get done grooming the horses. I don't have time."

"Then you can begin tomorrow. Princess Wren will meet you here after her breakfast tomorrow."

"But..."

"I said you will begin tomorrow, Aleric." Mrs. Pendelin's face was as stern as my mother's face had been the day I forgot her birthday. However, her eyes, unlike my mother's, remained warm.

The boy sighed and kept brushing, though a bit more vigorously than before.

"Come along, Princess Wren. You can help me gather herbs and vegetables for our lamb stew this evening."

3

The next morning Mrs. Pendelin shooed me away from the kitchen after I had eaten one of her cinnamon rolls. She insisted that overnight her son had grown eager to show off his skills to me. So, I headed out to visit Aleric at the stables.

I walked slowly through the cool morning air, wishing I could just go back to my room without offense. I wanted to be with Aleric about as much as he obviously wanted to be with me. A picture of my father's face rose in my mind and I could feel my steps quicken. I would do anything to get his attention - even if it meant I had to spend time with some obnoxious boy.

Aleric was nowhere to be found when I entered his domain. The horses stood in their stalls, eating from buckets of oats and grain, snorting as I walked by. At least they acknowledged my presence.

The sweet-sour scent of hay and the pungent smell of horse manure was strange in my nose. I wasn't sure if it offended or engineered interest in me. I checked each stall for the boy, but no one was there. I came to the last stall and found a beautiful chestnut stallion just staring at me with large, brown eyes. Not able to help myself, I reached out and touched the silky mane that fell from his regal neck. He was amazing. I hoped I could ride him one day.

After inspection of the last stall, I was ready to turn around and leave the stables. It was then that I noticed the door leading into the barn was cracked open. I tugged the heavy wooden door open wider and stepped inside.

A lantern sat on the dirt floor of the barn, illuminating the stashed hay piled nearby. I heard a swishing sound coming from my left and turned to see what caused the sound. There stood Aleric, his back facing me. He held a sword above his head with both hands as he leaned forward on his right leg, slicing the air with the sword as he brought it down. He took a step forward with his left leg and carved through the thick air, moving from the left to the right.

The sword gleamed silver in the shaft of gray morning light coming through a window above the barn loft. It stirred the specks of dust floating in the fragrant air, which lifted from the sweet smell of hay and the pungent, earthy scent of the horses nearby. Aleric had no idea I was there, so I moved into a shadowed corner of the barn to watch.

He moved back and forth, taking two steps forward and then one step back, raising the sword above his head and then side to side in an arc. All was silent except the swooshing sound of his weapon. It was as if I were watching a dream with my eyes wide open. His movements were so precise and graceful that I wondered if this could truly be the same rude, blundering boy I had met yesterday.

Aleric began to move more quickly now, thrusting the sword out in front of him as if he were stabbing an imaginary foe. His feet kicked up the dust on the barn floor. The dust went straight up my nose and I held my breath, fighting against the burning itch. Try as I might, I had no power over the sneeze that erupted.

Aleric spun around in an instant. His sword thrust forward. "Who is there?!" He demanded. I quickly stepped from the shadows into the shaft of morning light, fearing Aleric would cut my throat if I didn't identify myself immediately.

"It's me! Look! I'm Princess Wren."

Aleric sighed and dropped his sword to his side. "Oh, I thought you were an intruder." He seemed almost disappointed that it was me and not some violent criminal. He was obviously stirred for a fight.

"Your mother told me I would find you in the stables. You weren't there, and I noticed that the barn door was slightly open so I assumed you were in here."

"How long have you been here?" Aleric's voice held a tone of irritation.

"Not very long. You're very good with the sword."

"Not good enough or old enough to be a soldier, so what good is it?" There was no mistake. Aleric was angry and I wished I had never come to the barn.

"Maybe I should come back another time," I whispered, turning my back on him and heading for the door.

"No, no! Don't go! I'm sorry. I'm not used to people sneaking up on me."

I spun around to face him. Now it was my turn to be angry. "I was not sneaking up on you. I was admiring your skill, you thick-headed peasant!" The words came out before I had a chance to stop them, much like the sneeze that had caused all this trouble.

"I do apologize, Princess Wren." He walked toward me with a worried look dulling his bright eyes. "Please don't tell my mother how I have behaved. She will take away my sword privileges. It's always the first thing to go when she's angry with me."

My eyebrows raised in consternation. "I won't say anything. Can we please begin my horse riding lesson?"

"But of course, your highness." Aleric ran ahead of me, pulling the barn door open to let me through. Sword fighting was obviously important to him.

The horses stood silently in their stalls, staring at us as we walked by. I wondered what they thought about all day when they were confined to their stalls. I didn't yet understand that a horse is taken out of the stable at least once or twice a day. I felt sorry for them, thinking about being locked up all day long. I knew what that was like. I wished I could ride them all to give each one a chance to escape, even if it was for a very short while.

"Have you ever ridden a horse, Princess Wren?" Aleric stopped in front of the stall of the chestnut stallion.

"No. My father said he was going to teach me but never had the time." I wondered again if this would bring us closer together. Maybe if I already knew how to ride, my father would want to go riding with me. Something inside told me not to count on it.

"Princess Wren. Princess Wren. Princess Wren!" Aleric was shouting at me. I had been day-dreaming that my father asked me to go riding in the woods, the forbidden realm I had yet to explore. My mother always got angry with me for daydreaming.

"Sorry. I'm listening now."

Aleric handed me a saddle that he had brought out of a small room beside the stables.

"Put that over the horse."

The horse snorted and whinnied a bit as I gently laid it across his back. Aleric showed me how to cinch up the saddle and grabbed the reins to guide the horse to the arena area outside the stables.

The arena, empty now, was typically full of people on Friday evenings when the king's knights would joust and sword fight. It was the highlight of the week for most of the residents of my father's kingdom.

I had watched the competition many times myself. It was something to behold. The knights wore their gleaming suits of armor and fought as ferociously as if they were in a real battle. I had wondered if they ever felt fear. Their fighting looked so brutal and violent, so completely different from what I saw in the barn with Aleric.

He walked the horse to the center of the dirt arena. It was late summer, almost fall, so the floor of the arena was dry. It was often a thick mud. I was almost disappointed. Part of me wanted to get covered in mud the way the knights would while fighting in the arena.

The cook's son motioned for me to join him in the center of the arena. "You have to ride sidesaddle since you're a girl." He helped me up into the saddle designed specifically for this type of riding. "Your feet go on that wooden platform attached to the saddle."

I placed my feet on the small wooden shelf-like object toward the bottom of one side of the saddle.

"Now, I want you to hold on to the horn of the saddle, the part sticking up in the center, while I walk you around the arena. Hold on tight because this is going to feel very strange at first."

I grabbed the saddle horn with both of my hands. I felt nervous, afraid of what would come next. The leather of the saddle was cool and smooth while the body of the horse against my legs felt warm and alive.

Aleric slowly pulled on the horse's reins, leading the animal from the center of the arena to the outer ring and then slowly around the outer ring.

I began to smile. The rhythm of the horse beneath me was calming. It made me feel like I was walking on the wind.

Aleric picked up the pace and did a slow walk-run next to the horse, causing the animal to trot beside him. My eyes grew large as I tried to observe everything that was happening. My smile turned giddy and I was less apprehensive as we made our way around the arena for the third time.

The boy began to walk once again and then came to a stop. I nearly fell forward from the sudden jolt as the horse came to an abrupt stop.

"Very good, Princess Wren. You ride like someone who has some practice." Aleric smiled up at me and I could feel myself blush. I had never been told I was good at anything. It felt good to hear the compliment.

We went around the arena the same way, walking and trotting until Aleric decided it was time for me to take the reins.

I nodded, my hands trembling as I grabbed hold of the smooth leather. I pulled gently on the right rein and the horse began walking to the right. I tugged on the left rein, turning the horse to the left.

"Pull on both reins when you want to stop," he called out to me.

I pulled both reins and the horse immediately stopped in his tracks. This was getting to be more and more fun. I had never experienced this kind of control over another creature. I felt heady with power.

I snapped both reins the way I saw Aleric do and the horse began to trot. I turned the horse to the left and began to ride along the outside circle of the arena.

My heart pounded with excitement. As I rode, the arena became a secret passageway in my imagination, transporting me to another land. I had never felt so free. I wished my father was here to see me, certain he would be proud of me.

I rode around in circles for a good while. Aleric sat in the arena seats and watched. Finally, he walked out into the middle of the arena and motioned for me to stop.

I gently pulled on the reins and the horse came to a stop in the middle of the arena next to Aleric.

"Our lesson is over for today. You're a natural. You ride almost as well as any soldier..."

When I glanced at him, he added, "any soldier's first time in the saddle!" Aleric was acting toward me. This was a different person than the one whom I'd met yesterday. He looked at me differently.

Aleric held out his hands and I grabbed them with mine, allowing him to help me down off the horse. We walked the horse back to the barn stall, where he handed me a brush.

"Time to learn how to take care of the horse," he said, smiling.

I looked at the brush and frowned. "What do I do with this?"

He grabbed a second brush and began pulling it down across the horse's side. "You brush the horse like this. Doing this keeps the horse's coat healthy and shiny."

At first I was annoyed that he expected me, a princess, to do the work of a stable boy. If my father knew I was doing the work of a servant, he would be none too pleased. I went along with it because I wanted to keep Aleric happy and I didn't have anything better to do. I hoped that if I stayed in Aleric's good graces, he might teach me how to fight with a sword. Ever since I saw him practicing in the barn, I wanted to learn. I couldn't get it out of my head.

Aleric continued to show me different techniques with the horse throughout the week. I soon had the horse prancing and trotting at my command. My time with Mrs. Pendelin's son was the highlight of my day. I no longer spent time in the kitchen after breakfast, but went straight to the stables where Aleric waited for me.

On our fifth day of practice, he decided we would do something different.

"Today we will ride in the forest beyond the castle walls." He hoisted a regular saddle, one with boot straps, on top of the horse and looked at me for my reaction.

"I can't do that. I am forbidden me to leave the castle walls."

"Never fret, Princess Wren. I have a way."

He handed me a long cloak that was too big for me. "Put on the cloak."

I did as he said.

"Now lift your dress above your knees and put your left foot in the stirrup."

I did as he instructed. Holding my dress up with my left hand, I slide my left foot into the stirrup.

"Now pull yourself up with your right hand and swing your right leg over the horse."

I felt my face grow hot at the thought of riding the horse like a man while wearing a dress, but the desire to embark on an adventure overruled my embarrassment. The cloak covered my bare legs and shoes.

"Now take the horse out of the barn and I will be right behind you."

I led the horse into the cool, morning air. The sky was filled with light gray clouds, blocking out most of the sun. I knew the clouds would disappear by mid-afternoon as they always did in the fall. The heat of the ever-waning sun would burn them off.

Moments later, a good-humored Aleric saddled up beside me, mounted on another horse. "Are you ready for an adventure, Princess Wren?" He grinned, and I was pleased that he wanted to take me somewhere new.

"Yes!" I couldn't wait to get started.

"Let's go." He trotted the horse out ahead of me and I rode behind him, keeping the same pace as him. He came to a stop as we reached the road that led to the castle gate.

"Don't say a word," he instructed. "The gatekeeper will think you're my traveling companion as long as he doesn't hear your voice."

I nodded. We rode slowly to the enormous wooden gate that blocked the entrance to the castle road and surrounding land. My heart began to pound. I had never been outside of the gate. Fear and excitement coursed through my veins.

"Good morning Valderon," Aleric called to the guard standing next to the high wooden gate.

"Good morning Aleric. Out for a morning hunt in the forest?"

"Just a morning ride."

"Who is this with you?" Valderon asked, looking at me. I kept my head down, fearing that if I looked at him directly, he would recognize me and I would be banished to my room forever by my father.

"He's my cousin visiting from Shaw."

"What's your name lad?" I could feel his eyes boring into my downturned head. I couldn't breathe. I wasn't supposed to talk but I knew I couldn't just ignore the man. Luckily, Aleric knew what to say.

"His name is Terin. He's very shy and has trouble speaking to people he does not know."

"I see. Well, Terin, you will have to learn to be brave and speak up, or life will just pass you by."

"We are working on that," Aleric jumped in once again.

I nodded in agreement, still holding my breath, hoping he would just open the gate and let us pass.

Valderon did just that. Walking over to the giant iron latch on the right side of the gate, he slid the iron bolt to the left and unlatched the gate.

Aleric passed through and waved. I did the same, still refusing to make eye contact. It wasn't until we rounded a corner in the road and could no longer see the gate that I started to relax. For the first time in my life I was outside the castle walls, beyond the reach of my father and my mother. I felt as free as the red breasted robins and blue jays I used to feed in the castle garden.

My willing conspirator led us down the road, and it curved into the woods. The path suddenly became narrow, with giant trees sprouting up on either side of the path.

I inhaled deeply and could smell the moist earth beneath us and the tart, clean scent of the trees. This was a new scent to me, something I had only caught briefly on the breeze while bound within the castle walls. It was one of the most intoxicating fragrances that I had ever smelled, and it made me want to push my horse a little faster.

The boy must have been affected the way I was by the clean, open air because he started to ride faster and faster. The trees on either side of us were becoming a blur as we

rode. We came to a tree that had fallen across the path and
Aleric sailed over it with ease, his horse leaping across the
barrier gracefully. Without thinking, I dug my feet into the
sides of my horse, while gripping the reins tight. My horse
leaped through the air, barely missing the fallen tree.

My breath caught in my throat as I realized how close to
danger I had come. I could feel a hot anger rise inside my
chest.

Aleric looked back at me after bringing his horse to a
slow trot and smiled. "That was excellent, Princess Wren!"

Instead of shouting, I gave him a weak smile. I couldn't
stay mad at someone who was telling me how good I was.
This was my weakness and it seemed that Aleric could get
away with anything just by tossing me some kind words.

We rode until the noonday sun was high in the sky. We
veered off the trail on a smaller path that led to an open
glade. Aleric stopped next to a giant rock in the glade
surrounded on all sides by dense forest. Purple-blue
bluebells and milk-white snowdrops sprouted here and there
around the rock and throughout the verdant green field.
More large rocks were scattered across the glade. Mountains
rose high and majestically to the west of the field. I felt as if I
were riding in a painting.

"We'll have our noonday meal here."

I nodded and felt my stomach rumble at the thought of
food.

Aleric reached into the bag attached to the side of his
saddle and pulled out a small loaf of bread along with a
block of yellow cheese wrapped in a white cloth. He walked
around his horse and pulled out two metal cups and an
earthen jug with a wooden stopper from the bag on the other
side of his saddle.

I followed him over to the rock. Setting the food on a
level space in the middle of the rock, he scrambled up one
side and sat beside the food, motioning for me to join him. I
pushed myself up on and sat on a smooth, level space beside

the food. The rock made a perfect table and I wondered if men had carved it this way. It was difficult to believe it was made this way by nature.

Aleric sliced off a piece of bread and cheese and handed them to me. Next, he pulled the cork out of the jug and poured cool water into one cup, and then the other.

"Here you are, Princess Wren." He smiled and handed me the cup.

Everything tasted so wonderful. I didn't know food could taste this good. I had eaten bread and cheese in the garden, but never in the woods. The air seemed to make me hungrier and I devoured the food in just a few bites.

I couldn't tell why Aleric kept glancing over at me, except that he seemed greatly amazed by how quickly I devoured my food. "Riding a horse will make you more hungry," he said, taking a large bite of his bread and then cheese.

I nodded and eyed the loaf of bread and block of cheese in the center of the rock. Aleric smiled, withdrew the knife from the leather pouch at his side, and cut me another slice of both things. I thanked him and ate this just as quickly as I had the first pieces he gave me.

I wished we could stay here forever in this place and time. Everything was perfect, the blue sky, the gentle breeze and the wildflowers swaying gently to and fro. I couldn't believe it had taken me twelve years to find my way out of the bonds of the castle.

"We'd better head back soon. Someone will start to wonder where you have gone."

I just smiled because I knew there was no one to wonder about me except maybe Aleric's mother. I stared at him and worked up the courage to ask him what I had been waiting to ask for a while. "Will you teach me how to fight with a sword?"

His eyebrows raised in surprise. "Princess Wren, sword fighting is not something for a lady to do, not to mention that you're a princess."

"Why not?" I was not about to be told "no".

"Swords are dangerous and ladies aren't skilled enough to fight with them. And, fighting is a man's job, not a woman's."

"You said yourself that I ride a horse as well as any man. Perhaps I would handle a sword just as well."

"No, Princess Wren. I will not do something so unnatural. Your father would have me in shackles. You must act like the lady you will become someday. There will come a time when you will be queen like your mother."

"I don't want to be anything like my mother!" I shouted, surprising myself as well as Aleric.

My young teacher seemed to regret his decision to break any rules at all now. "It's time to go. There will be no more discussion of sword-fighting." Aleric stood, gathered the bread and cheese, wrapping them in the cloth, and then returned the food to his saddle bag.

I took another gulp of the cold water, which tasted bitter to me now, and handed Aleric my cup before mounting my horse for the ride home. The cool water did nothing to soothe the words burning in my throat. I wanted to scream at Aleric and tell him he was being unfair. Deep down I knew he was right, that ladies were not permitted to fight. Thoughts of my future smothered the buoyant spirit that had been mine as we had lunched earlier. I could hear my mother's words ringing in my ears, "I will make a decent princess of you yet." I whispered under my breath, "Are you pleased Mother?" I knew if she were still at home in the castle, she would be.

We rode home in silence.

Aleric was nowhere to be found. For several days, I came early to the stable only to find the stalls empty. I checked the barn each time and all I could see was straw and mice scurrying here and there when I opened the door.

On the fifth morning of not finding Aleric, I went to Mrs. Pendelin and asked her where he was.

"Why, he's away with the men on a hunt. Winter will be here soon enough, child, and we will need meat for the castle reserves. He has gone with your father and most of the men from the kingdom. They will return soon enough." She smiled at me and patted a lump of dough with a plump hand. "Wash your hands, child, and help me knead this dough."

I did as she said, rinsing my hands in a bowl of fresh water I poured from a pitcher sitting on the table next to the bowl. I stood beside Mrs. Pendelin and kneaded in silence for a long while.

"That should be good enough, Princess Wren. Shape the dough into small, round rolls and we will put them over the fire when you are done."

I began pinching off small lumps of dough, rolling them in between my hands until they formed a ball. Mrs. Pendelin rolled the dough between her thick hands and hummed a song I'd heard her sing many times. She paused.

"So you and Aleric seem to be good friends these days."

I nodded, not sure what to say. After our last conversation, I wasn't sure if we were friends any longer. We parted ways after our trip to the forest without saying a word to one another.

"He says you can ride a horse as well as any man."

I looked at Mrs. Pendelin, who was looking down at the dough in her hands. "I really enjoy riding," I said in a quiet voice, pleased that Aleric told someone else about my skill. Maybe I really was as good as he said I was. I thought perhaps he was just telling me that to be kind, but since he had said the same to his mother the words held more weight.

"I am glad you two are such good friends," she continued. "Aleric needed someone and so did you. We all need someone we can count on to be there for us when other people let us down."

If only she knew how Aleric had let me down when I asked him to teach me how to sword fight. I couldn't tell her because I knew her response would be much like his. I just wished someone would understand how much I wanted to learn. More and more I found myself standing in front of the mirror in my room with a stick, trying to mimic the moves I had seen Aleric perform the day I watched him in the barn. That seemed so long ago now. I sighed.

"He'll be home soon enough child."

I nodded again. Let her think I was sad that he was gone. My secret would never be told to anyone but Aleric.

It took another week before Aleric returned to the castle. By that time I had quit going to the stables to look for him. The only way I knew he was home was because Mrs. Pendelin told me when I came down in the morning to help her make bread. While Aleric was away, I had gone back to helping prepare food. I didn't find baking bread nearly as exciting as riding a horse, but at least I was not alone. Being alone was one thing I couldn't tolerate.

"He has returned, Princess Wren, and he asked about you before he went to the stables. I told him I would send you to him if I saw you this morning. He told me to have you come to the barn."

"The barn?" I tried to keep the excitement out of my voice but some spilled out before I could stop it.

"Yes. He said he needed help moving a litter of kittens into the barn loft where they would be safe."

"Kittens? I see." The disappointment spread through me like a disease and I walked slowly to the door that led me out of the kitchen and on to the path leading to the barn.

"It's a beautiful day, Princess Wren," Mrs. Pendelin called after me. "Be of good cheer."

The air outside was chilled and damp in the early morning sun that was just now rising in the east. I didn't see anything beautiful about the day and considered returning to my room to sleep away the morning hours. Still, I had missed being with my friend and had a faint desire to see him, even though I was still angry with him. I trudged onward until I came to the stables and the open door leading to the barn.

There was Aleric, standing in the shaft of light, swinging his sword from left to right, both hands on the handle of the weapon. He didn't hear me when I entered the barn so I stood watching him for a while, wishing he would turn around and hand me the sword and show me what to do.

"Are you just going to stand there or are you going to joust with me?" Aleric spoke without turning around. Somehow, he knew I was there. That's when I spotted a second sword laying on the ground by the door. I had nearly stepped on it, not realizing it was there. I picked it up and examined it in the dim light floating through the barn window.

It was small, much shorter than Aleric's Claymore, and the handle was made of what appeared to be silver. Dark green stones were inlaid in the silver, smooth and cool to the touch. I couldn't stop staring at it. At the bottom of the handle were two raised letters, A and T, made from a darker shade of silver.

"That is a sword given to me by my father when I was a small boy. That's the only thing he's ever given me, so don't lose it. Handle it with care. My father is dead and that's the only thing I have to remind me of him."

I wanted to drop the weapon and run. It felt so heavy in my hand. The responsibility made it almost too much to hold but I gripped it tightly, determined to overcome my fear. I had been waiting for this moment for days on end and I wasn't about to let it pass me by.

"Come over here, Princess Wren, and follow my steps."

I stood beside Aleric, holding the sword in both of my hands as he did, moving it from the left to the right. We sliced the air with our weapons, then brought them overhead to crash down upon our invisible opponents.

My body was covered in goosebumps; so thrilled was I to finally be doing the very thing I'd been dreaming of ever since I had watched Aleric practicing in the barn. I wondered what had changed his mind. I thought it better not to ask for fear of irritating him, causing him to change his mind. As if reading my mind, he spoke.

"I went on a hunt with the rest of the men from the kingdom," he said, drawing the sword above his head once again and bringing it down with a thin swish of the blade. "One day we were hiding in the forest and a family of deer walked by. The mother immediately sensed our presence and ran, two of her fawns leaping after her. Her third fawn, who seemed to be the youngest, stood there eating berries from a bush. He became an easy target and we shot him without hesitation." Aleric stopped, dropping his sword to his side, and stared at me.

"I thought of you as I watched the fawn fall to the ground, dying before my eyes. It was so helpless and naïve like you, Princess Wren. I knew then that I had to teach you how to defend yourself. That is why I changed my mind."

I continued to move the sword from side to side the way we had been doing for the last few moments and remained silent. I wasn't sure what to say, especially after he called me helpless and naïve. I knew he was right, but I didn't want to admit my weakness. I hated feeling so vulnerable.

"I want you to do the same moves I've been showing you over and over until the sun is shining full and bright through the barn window. Go side to side with the sword and then overhead and down. I will show you more moves tomorrow and, in a couple of days, we will spar. Sparring is where you will learn the real technique of sword fighting. Fancy moves count for nothing if they don't protect and defend you."

I nodded, caught up in the movement of the blade through the air. I didn't even notice that he had left the room until the sun was blazing through the barn window. My shoulders ached and my arms trembled under the weight of the sword. I had done as he said and continued to joust beyond the amount of time he told me to take. I was completely exhausted. It felt wonderful!

We continued this routine for the next couple of weeks. Aleric would show me different techniques with the sword. He would stay for a while, making certain I was performing them correctly, and then he would leave while I practiced the techniques over and over. He would often repeat moves we had learned the day before, coupling them with the new moves to create a series of motions that mimicked a sparring match. By the end of the two weeks I could put together at least seven moves.

On the morning of the first day of the third week, Aleric waited in the barn, holding a breast plate and helmet which he handed to me as I entered.

"Today we spar," he said, placing a metal helmet on his head after strapping on the heavy metal breastplate.

I buckled the leather strap that held the breastplate around my neck and then the strap that hung next to my waist. Slipping on the metal helmet, I picked up my sword from where it sat, leaning against the cool wall of the barn, and held it out in front of me. Aleric hit my sword with his own, causing it to clatter to the ground.

"Hold it tighter than that, Princess Wren."

I picked up the sword from where it lay in the dust of the barn floor and gripped it tightly between my hands.

Slam! Aleric's sword came crashing into my sword once again, but this time I held the weapon firm. Sparks flew off my sword as his made contact with mine. My hands tingled from the blow and I wondered if I was strong enough to fight back.

Crash! Aleric's sword clattered against my own once again. Instinctively I raised the sword above my head and slammed it down against his weapon. The past two weeks of practicing certain moves over and over again were paying off. I moved the sword from right to left and then back, causing Aleric to back away from me as I advanced toward him.

His sword clamored against mine as I continued to press forward, surprised by the rage that was ignited by his initial advances against me. I had enough of being on the defensive and had clearly taken on an offensive stance against him.

My opponent continued to retreat as I delivered blow after blow, moving as I had over the last two weeks, the sword and my steps synchronized by the repetition of my diligent practice. I delivered a blow with all my strength brought from the sword's position above my head. Suddenly, Aleric's sword dropped to the floor. He had a bewildered look on his face that I was certain matched my own. I was as stunned as he was by my ferocious performance.

"You seem to know what you're doing, Princess Wren," he said, his face downcast as he retrieved his sword from the straw covering the barn floor. I wasn't certain, but I thought I heard an edge of agitation in his voice along with a hint of humiliation. During our many hours of practice, he had told me that no one had ever been able to remove the sword from his hand during a sparring round. I smiled in the bright light streaming into the barn, realizing that I was the first to have done so.

Our lesson ended early that day. Aleric said nothing as he removed his breastplate and helmet. He motioned for me to remove my equipment. After I handed it over, he walked swiftly to the barn door.

"Our lesson is done for the day," he muttered, running like a spooked horse from the barn.

I stood there for several minutes and then lifted my sword in the air, determined to keep practicing. I had never felt quite so inspired to do something in all the days of my short life. I had finally discovered what I was born to do.

I was unprepared for the pain in my forearms, my thighs, the core of my body, and my upper arms. Everything blazed with pain. Thankfully, Aleric was not in the barn the next morning or the morning after that. I asked Mrs. Pendelin where he was. She said he was helping his uncle cut firewood for the winter. The days were growing cooler with fall upon us and winter would be here in a moment's notice. Still, I wondered if it was the firewood that kept him away or the fact that I had defeated him in a sparring match. The thought made me smile as I practiced by myself in the barn that morning. I was not about to stop perfecting my skills. I had come too far and was too good at sword fighting to give up.

On the third day, Aleric was already in the barn before I got there. He wore a helmet and breastplate and motioned for me to put on my armor. I strapped on the helmet and chest piece and stood across from him. He advanced immediately, and I was on the defensive, protecting myself from his attacks with my shield and sword.

He wielded his sword with such speed and accuracy that I could barely keep up. In no time I found myself backed against the wall with nowhere to turn.

He virtually growled as he slammed his sword into my sword. I could only watch as the sword fell from my hand, flying through the air a few feet from where I stood. It clattered to the ground. I looked back at Aleric, who had his sword pointed at my throat. A flash of fear ran through my chest and out my limbs as I wondered if he would finish me off then and there.

Instead, he dropped his sword to his side, breathing heavily. Between breaths he spoke. "That was a good duel, Princess Wren."

I took my eyes off the sword in his hand long enough to glance up at him. His face was flushed red and sweat lined his upper lip. He smiled, and I tried to smile back, but it would not come. I discovered that I didn't like losing a battle.

"You fought well, Princess Wren. Don't look so dejected. I gave you everything I had. Most of the knights in your father's command would not have fought so well." He pushed away dark, sweat-laden hair from his eyes and stared at me. I knew he was telling the truth and it made me feel a little better.

"Besides, Princess, you can't always win. I'm the one teaching you. remember?"

I smiled and blushed. I knew I was lucky to have him as my teacher. Not many would be as patient and kind as he.

Aleric continued to teach me all that he knew. Days turned into months and months became years and soon, five years had passed. Aleric became a soldier in my father's army and I became a very lonely seventeen-year-old. My father and I rarely spoke, and my one friend was always away escorting his king on his many quests for land, knowledge and power. My father was relentless in his pursuit of more. Nothing seemed to satisfy him. And so, my friendship with Aleric, my life line, came to an abrupt halt.

Before he became a soldier, I convinced Aleric to give me some of his clothes so that I would have a way to escape the prison of my castle. We had snuck out of the castle walls for the hundredth time, it seemed, to the meadow we had gone to the first time that we left the confines of my home. I rode quietly beside him through the forest. When we reached the flower-laden meadow, I was struck by the brightness of the sun. It was at that moment the idea came to me.

"Aleric, there is something I must ask you to do for me, a favor of sorts."

"What is it, Wren?"

He had long ago stopped calling me Princess Wren, which suited me just fine. I was not his princess, but his closest friend.

"I need you to give me a pair of your pants and one of your tunics."

"Whatever for?"

"I need something to wear to disguise myself if I am caught outside the castle walls."

"You must never leave the castle unless you have an escort."

"You know as well as I that you are my one and only friend. There is no one else who will escort me. Now that you will be gone, I will have no way to leave this prison. I cannot bear the thought of spending my days as a prisoner within these walls."

"Wren, you know you cannot venture out alone. It is too dangerous."

"What is even more dangerous is if I am kept locked away from the world in that castle. I will die, be it ever so slowly. Please help me."

He stared at me, the conflict of keeping me safe and the desire to let me live at war within his eyes. "I will do as you wish, Princess Wren, but only because I know you can wield a sword as well as any man."

The name "Princess Wren" caught my attention. He hadn't used my official title in years. It made me feel distant from him.

"I also need you to get me the best sword available before you leave. One like yours, a Claymore. I'll be giving you back your prized possession from your father." I looked hard into his eyes. "Thank you for everything. You have saved my life."

We ate our lunch that day in silence, both of us knowing that this would be the last meal we would have together for many years to come. As a soldier, Aleric would be required to travel to distant lands with the rest of my father's military. The sun went behind a cloud, casting a fitting gray shadow over the moment. I could hardly eat as the reality of what was going to happen set in.

"You must promise to come visit me, Aleric."

"Of course I will. I have to come back once in a while. We will see each other again, Princess Wren."

Somehow I knew this was not true. I knew we were actually saying good-bye and I could not bear it.

"I have some pressing matters at the castle tonight, so I must get back." I didn't want him to see me crying and figured it would be easier to conceal if we were riding.

"As you wish, Princess."

This was the third time he had used my official title. This was obviously difficult for both of us.

That evening we met for the last time in the barn. Aleric stood in the moonlight streaming through the barn window, with brown pants and a red tunic in his hands. He set them on the ground and stood, staring at me.

I bent to retrieve the bundle from the floor and he reached out, grabbing my shoulders and pulling me upward to stand straight once again.

"I will miss you, Wren." His words were a whisper, but his embrace was strong and almost demanding. I could feel his lips move on the top of my head as he kissed its crown. I felt my own arms tighten around him and we stood that way for a long while. I wanted the moment to carry on into the future, perhaps for an eternity, but then Aleric whispered, "I must go."

He pulled back from me and I saw him wipe his cheek as he strode out the barn door into the stables and then out into the blackness of night. I picked up the clothing from the floor and kissed the top of the soft heap. This was my ticket to freedom, the way to endure the long period of waiting for Aleric to return. My legs trembled as I made my way back to my room in the castle. Life was changing quickly. I knew it would never be the same.

That night I dreamt of my mother. I had not dreamt of her in many years. When she first disappeared, I dreamt of her often. In my dreams she was always either angry with me or pleading with me to help her in some way. This dream was different. She stood at the castle gate, looking much the same as she had five years ago when I was twelve and she disappeared. Her auburn hair hung loose and shone in the sun. Her gray eyes stared down at me from her high post at the gate. She wore a light blue dress, the same one she had been wearing when she vanished so long ago.

"Where are you going, Wren?" Her voice was as cold and accusing as her gray eyes.

"I am only going out for a short while to explore the world," I answered.

"How dare you leave without permission! Why must you continue to harm me, Wren? All I have ever done is try to care for you and look after your wellbeing."

I looked up at her, but found I had no words to speak. She was right and I was wrong.

My mother climbed down the ladder and walked over to me. Standing only an arm's length from me, I could see a small circle of blood on her blue dress growing larger and larger by the second.

"Look at what you are doing to me! You are so selfish, Wren. Every time you leave this castle you inflict a wound upon me! Curse you! Curse you for making me so wretched! May you suffer as I have suffered since I gave birth to you. May you know the pain of unrequited love. May you feel the loneliness you have brought upon me."

The blood spread and thickened, covering her waist. I felt my legs go weak and my head swim with dizziness. My face was moist and cold. Just as I was about to collapse to the ground, I awoke.

Morning spread through the curtains covering my bedroom windows, casting aside shadows with golden rays of light. My hair stuck to the sides of my face. I was still gasping for breath, struggling to repair my composure. Throwing the covers from my moist body, I quickly stood, yanked off the wet sleeping gown I had been wearing, and grabbed the fur robe lying at the edge of my bed. I walked to the hearth inside my room, poking the coals still glowing from the night before. Laying a small log on top of the coals from the pile that sat beside the hearth, a warm fire blazed into being, chasing away the chill that had come over me.

Staring at the fire, I considered what I should do for the day. I had to try out my means of escape to make certain it would work. The dream of my mother made me more determined than ever to break the bonds this place held over me. I made my way to the barn, carrying the clothes Aleric had given me along with a set of boots and a long cloak, all of which were tucked away into a leather satchel. The satchel was a gift from Aleric for my sixteenth birthday. If it were not for him and his mother, I would have received nothing to celebrate my birthdays since my mother's death. I don't think my father even knew when my birthday was, nor did he seem to care.

I climbed the ladder to the barn loft and walked to a far corner where I knew no one would see me. My hands trembled as I took off the dress and pulled on the pants and tunic. What if this did not work? I would be stuck in this place until Aleric returned. I knew I would rather die than see that happen. The clothes were too big but I figured I could hide them under the cloak. The days were becoming warm once again as spring melted into summer. I would have to endure the heat, at least until I reached the forest.

The soft boots Aleric had provided along with the clothes were also too big. Although I was almost as tall as him, my feet were half his size. I tied them as tightly as I could over my sandals. Stuffing my dress and shoes into the satchel, I stood to make my way across the loft. I tripped and nearly fell because of my oversized boots. I knew climbing down the ladder would be a challenge, but I was determined. This was a matter of life and death and I was not about to waste away inside these castle walls.

My determination carried me down the ladder, the long cloak tucked securely under one arm. I looked around the corner, into the stables before entering to make certain no one was there. The way was clear, so I stole into the stall where my horse stood waiting.

After mounting the horse, I pulled on the cloak and placed the hood over my head, concealing my hair along with most of my face. With my heart racing, I rode to the castle gate.

Valderon, wearing his soldier's armor and royal tunic, stood at his post as usual, guarding the entrance to the castle. He looked down at me from his perch and commanded me to halt.

I glanced up at him and then quickly put my head back down so he wouldn't be able to see my face.

"Ahh, Terin. I thought you would have gone with Aleric on his military quest."

I shook my head from side to side, staring at the ground.

"There you are again wearing too much clothing for such a fine day." Valderon was not making this easy.

"The sun," I said in as deep a voice as I could muster, trying a growl. "Hurts my skin."

"I know. You're one of those pale fleshed creatures."

I nodded vigorously, hoping he would allow me to pass.

"You drew quite a lot in life son, both shy and pale. If I were you, I would not venture too far from these walls. There are ravenous wolves out there ready to devour someone like you."

I despised this man. He was becoming a hindrance to my freedom.

I nodded again. I heard the gate begin to open. Freedom was only a few steps away. I could almost taste it.

Keeping my head down, I waved to Valderon and rode through, seeing my mother once again as she had appeared to me in my dream. Her gray eyes flashed as I rode through the open gate. I could see her lips move over the words of her curse but could not hear her voice as I had in the dream. I rode along the path leading to the forest and my mother quickly vanished from my mind. I was free.

5 |

As soon as I reached the forest, I pulled off the cloak and shoved it into the satchel along with my other clothes. Flynn snorted and stirred as we stood beside a large tree a few yards from the path. Before pushing the cloak into the bag, I retrieved my shoes from where they lay hidden beneath my clothes. I could no longer bear to wear these oversized boots. Having dismounted my horse, I stood on the spongy ground of the moss-covered forest floor and slipped into my shoes.

The satchel was just big enough to hold the large boots, the cloak and my dress. I would have to change back into the boots before entering through the castle gate once again and so decided to make this thicket my regular spot for changing my clothes.

The sound of voices and the thump, thump of horse's hooves quickly caught my attention. I peered around the large tree toward the path and could see two of my father's soldiers riding in the direction of the castle. I held my breath, drawing my horse close to my side, and stood as still as I could possibly make myself.

"King Belodawn is a fool," I could hear one of them say. "He thinks he has the strength to conquer any kingdom that gets in his way but he does not realize that his men are weary and need to rest. He never allows them to return home. He sends us to retrieve supplies not giving any thought to the men and their families. They will begin to desert him eventually."

When my stallion snorted, the two soldiers pulled up their steads, peered about the spot where I stood without noticing me, and galloped off. When I could no longer hear their horses, I climbed back onto my stallion and rode back to the path, turning in the direction the men had come from. I knew my uneasy stomach was because of what the soldier had said. My father would not allow the men to come home and rest. That meant I may never see Aleric again.

I rode to the meadow, sweating beneath the heavy shirt and pants I wore. I decided in that moment that I would mend these clothes to make them fit me. Perhaps I could buy a pair of boots that fit me from the village shoemaker. If I was going to be leaving the castle grounds regularly, I would need to make myself more comfortable.

I climbed off my horse and stood in the middle of the meadow. A cool breeze blew through the wildflowers, drying the sweat that covered my body. I pulled out the sword from where it hung at my side and began to move, slicing and jabbing the air, slowly at first and then gaining speed as I went along. I don't know how long I practiced, but by the time I fell to the ground in complete exhaustion, the sun was high overhead.

I sat on the rock where Aleric and I sat the first time we had come to the meadow and looked out across the field. It was surrounded on every side by dark forest. I wondered who else knew this place existed. I hoped not many. In all the years I had been coming to this place, I had never seen another person. Most people stuck to the path leading through the forest. This meadow was at least half a mile off the path. Aleric had marked a few trees with notches to show us how to find it. We were always careful to take a slightly different route near the marked trees to keep from wearing the ground thin and making an obvious path to our secret place.

I felt most at ease and free here. If I could have, I would have lived here. Butterflies danced from one blue or white flower to another. The warm sun made me drowsy. I took the water, grapes and cheese I had brought from my saddle and sat back on the rock to eat my noonday meal, hoping this would chase away the fatigue I felt.

As I popped one sweet and juicy grape after another into my mouth, noticing muscles flex in my arm, I thought about Aleric. He had only been gone one day and already I missed him. I wondered what he was doing and whether or not he missed me. He had lingered as we said good-bye yesterday. I thought he might even kiss me, but he only lifted my chin so that we were looking at each other. We said nothing and then he let go and walked away. I wondered what it all meant. Perhaps it did not matter because we could never marry as long as my father was king. He would not allow it.

A terrible sadness crept through me and I wanted to cry but couldn't. The tears caught in my throat and I ate a piece of cheese to push them down. I had spent enough time crying over him. I had to be strong. I could hear Aleric's words to me when he told me he would be leaving with my father's army. "You must continue being very strong and brave, Wren, the way you've always been."

I had never thought of myself as strong and brave but perhaps he was right. Aleric could see things in me that I could not see in myself. This was one of the reasons I loved him so much.

I left the meadow that day with a new resolve. I would be the person Aleric saw, someone who was strong and brave. I was alone, but not without purpose. I would become who Aleric said I was.

6

This is how I spent my days over the next two years. I would venture out to the meadow every two or three days to keep Valderon from asking too many questions at the gate. As far as he was concerned, I was responsible for hunting rabbits in the forest, helping to feed the remaining castle staff. My alleged father was away exploring new lands with the king, and being too weak, I had stayed behind to help manage the king's hectares under his charge. This is what I had written in the note I handed to Valderon that first day when I had approached the gate alone. Incidentally, I had also handed him one of Mrs. Pendelin's fresh meat pies. He had looked at me curiously, then nodded, hopefully assuming I was too shy to speak these words. I constantly wondered how long I could push my luck with the guard.

One day flowed into another. I had a routine for helping Mrs. Pendelin in the morning baking bread for the day. Doing chores gave me a sense of purpose at least. I would help her prepare the dough, eat a bowl of porridge, and then make my way to the stables where I would feed the few horses that remained, a mare, a couple geldings, and my stallion. After feeding and grooming them, I would climb the ladder to the barn loft and retrieve my sword from under the hay where I had it hidden. I practiced for hours until my arms ached and I could barely hold the sword. Then, I would put the sword back under the hay, grab some cheese and meat from the kitchen and wander through the castle garden until evening.

With my father gone, there was no one to tell me I could not spend time in the garden. There was no one guarding the entrance to the garden and no one tended it any longer. There was little chance I would be caught doing something my father had forbidden so long ago. He was too busy finding new lands to conquer. I was free to roam the garden grounds.

Roses still bloomed and grew wild. Grasses and weeds stood waist high and wildflowers bloomed among them. The fruit trees produced large, juicy cherries and plums. I could feast on them each day. There was a never-ending supply of fruit in the summer.

I once again began making houses for the birds as I had done long ago. Although I hated that Aleric was gone, it was wonderful to have my father at such a distance. I was free to do almost anything I wished. Still, I was careful to practice my sword skills in the barn to keep from being discovered. I wouldn't risk my father finding out about that.

In the evening I would retire to my room with a piece of chicken or some bread and read by the fire. I had found some books on sword fighting techniques and others on the strategies of war in the castle library. I was fascinated by the details of war. I could understand why my father was so driven to war. There was something life-giving about a cause worth dying for.

I also read the leather-bound holy book. I wondered about this man called the Christ. He was so different from other men I had known; primarily my father. He had many followers, so he must have been a charismatic leader, but he also taught peace and love. I wished I could talk to him about this life of royalty and loneliness. My questions about

the paths I was considering were left unspoken. There was no one to really talk to about them. I had been lonely most of my life until Mrs. Pendelin had paired me with her son.

Two years passed and Aleric never came home. His mother and I missed him terribly. We spoke often of how difficult it was to be left behind to wait. I grew more and more restless, taking trips outside the castle walls more frequently. I would ride beyond the meadow, following the path through thick woods. I came upon a mountain cliff with a waterfall that descended into a pool of emerald green water. I would often remove all my clothes and plunge into the pool, drinking in its delicious coolness on a hot summer day.

It was on one of these days that I found the proclamation. The white piece of parchment was nailed to a tree along the path leading to the pool. It announced an upcoming sword fighting contest in the land of Shaw, at the castle of King Olerion. I had heard of this kingdom. Aleric spoke of it often, of its beauty and plentiful supply of deer. The king sometimes granted people from other kingdoms access to his land to hunt. Aleric had attended many of the hunts and came home to tell me about them, about the splendor of the land and his many successes during the hunt. I longed to see this place.

I ripped the announcement from the tree and tucked it inside my shirt to read later on. I knew, before reading any further, that I would enter the contest. This was what I had needed for so long. The days were blending together, like one long day that never ended. This would take my attention away from how much I missed Aleric and give me something to brood about.

I stripped, careful to fold the announcement inside my clothes. Goosebumps spread across my naked body as I eased my way into the icy, emerald water, tiny pebbles rolling against my feet with each step. Fully submerged, I relished the piercing cold against my skin. It reminded me that I was alive. So often I felt numb, bored with the mundane motion of my days. The cold and risk of being seen naked brought a clarity to life. It reminded me that there was more to my existence than just being the daughter of a man who could care less that I existed and a mother who was no longer in my life.

I laid back, floating on the water with the sun high in the blue sky overhead, and thought of Aleric. If he ever returned, I would show him this pool. Perhaps we could swim here together. The thought made my heart beat faster and caused a stirring deep inside me. How I longed for him.

I sprang to my feet when I heard the horse's hooves thundering down the path just a stone's throw from the pool. I wrapped my arms around my chest, hoping to conceal my nakedness. The lone rider slowed as he approached the section of the path that passed by the pool and looked in my direction. I held my breath, hoping he would continue on his journey. He did not.

"Aye there," he called, leaving the path and trotting his horse toward the pool. "Are you in distress?" He dismounted his horse and tied the beast to a tree next to my horse.

"I am fine," I said a little too sharply as he walked to the edge of the pool. "I'm seeking refreshment on this warm summer's day."

The man looked up at the sun. His dark hair and beard shone in the light and I could see a reddish tint to them. He looked back down at me and smiled. I shivered. There was something unfriendly in the smile.

"Perhaps I will seek refreshment with you." He began to remove his shirt and I quickly spoke.

"I have soldiers waiting for me just a stone's throw down the path. I can call them at any time and they will defend me."

The man pulled his shirt back down over his chest and stomach and stared down at me. His dark eyes were cold and hard against pale skin, so opposite of Aleric's golden face and gray eyes. I felt a desperate need for Aleric to be here at this moment.

"We shall see if this is true," the man said, turning to walk toward his horse. As soon as he mounted the beast and rode down the path, I sprang from the pool, grabbed my clothes and yanked them on over my wet, trembling body. Pulling on my shoes, I ran to my horse and rode as fast as I could in the opposite direction of the man.

After a few minutes, I turned my horse off the trail, stomping through the thick forest on my left. We walked slowly for several minutes until I came to a spot where the trees formed a rough circle around a patch of bare ground. That is where I stopped and waited, listening for the sound of hooves in the distance, every fiber of my being on alert for the stranger.

A cool breeze caressed the trees, carrying the sharp scent of pine and earth to my nose. I inhaled deeply and heard my heart begin to slow. The only sounds were the wind and my own breath with a backdrop of the beating of my heart. I lay my head against my horse, staying put in the saddle just in case I had to flee.

The woods were growing dim when I awoke. The fear that had driven me into a frenzy had also exhausted my body and I slept more deeply than I had in a long while. I patted my horse and rubbed the side of his neck. "Thank you for being a true friend, Flynn," I whispered in his ear. He whinnied and snorted in response.

I looked around me and saw the piece of rope I had tied around a tree to help guide me in the right direction toward the path that would lead me home. It was easy to get lost in the woods. I had experienced a few adventures in my wanderings outside the castle. I nudged Flynn forward, past the rope, and could see the trail of crushed vegetation that would lead me to the path.

In no time I was on the path, my heart beating a little faster as I remembered the man who had so rudely interrupted my swim. Perhaps he would still be waiting for me along the path. I had to take that chance. There was no other way to get home. I shivered in the coolness of evening and trotted forward, my head darting from side to side as I surveyed the ever-darkening landscape. Eventually I forgot about the man and his cold, dark eyes that stood so separate from his empty smile and rode as fast as Flynn would go. Luckily the moon was full, spreading a milky white light through the trees; just enough light to see the trail ahead. I had never ridden at night and it took me twice as long to reach the castle gate.

Valderon yawned as he opened the gate. "You're back late, Terin. You never tarry this late."

I nodded, hoping he would remember that I was shy.

"It must have been a difficult day hunting," he said, a questioning tone to his voice.

I nodded again and waved at him as I trotted away from the entrance. "Good night," I called in as masculine a voice as I could muster.

"Good night shy Terin. Don't let the shadows frighten you."

I smiled. If only he knew who I was, he would eat his words. It had been a long day and I was anxious to study the announcement still resting securely in my satchel. I quickly tended to Flynn. Grabbing some bread and cheese from the kitchen, I ran to my room and locked the door, devouring my meal as I pored over the parchment.

"Hear ye, hear ye," it read.

"King Olerion does announce this day, the fifth of June, in the year of our Lord, 1542, that there shall be a sword fighting contest on July the fifth in the arena of King Olerion's castle. Any male aged 18 and up shall be allowed to compete. The winner shall receive a most handsome reward to be disclosed at the end of the tournament."

I could feel my pulse quicken. I was going to win this contest and prove that I was the best sword fighter in the land. I could not wait to tell Aleric that I'd won the contest. He might even convince my father that I would be a valuable asset to his army and then I could always be with Aleric and never alone again. This is what I longed for. If only dreams were real.

I had nearly a month to train. I would practice all day if I had to. This was my chance to escape these walls for good. I rolled up the parchment and stashed it away in the basket of yarn that was never used, as I had no interest in knitting. It would be safe there. No one ever came into my room except the castle maids who entered once a week to change the linens on my bed and clean out the fireplace. They never touched the basket of yarn.

I removed the pants and shirt I'd been wearing all day and crawled beneath the covers, completely exhausted. I dreamt I was fighting one man after another in King Olerion's contest until I faced a man with dark hair and a beard that shone red in the sun. His eyes were black and as cold as the deepest part of a mountain lake. I awoke, still moaning from seeing the man in my dreams. After many deep breaths to calm my trembling body, I came to the realization that I dreamt of this man because of the frightening experience I had with him the previous day.

"He cannot harm me," I said aloud to the darkness. "He is nothing."

I was too wide awake to go back to sleep, so I rose from my bed, slipping into my light blue silk robe and slippers, and stoked the fire in the hearth. Grabbing the holy book from the table beside the bed, I took it over to the fire and opened to the place where I had stopped reading the last time.

"I will never leave you or forsake you," I read. Was this true? I hoped it was. I needed someone who would never leave me. It seemed like everyone I knew and loved had left me at one point or another; first my mother, then my father and now Aleric. This Christ promised to never leave or forsake his followers. How desperately I wanted to have lived during his time and have been under his protection. Perhaps his wisdom could somehow reach out from the past, from the pages of these ancient stories. I yearned to create a living form of this written Christ. Could he show me that he held the answer to the pervasive loneliness I felt?

Suddenly my mother's angry words, spoken so long ago, came rushing back to me.

"You are a little whining brat that no one would want to be with you. No one will protect you. You must learn to find a way to get what you want yourself. The world is a cruel, uncaring place."

I tried to remember why my mother had said those cruel words. It may have been the last day I saw her, the day I forgot my mother's birthday. Icy fingers of guilt spread across my chest, causing me to slam the book shut. I knew someone like the Messiah would never love someone like me, a person who caused her mother to disappear.

Although I had never said it aloud to anyone, deep down I believed that my mother would still be here if I hadn't been so selfish and forgotten her birthday. It was my fault my mother was gone. My father knew it and that was why he couldn't stand to be around me. Even Aleric had grown tired of me, probably because I was too selfish. The best I could do was win this contest and bring glory to my father's kingdom. Perhaps then both the king and Aleric would want to be with me.

7

I awoke as the first light of dawn filled my bedroom windows with soft gray. The knowledge that today was the day of the sword fighting tournament filled me with excitement and fear. Waves of anxious rumblings crashed through my stomach.

"Steady, Wren," I said, staring at myself in the mirror. "It's just a contest."

My hands shook as I dressed in the clothes I had so carefully sewn over the last month. I had to have men's clothes for the contest and Aleric's just wouldn't do. The black pants and white tunic fit just loose enough to cover my feminine form but not so loose as to impede movement. I already had boots which I had made to fit my feet, growing tired of tripping over Aleric's boots long ago.

The final step was my hair. I knew it had to be cut. I would say that I had to cut it because I caught it in the weaving loom. I took the scissors in trembling fingers and with one hand, holding the braid of hair out to one side, I began to cut through the thick strand. When I finished, I had cut off a length as long as my arm. The shimmering, blonde hair lay in my hands as I surveyed myself in the mirror. My blue eyes still looked the same, but the rest of my face looked larger without heavy locks of hair cascading down either side of my face. I wasn't sure what to think.

I was almost as tall as a man. As I grew older, my face became more angular, not retaining the soft shape of childhood. I hoped I looked masculine enough to pass for an eighteen-year-old boy. Grabbing the black cap I had made to match my tunic and trousers, I pulled it onto my head. Blonde hair stuck out from underneath it brushing the collar of my shirt. My mother might have glowed to see me going after what I wanted by my own cunning.

"You're a handsome eighteen-year-old boy," I said to the reflection in the mirror. This was going to work. I was going to make my father proud and Aleric would be amazed.

Opening the door to my bedroom very slowly, I peeked out to make sure none of the castle servants were lingering nearby. Clutching my red cloak covered with lions and trees in black embroidery, I crept along the stone hallway and down the stairs to the front door of the castle. The sun shone bright outside and I felt as radiant as the blazing light that surrounded me. Even though it was warm, I wrapped myself in the cloak, preparing for my meeting with Valderon.

Mounting my horse once we were outside the stables, I rode to the castle gate, nodding at Valderon as I stopped in front of the giant door.

"I don't know how you do it, Terin. It's blazing hot and it isn't even noon yet. You'll suffocate in that cloak."

I was most certainly suffocating. How I wished he would just let me pass. I shrugged, playing on Terin's shy nature in order to remain silent.

"Try not to sweat to death in that cloak."

I nodded once again and trotted through the opening, my willpower completely focused on remaining calm until I was out of Valderon's eyesight. As soon as I came to the bend in the road where it turned toward the direction of the forest, I dug my heels into the sides of Flynn and sped off toward the road that went through the woods.

The cloak pulled off my shoulders at last, and I crammed it in the saddle bag. Free of the burdensome layer, I raced along the familiar path. The wind dried the sweat staining my shirt. I relished the feel of it across my bare neck. Having short hair was so freeing. I never realized what a burden hair could be.

My freshly shorn hair and custom fitting clothes seemed to make me faster. I reached the waterfall and pool in no time. I thought of the red bearded man as I rode past the place I had hidden the day he approached me by the pool. The thought made me shiver in spite of the heat of the day. I hoped that was the one and only time I would see him. Sometimes I hated being a woman in a world where some men were dangerous. Actually, most men were dangerous, just in different ways. This made me think of the man, Jesus, spoken of in the holy book. Was he dangerous? Somehow, I didn't think so.

The dense woods grew sparse. I rode along until I came to an opening in the trees. Beyond the trees I could see the land slope downhill into a valley. In the valley below sat King Olerion's castle. Aleric had described it to me many times. There was no mistaking the golden spires on top of the numerous turrets extending from the castle roof. King Olerion was very wealthy and he spared no expense when it came to his living quarters.

Several houses dotted the hillside leading down into the valley. I rode past one cottage after another, chickens and dogs darting here and there along the path that ran in front of the homes. People nodded or waved and I began to relax, feeling more and more at ease. I don't know what I was expecting. I had been thinking of the red-bearded man and had started to believe all the people in King Olerion's kingdom were like him. These people were just like any other common folk except, perhaps, friendlier.

I descended into the valley and finally arrived at the entrance to the castle.

"State your business lad," the guard at the gate said gruffly. His voice matched his burly appearance. He was a large man as well as tall, and his girth was barely concealed by the clothing stretched across his massive arms and legs. He could squash me just by sitting on me. The thought made me quiver.

Clearing my throat, I spoke in as deep a voice as I could muster. "I'm here for the sword fighting contest."

The guard stared at me and then a smile broke out across his face followed by deep laughter. "You're here for what?!"

"For the sword fighting cont..."

"I heard you. I just had to make sure my ears did not deceive me. You don't have the normal sword fighter appearance and where is your armor?"

I felt my face flush red both with embarrassment and anger. I hadn't even thought about armor. I had never worn a full body of armor. Aleric and I always practiced in our everyday clothing, sometimes wearing a metal helmet and chest plate but that was all.

I raised up to my full height sitting in my saddle. "No armor! It slows me down."

The guard smiled once again. "Of course, O, Impervious One." At this the man laughed heartily once again and took his stance.

"Ha, ha, laugh if you like," I snapped. "No one will be laughing when I win this contest."

"No, no, of course not." The guard turned a wooden wheel and chains began to wrap around it, lifting the gate in front of me.

As I rode beneath the gate, I continued to hear the guard's laughter. Not bothering to look back, I quickly became amazed by the swarm of people wandering through the castle grounds. Many of them wore armor and carried long, heavy swords at their sides. I stared at the ground, embarrassed by my lack of proper attire.

"You're not going to wear that plain smock to see your father, are you?"

My mother's words echoed through my mind from days gone by. I used to love wearing a plain blue dress that made my golden hair shine in the sun. My mother hated the dress and said it was not fit for a princess. If only my mother could see me now. She would be horrified at the sight of her only child dressed in men's clothes with her hair cut short.

I couldn't help but take a bit of pleasure from the thought of causing my mother such a disturbance and I smiled. My mother had always been a source of criticism and gave me one memory after another of embarrassment and humiliation. It felt good to do something that would have so drastically gone against my mother's standards of behavior. Still, I wished I had some armor. I wasn't sure how I was going to compete without it.

Suddenly the sound of a horn bellowed out across the village that spread in front of the king's castle within the castle walls. The sound came from an upper balcony of the castle where one of King Olerion's men blew a trumpet. He was dressed as the guard at the gate had been, in purple pants with a squash yellow shirt on which was embroidered the king's crest in black and purple. His hat was adorned with purple and yellow feathers and I thought I had never seen so much color at one time.

My father's colors were gray and white and the royal crest, while intricate and lovely, was always embroidered in black. I wished I could wear King Olerion's crest, a symmetrical symbol of bears and deer. The animals were woven into a forest of green trees against a background of purple skies, so different from the ravenous wolves of my father's crest. The symbol of my father's kingdom seemed to speak of greed and violence while King Olerion's crest captured the peace and harmony in nature.

"Hear ye, hear ye!" The king's consort yelled from the castle. "The contest of swords will begin at high noon. All contestants must register at the entrance to the arena north of the village. We will place you into groups of four. You will then fight one man from your group. If you are the victor, you will fight the victor from the other pair of contestants in your group. The winner of the small group of four will then advance to the next level." The group of contestants murmured. "Further instruction will be given at the entrance to the arena."

I followed the crowd, dismounting Flynn and leading him by the reins as I walked ahead of him. As I drew nearer to the arena, I discovered long rows of watering troughs for horses and a fence post for securing the beasts. I left Flynn there to refresh himself and await me.

I felt naked without the full body armor that most of the contestants wore. I wanted to hide but forced myself to stand in the long line leading into the arena. I was the only girl standing in the line and I wondered if my disguise would be enough to conceal my true nature. I was grateful none of my father's men were around to participate. They were all off in a distant land, fighting for additional territory for my father's kingdom. No one knew me here, so they just assumed I was a young man participating in the contest.

"State your name and the kingdom you represent," said the baronet seated at a wooden table outside the arena.

"My name is Wre..I mean Remberdon and I represent King Belodawn's kingdom."

"Ha-ha, are you sure that's your name, lad?"

"Yes, sire," I quickly nodded, as a cool sweat broke across the back of my neck. I was already making a mess of things and the contest had yet to begin.

"Where is your armor?" The guard's eyes traveled up and down my body. Such scrutiny made me nervous.

"I prefer to forgo the armor, Sire. It weighs me down."

"Suit yourself. You'll compete at your own risk. These are real swords we're using today, you know."

"Yes, sire. Of course, I'm aware."

"Stand yourself over to the side, there." The man pointed to a group of young men standing to the left of the table. "You're part of that group. Those are the swordsmen you will compete against first."

I felt the sword sheath hanging comfortably at my side as I walked over to the group of young men chatting in the late morning sun while they began to don their armor. They were all a little taller than me. I hoped they wouldn't notice me standing outside the circle.

"Are you here to fetch us some water, boy?" One of the contestants took notice of me, assuming I was a servant. I could tell he meant me no harm. His green eyes danced merrily beneath black locks, and he smiled at me.

"I am here for the competition." I gave him a weak smile, hoping I concealed the quiver in my voice. My heart was pounding in my ears and I felt like I was going to faint.

The man stared at me and I was sure I had somehow blown my cover. He smiled again and threw his head back, laughing wholeheartedly. The other two men standing in the circle burst out laughing as well.

"What kid have they sent to us?" He bellowed. "Sorry, lad. You must understand. You do not ...

"Look like a sword fighter?" I finished his statement, an edge ringing in my voice. My eyes hardened. I wasn't smiling now.

"Well, yes," he continued. "Where is your armor?"

I put my hand on top of the Claymore at my side, the same sword Aleric let me use from the very beginning. "This is all I need. Armor slows me down." The more I voiced this defense, the more I realized it had always felt true to me. I had always practiced in my riding leathers. I began to lean into confidence of my experience.

"I see. Does your mother know you've entered the arena today?" Another generous smile spread across the man's face, this time showing a hint of respect when I did not respond. "Well, good luck to you. At least the contest isn't to the death, or you would be finished."

"Heaven knows you will need it," said one of the other swordsmen. He raised one of his dark, bushy eyebrows and stared at me as if sizing me up.

The trumpeter at the table in front of the arena blew a horn and the crowd quieted.

"It's time for the contestants to enter the arena. Stay in the group of four you were assigned to and line up."

Groups of men formed a line in front of two soldiers. A strong man opened the huge wooden door to the arena and I could see a large crowd of people sitting in the stadium benches surrounding the arena.

"What trouble did I bring upon myself?" I thought, my breath moving in and out in short bursts. My hands tingled and felt numb. I walked beside the men in my group and tried to breathe, pretending I was back in the barn at home, practicing my sword fighting skills.

The noise of the crowd grew louder as I got closer to the arena's entrance. This was going to be one of the most frightening and exhilarating moments of my life. Somehow my breathing calmed, and I regained my confidence. I was ready. This was the day I'd been working so hard toward this past month.

The sun was high in the sky, announcing it was noon and the contest would begin. The noisy chatter of the crowd seemed to fade into the background as I strode across the arena. It was replaced by something deeper and stronger; determination.

The trumpeter's horn blew once again, this time from one of the box seats that sat above the other stadium seats. A steward dressed in regal clothing of scarlet and royal blue shouted at the crowd. "All contestants must move to the center of the arena. Please move quickly as it is time for the contest to begin."

I moved with the three men in my group to the outer circle of the arena. My group was the seventh out of sixteen quads of would-be knights. I had a little time before it would be my turn to fight.

The group of men in the center of the arena was placed in a straight line by another soldier. I could hear the soldier assign a number to each man. "You are one, two, one, two..." Once numbers were assigned, the men paired off, the "ones" facing each other for combat and the "twos" as well.

The steward in the royal clothing continued. "You will be judged by the variety of sword skills used and by the way you execute these skills. If you cause your partner to drop his sword, you win the duel automatically. You will be given three minutes to compete. Whoever has the highest score assigned by the judges at the end of the time allotted is the winner of the duel. The winners of the first two pairs will then pair up and compete."

I wasn't sure I understood the way the contest worked, but I knew I had to make my opponent drop his sword.

"We will have one winner from each group. Those sixteen group members will then compete against each other. At the end of the day, there will be one winner who will be granted the reward promised by King Olerion. The reward will be revealed at the end of the contest."

I began to wish I had been placed in the first group. The hardest part of the contest was now this tense apprehension.

Being forced to be patient for answers was not the same thing as waiting for a contest of might and cunning. The stillness unnerved me, making it hard to breathe.

Horns blasted in choir.

The first two contestants into the amphitheater wore metal armor. When I looked into the openings of every passageway under the tiers of standing spectators, every readied swordsman wore body armor. The sun reflected off the shiny metal, setting the contestants ablaze. I touched the sword at my side once again and closed my eyes. I imagined every man wearing bedclothes. My fingers found the hilt of my Claymore, and I grasped the familiar architecture through my well-worn leather gloves. When I opened my

eyes I smiled, my confidence rising full and strong. I would not allow mere pieces of metal to leave me shaken.

Crash! The swordsmen began their battle performance, swords slamming against each other as they danced around the center of the arena. The taller man thrust his large blade through the air, nearly catching his opponent's throat. I swallowed and rubbed my neck with my hand. The confidence that had just risen up was now falling fast. I had to get some armor somehow. I was absolutely crazy to think I could compete without it. I had never used it with Aleric. We had always used shields for protection. I had a shield slung across my back, but watching the ferocity of the other fighters now, it felt like a sheet of parchment. It wasn't enough.

A trumpeter in gilded clothing blew his intermediary signal for the first two contestants to cease swordplay. The judges made marks on parchment and announced the score they gave to each man. The taller swordsman got a higher score than his opponent. He waved his arms in the air, his sword slicing the air above his head. I had been watching him. He was a good sword fighter, but not as good as Aleric. I recognized many of his moves and knew just how to counter them.

The next two opponents began their battle at the sound of the trumpet. I studied them, finding that focused observation seemed to calm my nerves. These two were equally matched. One would make an aggressive move, shuffling forward, and then the other would move in, as if they were taking turns. This went on for the first couple of minutes and then the man with the crest of a lion inlaid in the breastplate of his armor ran at his opponent, knocking the sword out of his hand. The trumpet blew, signaling that the man had immediate victory because he had knocked the sword from his opponent's hand. His opponent kept looking back and forth between the sword laying on the ground and the man who had just defeated him.

I thought of all the times I had disarmed Aleric. Another smile crept across my full lips as my confidence grew once again. I didn't need armor. I would just disarm every opponent until I won the contest. It was that simple.

The two victors from the first two matches paired off. The man wearing the lion's crest was much shorter than his opponent, and he rushed at the man with the speed of a fox. His smaller form proved an advantage over his opponent's long, lanky body. Before the tall man knew what was happening, his sword was flying through the air, landing in the arena dust with a thud. That was it. The smaller contestant was the victor of the first group of four men.

The other matches sped by in a blur, and I found myself in the middle of the arena lining up next to the other contestants. I was paired with the man of black locks whose green eyes danced in merriment even now. He obviously loved life, and I found it difficult to work up the desire to compete against him.

The steward in gilded clothing spoke to me as I stood across from my opponent. "Lad, you do realize that without proper armor you put yourself at great risk of injury?"

I nodded, acknowledging that I understood this.

"You really should wear armor. There's no need to endure serious injury because of the contest."

"I will be fine," I answered. "I can't move very well in armor."

"Very well. You are taking your life into your own hands."

I nodded. I stared at the laughter in my opponent's merry green eyes. It was no longer difficult to want to compete against him.

Moving my sword from side to side, and with a swift flick of my wrist, I caught the man's sword from underneath, pushing the weapon up and out of his hand. In a matter of seconds from the time when the trumpet sounded, I had defeated my opponent.

The man picked up his sword and then extended his hand to me, nodding at me in amazement. He shook my small hand and said, "That was an incredible move. No one has ever been able to take my sword out of my hand that quickly."

I could only whisper "Thank you." I wasn't used to such words of affirmation. Aleric was the only one who ever told me I had done something well. He had been gone so long now that I had almost forgotten how it felt to hear words of praise. I wasn't sure what to say.

"You are going to win this contest," the contestant continued.

I replaced the sword in the sheath at my side. "We shall see," I said quietly, hoping no one had overheard the man. His words embarrassed me.

The other two men in my group fought next. They moved back and forth, advancing and retreating as if in a dance. When their time had expired, the judges declared the man with dark hair and blue eyes the winner.

He and I had to spar to declare a winner for my group. I stood across from the man and stared at his face until it changed into Aleric's boyish features. The arena became the barn and I was ready to practice sword fighting.

The victor charged at me. I gently stepped to the side at the last minute, my sword crashing down upon his weapon. The force of my blow on top of his sword brought it clamoring to the ground. I had defeated him just as I had the man with the green eyes, knocking the sword out of his hand. The trumpet sounded, and the crowd cheered for me. I was beside myself with embarrassment and elation. I looked around the arena. I had never been the center of attention like this. It felt oddly exhilarating and terrifying at the same time. I wanted to leap into the air and ride my horse back home as fast as I could.

From the corner of my eye, movement distracted me. Approaching quickly was a flank of guards. "What's your name lad?" the master of ceremonies asked.

"Remberdon" I answered, almost forgetting the name I'd given the man at the table outside the arena.

The royal director grabbed my hand and held my arm in the air shouting, "Remberdon." The crowd cheered my name until the man blew his trumpet calling forth the next group of contestants. I moved to the outer circle of the arena and was directed by another soldier to sit in a front row of stadium seats where the other group victors sat. The man wearing the bear and deer crest on his armor was at the end of the row. He had his helmet off and I could see his dark red-tinted beard glisten in the sun.

My breath caught in my throat. I hoped my eyes had tricked me. I stole another glance at the man. His long, straight nose and firm jawline gave him away. I knew if I could see his eyes, they would be as dark as midnight. This was indeed the man who had approached me at the waterfall.

Apparently, the man could feel my eyes on him, and he looked my way. I quickly looked away and was careful to keep my eyes on the center of the arena. I could tell he was studying me more closely and this made me nervous. What if he recognized me? I stole another glance at him and found that he was no longer looking at me.

I began to breathe easily once again. He must not have recognized me. I was still unknown. I settled in to watch the last group of contestants compete. By the time the last group entered the center of the arena, I felt like I was going to fall asleep. The heat of the day was at its peak and I was grateful that I wasn't wearing any armor. I could see the men in the victors' row slowly removing piece after piece of armor. They looked like they'd been swimming, they were sweating so much.

When all sixteen group victors were sitting in the victors' row, the trumpeter counted them off into groups of four. I was in group three. Luckily, the man who had come close to molesting me at the waterfall was in a different group.

I devoured a bit of cheese and bread I had in a pouch at my waist. Then I noticed the men in my group eyeing the morsels hungrily. I split the rest of my food three ways and offered each man a bite, which only left me with a bite of both bread and cheese. They all thanked me and appeared grateful to take advantage of a lad they were prepared to harm soon. It felt just as good to me to make friends with those whom I would later defeat.

"Group three in the center of the arena," called the squire. I stood side-by-side with the men in my group as the steward in gilded clothing once again assigned us either number one or two. The number ones would fight each other, the number twos would go next and then the two winners would compete against each other. I was assigned number one, so I fought first. In three moves I had disarmed my opponent. He shook my hand in a congenial manner, remembering the food I had shared with him.

My second match proved to be more challenging. This man was only a little taller than me and moved swiftly, making it difficult to advance on him. I used a move Aleric taught me right before he left. I pretended to jab my sword at the man's chest and quickly moved my sword to the side, which allowed me to push the weapon out of my competitor's hand. The crowd went wild once again.

The competition was now down to four contestants. We lined up in the center of the arena. I was paired with a tall man that wore his thick, black hair in long waves. I was relieved to see the soldier with the bear and deer crest paired with the knight who stood beside me. I hoped I would not have to fight against this man who had filled me with such terror.

I watched as my nemesis advanced on his opponent. He was much smaller than the knight he fought against. I was sure he would be overpowered. The battle lasted the full amount of time. I held my breath as the judges deliberated. Finally, the officiator walked over to the soldier wearing the bear crest and raised his hand in the air. I groaned quietly. My worst fear was being realized.

Now it was my turn to fight. I tried not to think of the fact that I would have to fight that dreadful creature if I was able to defeat the man who stood before me. The trumpet blew and I was still deep in thought about this predicament when my opponent advanced upon me, his sword swinging wildly above his head. I lifted my shield just before the man delivered a crushing blow to my shoulder. My sword teetered as the man sliced at my right hand that held the sword. I dropped the shield in order to grab the sword before it clattered on the ground. My opponent kept advancing, delivering one blow after another.

Out of the corner of my eye I could see the man wearing the bear and deer crest armor laughing, mocking me, dropping his shield and grabbing his sword with both of his hands. Anger tongued up, a fire spreading from the middle of my gut to my arms and legs and all the way to my fingertips. I gripped my sword tightly, my knuckles turning white, and charged my opponent with all my strength. This anger was a mixture of old and new emotion. It was more than just the man mocking me. It was my mother disappearing, my father abandoning me, Aleric leaving. It was everything wrapped up in a fiery ball. Heat traveled through my veins.

I thrust my sword forward and it sunk into the space between the body and leg armor, into the area of his groin. I was in shock when the trumpet blew. I looked down to see the man I had been fighting laying on the ground with his sword beside him, blood oozing from where I had made a gash in his pale white flesh.

"Oh!" I cried. "I'm so sorry!" In the shock of what I had done, I used my normal speaking voice and regretted it as soon as I had spoken. The soldier with the bear and deer crest on his breastplate looked up, staring at me as if in recognition. I could feel his eyes on me, but I refused to make eye contact. I was not going to let him intimidate me.

I had been kneeling beside my opponent, but jumped to my feet. "Get this man some assistance," I said through clenched teeth to the officiator, trying to sound masculine.

Two soldiers rushed to the center of the arena and lifted the knight to his feet. They helped him walk outside the arena where the town medicine woman tended to him. The officiator walked to where I stood, raised my arm in the air and declared me victor.

He called the other victor to his side. "This is the final battle. This will determine the true winner of the entire competition."

I tried to control my shaking body. Being so close to this horrible soldier was unnerving. I wasn't sure how I would make it through this final fight.

The soldier stared at me. "Don't I know you?" he whispered as he walked to where the officiator pointed, directly across from me. "You look very familiar."

I shook my head. "I've never seen you before," I lied. He continued to study my face. I kept my eyes on the ground. I had to keep my focus.

The trumpet blew, causing me to jump as if someone had hit me with an arrow. Immediately the soldier began advancing upon me, moving his sword as swiftly as I worked mine. Only a little taller, he was able to move quickly.

I took a few steps forward, utilizing some of the moves that had worked earlier in the day. Yet, I couldn't seem to get under his sword to flip it out of his hand. His technique was fast and sure. He reminded me of Aleric and his sword fighting style.

My thoughts distracted me and I didn't see the blow to my shoulder. His sword ripped through my shirt, scratching the skin of my shoulder. My shoulder was now bare and bleeding.

I could feel tears spring to my eyes and I quickly blinked them away to clear my vision. The man's blows kept coming, one after the other, and I could barely keep up with him. My shoulder burned and throbbed, making it difficult for me to fight back.

"I know who you are, fair maiden of the wood." The man smiled and continued to press forward. "I would know that shoulder anywhere. You are the one I met at the waterfall not long ago."

I was infuriated that he would know any truth about me. He had made me feel so small and vulnerable. I was not about to let him do it again. My rage replaced my awareness of the pain and I swung my sword wildly, moving faster than I had ever done before.

My opponent tried to run backward, moving away from my vengeful swings. He wasn't able to run as well as he could swing his sword and tripped. I seized the opportunity and slammed my sword against his weapon, knocking it out of his hand as he fell. I stood over him, the point of my sword against his throat. The crowd cheered wildly, and the noise was so loud that it sounded like a stampede of horses had run into my ears.

"I know who you are!" the man yelled, spinning as he screeched. "I know you are no lad, but a lady."

I backed away from him. He rose to his feet, his finger pointing at me. "This is a maiden! Don't let her fool you!"

The officiator ran in between us at that moment and lifted my hand in the air. "The winner of King Olerion's sword fighting contest is Remberdon of the land of King Belodawn."

I stared at my accuser, who continued to yell and scream. "She is an imposter! The lad is a lady! Look at her! She had long hair only a few short weeks ago. I saw her bathing at the waterfall at the edge of the forest."

The crowd grew quiet. The officiator dropped my thin pale arm and stared. "Is this true?"

I looked out at the crowd. Everyone was staring at me. I glanced at the soldier who had called my bluff and then, holding my sword like a baton before me, I ran as fast as I could toward the passage from the arena.

Two of King Olerion's guards stepped out of the shadows and seized me by the arms, forcing me to stop. I ceased to struggle. I had no strength left. The fury that had driven me to defeat my opponent had been replaced by cold, hard fear. It lay in the center of my stomach, weighing down my spirit.

The officiator walked over to where the guards stood holding the defeated version of me. "Take her to the king."

8

The guards practically carried me out of the arena, across the road that ran through the village outside the castle, and into the castle itself. They left me in a huge waiting area with a marble floor and stone fireplace which took up half of one wall. The mantle above the hearth was made from a giant slab of marble. Gold and silver statues of bears and deer were scattered across the mantle. Above it hung a tapestry of King Olerion's crest of bears and deer. I wished once again that this crest was a symbol of my kingdom instead of the hungry lions portrayed on the crest of my father's kingdom.

I stood with my back to the hearth and enjoyed the feeling of warmth on my legs from the small fire that crackled there. Despite the heat outside, the castle was dark and cold, and the fire was a welcoming source of light and heat in this foreboding place. I surveyed the room. A giant crystal chandelier hung from the ceiling. Candlelight flickered against the ceiling, which was painted like a great forest with more deer and bears. Long, forest-green velvet curtains hung across giant windows that looked out over the village. A bearskin rug covered a portion of the white and black marble floor in front of the hearth. Two red leather chairs, both with a high back, sat on top of the bearskin rug. A small table in between the chairs held a candelabra that cast a warm glow. I was about to have a seat when a guard walked back into the room and summoned me.

"The king will see you now," the guard said, pointing toward a long hall attached to the room. I walked past the guard and he followed me, taking the lead halfway down the passageway. I followed him to a room at the end of the hallway. We stood in front of a large, dark wooden door that led into a room half the size of the one I had been in just moments before. In this room, another fireplace filled a far wall. A small table was placed in front of the hearth with four wooden chairs surrounding it. The chairs caught the light of several candles lit here and there around the room. The chairs were painted dark green with a gold swirling pattern on each seat. A harp stood in one corner and a round stool sat beside the instrument. A large green chair and a footstool decorated with a tapestry of forest scenes sat in front of the harp. I wished that there was someone playing the harp. I needed its soothing sound to calm my rattled nerves.

A man in a purple robe edged in white fur sat at the table. He wore a gold crown on his head and I could easily see this was the king. He stared at the fire and then turned his head to look at me. His brown eyes were the color of the forest floor and his hair and beard were darker still. His long, straight nose and high cheekbones gave him the look of royalty. I was struck silent by his handsome features.

I searched his eyes to see if there was anything welcoming or friendly there. I couldn't read him. He was mysterious. I didn't sense I was in danger, but I also knew that I was an imposter in his kingdom and this didn't make me favorably disposed to him. I shivered in spite of the warmth in the room.

"Are you cold my lady? Or should I call you lad?"

I looked down at the marble floor. I suddenly felt ashamed of my short hair. "Lady is the proper word. I am Princess Wren from King Belodawn's land."

"Princess Wren, daughter of the wicked King Belodawn. How could I be so fortunate?"

I frowned. "What do you mean?"

"Your father has tried to attack my kingdom and take my land more times than I can recall. When he finds out I have his precious daughter, he will beg my forgiveness."

"I don't think so," I said, clasping my hands in front of me. "He hardly knows I exist."

"So that's how it is? He's too busy stealing and spreading destruction to notice his daughter has cut her hair like a man and is fighting other men with a deadly weapon. You're not what I expected. I would have thought you would be like your father -- spoiled and greedy. Instead, you're just a liar and a thief. I suppose in that regard you are like your father."

I dropped my hands to my side. "I am nothing like my father!" I cried.

The king chuckled. "Okay, Princess Wren. I can see I'm insulting you, much like the way you've insulted my competition by pretending to be something you aren't."

"I'm just as much a sword fighter as any of these men."

"I'll give you that. You won the contest. I have to say I'm impressed. Where did you learn to fight like that?"

"One of my father's soldiers began teaching me when I was just a young girl. I've been practicing for six years. It's what keeps me alive."

"I can see that." The king studied me intently. "You are very brave, Princess Wren. Because of your skill and bravery, I have a proposition for you. You have two choices for the crime of deception you have committed against my throne. You can either be held in the dungeon for the next ten years, which is the normal punishment for what you've done, or you can help me protect my kingdom."

I frowned. "You want me to fight in your army?"

"No. I want you to do something much more dangerous than that. I want you to rid us of the dragon that torments my people."

"Dragon?!" My eyebrows rose as I looked at the king in shock. "I've never seen a dragon. I didn't know they were real."

"Oh yes! This one is very real and has been killing my people and stealing livestock for many, many years now."

"What do you want me to do?"

"I want you to slay the dragon, of course." He stared at me again without looking away.

"So I must slay the dragon or be put in your dungeon for ten years?"

"Yes, Princess Wren. You're catching on quickly." His dark eyes seemed to dance like the candlelight flickering around the room.

"It seems I have no choice but to slay this beast."

"I am pleased that you have not disappointed me, Princess Wren. I am almost glad you decided to try and deceive me."

"I was not trying to deceive anyone. I only wished to compete in the contest and I knew I wouldn't be allowed to as a lady."

"And so you decided to be deceptive by pretending to be something you aren't." The king looked away from me, staring at the fire flickering beside the table. "I admire your courage, Princess."

"Thank you." I fixed my eyes on the marble floor once again.

"You may go now, Princess. You will receive further instruction about slaying the dragon tomorrow. Tonight, you will stay in one of my guest rooms. My courtier will be placed at your door, so don't try to escape. You will be caught and carried to the dungeon if you do."

I nodded, not knowing what to say.

"Take her away," the king said, shooing me away with a swift motion of his hand.

The soldier, or the dark-haired young man whom I thought was a soldier, had been waiting by the door. I finally realized that this was no soldier but the king's courtier when he grasped my body and forcefully prodded me out of the room and down the hall. Our strides fell into comfortable unison, then, as I complied, and we walked toward the great room where I had earlier waited for the king. Instead of continuing into the room, however, we went up the stairway at left. At the top of the stairs, we went left again down a dark hallway and into a well-lit room at the end.

In the guest room, there were two windows looking out over a courtyard that spread through the back of the castle. Wind rustled the thick foliage of the lilac bushes planted at the far end of a giant fountain. I longed to walk along the pathway next to the fountain. Instead, I stood obediently by the windows, remembering the king's words that I would be imprisoned if I tried to escape.

The cool evening breeze wafted through the open bedroom windows. The scent of lilac swirled through the air, giving me a heady sensation. It was everything I could do to not crawl out of the windows in order to stroll through the courtyard in the shroud of darkness. I had an idea.

"Guard! Guard!" I yelled, struggling to get my escort's attention. I knew he was no guard but wasn't sure what to call him. The man finally appeared.

"Can you please accompany me to the courtyard in the back of the castle?" I asked. I was tired of waiting and hoping to get at what I wanted. It was time to start asking until I got what I wanted. No one was going to do this for me.

The king's steward looked at me and shook his head. "The king instructed that I should control you, Princess."

"Please. I just want to stroll through the courtyard below to calm my nerves and get a breath of fresh air." I stood by the window

looking down into the courtyard. I had no intention of trying to escape but needed something to help me relax.

"We cannot stay long," he warned. "If the king discovers that I let you out, he'll lock me away, even if I didn't disobey a direct command. He's a very hard man and does not tolerate any form of disobedience."

"I understand." I looked back at the man and smiled. I wasn't completely certain because shadows had fallen across the room making it difficult to see his face, but I thought he smiled back.

I followed the man to the door, still wearing the clothes I'd worn while competing today. I wished I had something to change into.

He turned around and frowned at me. "Wouldn't you like to change into the clean clothes the king has prepared for you before we take our stroll?"

"Clean clothes?"

"Yes, Princess. There are dresses laid out at the foot of the bed."

I realized I hadn't bothered to look around the room when I first entered. I had been drawn to the windows and gave little thought to the rest of the living quarters. I walked back toward the windows and looked to my right where a large bed stood, the head of which was pushed against the wall. At the foot of the bed, on top of the crushed purple velvet throw, were three beautiful dresses.

I walked closer to the bed and ran my finger over the pale green dress. Tiny pink and purple flowers were embroidered on the bodice of the dress above a green satin bow that tied around the fitted waist.

"Where did these come from?" I asked, walking back to the doorway.

"Why, from the king's daughter, of course."

I frowned. "These are her clothes?"

"Yes, Princess. She insisted on having them brought down to you. I'm surprised the king would allow it. You made quite a fool of him today."

"How did I make a fool of him?"

"The winner of the contest was to be given his daughter's hand in marriage. He's been trying to find someone for his daughter to marry for several years now. She's always been a bit wild and the king reasoned that whoever married her would have to be able to protect her at all costs. He wanted to find the most skilled swordsman in all the surrounding kingdoms so that he would no longer have to worry about her. Imagine his surprise when he discovered that the best swordsman was actually a swordswoman."

I shook my head. "I've made a mess of things. All I wanted was to prove myself by entering the contest and winning it. I wanted to show my friend and my father that I am as good as any man. I never meant to do any harm."

The man stood silently, looking at me. "I've never met a princess like you. You are nothing like the king's daughter who likes to spend her days dressing up and meddling in other people's affairs. She has a kind heart. If she didn't, she wouldn't have loaned you these dresses. She was in the crowd and saw you being carried off after winning the contest. She feels she owes you for keeping her from being forced to marry against her will."

"I should like to thank her for the dresses."

"You're not allowed to meet the princess. The king has strictly forbidden it."

"But why?" I questioned.

"He believes meeting someone like you would cater to his daughter's wild imagination."

I folded my arms across my chest. "That's ridiculous. I'm not wild. I'm just determined. Why is it that men think a lady is wild if they have focus and a strong will?"

He shrugged and shook his head. "I cannot help you there."

"I'll tell you. It's because they can't control women. This frightens men."

The attentive listener raised his eyebrows and smiled. "I believe you are on an enlightened path, Princess Wren."

"Yes." I grabbed the door and began pulling it closed. "I will dress now," I told him. He moved away from the door to stand in the hall outside.

Having shut the door, I walked back to the bed and selected the green dress with the flowers. Standing by the fire blazing next to the bed, I quickly pulled off my sweat-stained clothes. I ran my hand across my shoulder where the sword had scratched my skin. It wasn't a deep scratch, but made my shoulder a little tender. I felt grateful that this was the only injury I had acquired during the sword fight.

I slid into the beautiful dress that belonged to the king's daughter. A pair of pale pink slippers lay on the floor next to the bed. I walked across the cold marble floor and slipped them on. They fit as if they had been made for me. King Olerion's daughter must be about my size, I thought, because everything fit as if it were mine.

I surveyed myself in the full-length mirror. I liked how the lime-green dress made my eyes a brighter blue. "The princess has good taste," I thought.

Opening the door, I motioned to the man. "I am ready."

He gently clasped my upper arm in his hand and led me down the stairs and further down another hall to a door that opened to the back of the castle. The warm evening rushed through the opening as soon as he unlocked the door. I deeply inhaled the overpowering scent of lilac.

We walked down a stone walkway lined with torches to a courtyard outlined with well-manicured shrubs shaped into perfect circles. In the middle of the courtyard was a square white marble planter containing purple and black flowers. The flowers were arranged in such a way as to make the head of a deer and a bear, the symbols found in the king's crest. I was amazed by the artistry. The stone pathway ran along the sides of the planter and beside the circular shrubs. In the center of the planter was a three-tiered fountain. Behind the circular shrubs were lilac bushes the size of trees. This was the reason for the heavily perfumed air.

I walked beside the planter by the light of a full moon. Upon reaching the lilac bushes, I turned right and continued to walk down the path that ran alongside the bushes. I took a deep breath, almost tasting the perfumed air. That's when I heard a long sigh coming from the other side of the shrubs. I stopped and looked at the guard. He shook his head, indicating he had no idea who made the noise.

I could see through the bushes in places. A shadowy figure sat beside one of them. The figure sighed again and then a woman's voice floated on the breeze.

"My life is so dull. When will I ever escape this boring life? I must get beyond these castle walls."

"It's the king's daughter, Princess Lorenda. We must leave now. You are not supposed to be anywhere near her."

"Wait!" I wanted to meet the person I could identify with so easily. I knew what it was to be bored and feel stuck in a life you didn't want.

"Princess Lorenda," I called out into the night.

"No, Princess!" my escort hissed.

"Yes? Who's there?"

"It's Princess Wren. I wanted to thank you for the use of your dresses."

The shadowy figure walked through the space between the bushes. I could now see her in the moonlight, dark red hair cascading over her shoulders. Her deep blue eyes seemed to sparkle in the glow of the moon.

"Pleased to meet you, Princess Wren." The fair maiden extended her hand and shook mine vigorously. I was surprised by her strength. She seemed so fragile that I expected a weak, timid handshake.

"I'm not supposed to talk to you. My father has forbidden it. Of course this is not the first time I have done something my father has forbidden."

I smiled. I liked the girl already. I thought she was courageous.

"The dress suits you."

I looked down at the green satin that covered my body. "It looks as if we're the same size."

"Yes," Princess Lorenda agreed. "We could be sisters."

"I always wanted a sister." I smiled once again. I wished that I had met Lorenda under different circumstances. I could tell we would have been great friends.

"Let's walk among the lilac bushes."

I followed Lorenda through the gap in the bushes. The escort sighed and followed. I walked through a space in the bushes into a large lawn surrounded on every side by more lilacs. Lorenda began to skip across the lawn, grabbing my hand to get me to follow. She laughed, which made me giggle. We could hear the escort's noisy paces after us, his breastplate rattling as he ran.

"Princess Wren, you must stop!"

Lorenda let go of my hand and began to spin in circles. I followed, the heavy scent of lilac making me feel as if I'd had too much wine. I threw my head back and stared at the moon as I spun. The movement of my body made the glowing orb look like it had a long white tail. I had never felt quite this free, like anything was possible at this moment.

"That will be enough, Princess Wren!" He grabbed my arm and began walking me back across the lawn.

"Travin, you are such a bore!" Lorenda said as she stopped spinning and followed me across the lawn. "Can't you let us have a little fun?"

"Your father will have my head if he catches you two together."

"So dramatic, Travin."

I couldn't help but smile as my escort, Travin, pulled me through the lilac bushes.

"We shall meet again, Wren. We are friends now and that will not change no matter what my father says."

I knew it was true. We were friends and we would meet again.

9

Surprisingly, I slept extremely well. What I had anticipated to be a long night mulling over what I would have to do the following day, was of no concern. I fell asleep as soon as my head hit the pillow. My energy was drained from all the sword fighting I had done that day.

Sunlight streamed in through my bedroom window and a gentle breeze caught the curtains, causing them to billow into the room. I went to the window to inhale the scent of lilac one last time before I would be forced to leave and face the terror of trying to slay a dragon.

"Princess Wren!" Lorenda waved at me from below my window. "My father is still asleep. Meet me in the garden for breakfast."

I grabbed a dress. This time, it was the royal purple one with two swans, their necks intertwined, embroidered on the bodice. Running my hands through my hair, I ran to the door and opened it.

There stood Travin, his eyes bloodshot, staring down at me.

88

"Travin, would you please escort me to the garden?"

"The king will be summoning you soon and have you escorted beyond the castle walls. Look! You are hardly dressed to be your way to the home of Sinder!"

"Who is Sinder?"

"Why, the dragon of course. Have you already forgotten that you've agreed to slay the dragon in exchange for your freedom?"

"How could I forget something like that? I was hoping to walk in the garden one last time in order to calm my rattled nerves."

"As you wish. Princess?" Gallantly, the courtier extended his arm to me and I took hold of it, allowing him to lead me down the stairs and out the back entrance.

Princess Lorenda sat on one of the walls of the square planter that held the purple and black flowers, eating a plum. Her long red hair floated on the breeze and her bright blue eyes danced with merry mischief as she grinned at me. "Good morning, Princess Wren! I must say, that dress, too, is a vision. You look marvelous in my clothes!"

"Thank you."

"How did you sleep?"

"Very well. I didn't realize how tired I was from all that fighting yesterday."

"I can only imagine." Lorenda handed me a plum and patted a space on the wall, beckoning me to sit.

I kept forgetting that I was probably going to die later in the day. It was hard to imagine that I would be face-to-face with a dragon in a short while. The sun and cool breeze scented with lilac, the juicy sweetness of the plum in my mouth, and the wonderful company of Lorenda made the day seem like one to celebrate and not to dread.

"Princess Wren, who taught you to sword fight? Your father?"

"Oh, definitely not him! He doesn't even acknowledge that I exist. He's never home and if he does happen to stop by for a short while, he never comes near me."

"I wish my father was that way."

"No, you don't." I shook my head. "At least your father cares about you."

"Yes. Far too much. I can't breathe from all his caring. What about your mother?"

"She disappeared when I was twelve and no one has ever seen her since."

Lorenda stopped eating her plum and stared at me. "That's awful!"

"Yes." I took a large bite of my plum, not wanting to talk about my mother. Mentioning her always made me feel sick inside. I still blamed myself for my mother's disappearance. If I had remembered my mother's birthday, perhaps she would still be here. She would not have gone to the garden that day and she wouldn't have disappeared.

"My mother is dead," Lorenda said in a matter-of-fact manner. "She died when I was twelve, killed by the horrible dragon my father has ordered you to put to death. That's one reason he won't allow me to leave these castle walls without a bodyguard."

"I'm so sorry." I wasn't sure what to say.

"It's behind me now." I lied. "That was six years ago."

"So, you're eighteen years old?"

"Yes."

"So am I!" I couldn't believe the similarities between the two of us.

"Oh no!" Lorenda stared at the space just over my shoulder. Turning my head in the direction of her stare, my stomach dropped. King Olerion was almost running down the path leading to the garden where we sat eating plums. His face was red and looked pinched.

"Lorenda, I strictly forbade you to be around Princess Wren! And you, Travin," he yelled, looking to his right at the man standing a short distance from the planter. "I will deal with you later. I told you to make certain Princess Wren stayed in her chambers until I summoned her for her task."

"Oh, father, don't blame Travin! Princess Wren came out for a breath of fresh air and I happened to be here."

The king shook his head. "It matters not how the two of you happened to be out here at the same time. The point is, both you and Travin have disobeyed me."

"I will return to my room." I stood, holding out my arm for Travin to take hold of it.

"Return to your room at once! I will summon you shortly. The mission you have agreed to carry out in place of serving time in my dungeon is upon you. Or have you forgotten why you're here, Princess Wren?"

"No, my lord. I am ready to fulfill my vow."

"And that you shall! Travin, escort the princess back to her room where I told you to keep her in the first place."

I looked over at Travin as we walked. His face was pale and he trembled.

"I am sorry, Travin."

He sniffed and walked silently. Perhaps he was too frightened and upset to utter his accusations against me.

"You must stop disobeying me, Lorenda." I could hear the king continue to yell as Travin and I made our way into the castle and up to my room.

I sat on the edge of the bed, staring out the window, listening to the king scold his daughter.

"Look at me, Lorenda!" The king sounded exasperated. I almost felt bad for him. "I'm trying to keep you safe!"

"You're trying to make me a prisoner," Lorenda yelled. "I've had enough of your so-called protection. Mom is dead and she's never coming back. I'm not my mother."

I rose from the bed to see what was happening in the garden below.

The king threw his hands in the air and stormed away from Lorenda. He entered the castle, leaving her sitting by herself with her half-eaten plum.

Lorenda looked up and smiled at me. I waved and she waved back. Hearing Travin at the bedroom door, I quickly backed away from the window.

"The king will see you now, Princess Wren."

I nodded and walked out of the room, my arm in Travin's warm hand once again.

The king was seated in the same room at the table in front of the fire.

"Have a seat, Princess," he said, gesturing toward the chair that sat directly opposite him at the table.

I took a seat and stared down at my folded hands.

"You are not to speak to my daughter ever again. If you do, you will be imprisoned for much longer than you would have been for deceiving me about the sword fighting contest."

"Yes, my lord." I was not about to oppose him. I had already pushed the king's limits by meeting his daughter in the garden. I did not wish to cause the king any more pain, especially since it would not bode well for me.

"You will be given an escort to the path that leads to the dragon's lair. It is a two-day journey from here. Once you get to the path you will be able to reach the dragon in half a day's time. I will give you six days from now to fulfill your vow. If you have not returned in six days, my men will hunt you down, and you will serve out your sentence in the castle dungeon."

I felt my eyes grow moist and I clenched my teeth, holding my breath, willing myself not to cry. If only I had listened to Aleric and stayed within the safety of my father's castle. It was too late to wish I had made a different decision. My fate was sealed.

"You will leave at mid-morning. I have asked the cook to prepare a hearty breakfast for you. You will dine here in this room where I can keep watch over you. I have other business to attend to, but there will be two guards standing outside this door. So, don't consider wandering the halls or asking them to take you to my daughter. They have strict orders and understand that they will be imprisoned if they disobey these orders."

I nodded and bowed my head.

"Don't look so forlorn, Princess Wren. I'm certain you will have victory. You were able to defeat the best sword fighters from the surrounding kingdoms. You should be able to deal with one little dragon." The king smiled then, a somewhat malicious smile. He was obviously angry with me for spending time with his daughter. If only I could disappear.

"Your morning meal will be brought in shortly. I will leave you to your thoughts." The king rose from his chair and walked through the doorway, leaving me to gaze at the fire. As soon as he was out of sight, tears ran down my cheeks. I buried my head in my arms and sobbed.

After crying for what seemed like an eternity, I wiped my face and looked at the table in front of me. In the middle was a large book with an ornate cover. It was a copy of the Holy Bible, much like the one in my room at home. Looking at it made me miss my father's castle. That life seemed so far from me now. I couldn't believe it, but I actually longed to be within the confines of my father's castle walls where I was free to roam, eating whatever and whenever I wished. My stomach growled.

Opening the heavy leather book with both hands, I turned to a detailed fanciful font, letters that spelled the name of a group of Roman people, "Ephesians." It appeared to be a letter to them. I read from the long letter to segment six, which talked about the armor of their God. Each piece of armor seemed to symbolize a spiritual principle. I wondered if the followers of the Christ used this sort of armor when they had to do battle. I flipped the pages forward, hoping to find more information about Jesus. My eyes fell on chapter thirteen of the book entitled Hebrews. These were words Jesus had supposedly spoken. "I will never leave you or forsake you."

I stared at the passage. How wonderful it would be to have someone in my life that would never leave me or forsake me! How wonderful it would be to have invisible armor, like the kind I had just read about, that would protect me! I wondered if it could be true. How I wanted it to be true. Footsteps sounded on the threshold of the room and a servant entered carrying a tray of food. I quickly closed the Bible, fearing I would be in trouble for tampering with the king's property.

The servant set the tray of food on the table in front of me and began to walk back out of the room without saying a word.

"Thank you," I called after him. The curly haired man turned around and nodded, his face like a stone. I was struck by how good looking he was. His dark brown eyes matched the color of his hair and his face was a shade of creamy olive. I wondered if the king purposely collected beautiful people to serve him. His guard, Travin, was also extremely good-looking. The king obviously was impressed with beauty.

I could smell the warm bread, which was wrapped in a white cloth on the tray. There was an assortment of fruits and cheeses along with it. Eggs sat in tiny silver cups. Two bowls, one with clotted cream and the other with raspberry preserves, sat next to the bread. My mouth watered.

I took the cloth off the bread, cut a piece, spread it with the clotted cream and raspberry preserves and took a large bite. Flavors exploded across my tongue, and due to the creamy, tart, sweetness that filled my mouth, I almost forgot that I would be facing a dragon in less than three days. I sliced another piece and then moved on to a second and third, nibbling on the eggs and fruit in between. I hadn't eaten like this in a long time; not since the day Aleric had left. Something was shifting inside me. I was discovering a world outside of my father's castle, a world I longed to explore and of which I longed to be a part. It made my soul hunger for more. The hunger permeated my body, awakening an appetite that had been stagnant since Aleric had left.

I bit into another juicy plum and stared at the large book sitting on the table. I wished I could talk to someone about the armor of God. Was it real? Was it really true that the Christ would never leave or forsake me if I believed in Him? I had read about Jesus' death and resurrection, and wondered if all these things had really happened long ago before I was born. I wished they were true. If so, I would be a Christ follower for the rest of my life. How could I not be totally committed to someone who would never leave? He sounded wonderful and I wished I could talk to him.

I sat quietly listening for footsteps in the doorway. I couldn't hear anyone approaching.

Swallowing another bite of plum, I looked at the space above my head and prayed. "Jesus the Christ, if you can become real to me in my world, show yourself to me somehow so I can come under your protection. I'd really like to believe the power of your words exist in my time. So, if you are listening, might you show me how to put on this armor of God? Oh, help me defeat this terrible dragon!"

As soon as I finished the prayer, I heard a knock at the door. "Come in."

"Princess Wren," Travin said, opening the door. "It's time for us to take our leave."

"I am ready, Travin."

"I will not be accompanying you." Travin looked full of fear. "The king has ordered me to stay within the boundaries of the castle until your mission is completed."

Aghast at my own constraint to loneliness, I admitted, "I'm truly sorry. It's my fault. My actions have caused problems between you and your king."

Travin shook his head. "If it wasn't you, it would have been something or someone else. The king is extreme when it comes to his daughter. He will not tolerate even the hint of something that could draw his daughter from his protective care. Things were very grave when his wife was killed by the dragon. The king has never been the same since that time. He was once lighthearted and joyful. Now he is a man full of fear. His fear causes him to be harsh."

I thought of my own father. I wondered if this was true of him as well. Perhaps it was a fear of losing me the way he lost my mother that caused him to abandon me. The thought caused the usual ache I felt when pondering why my father paid no attention to me seem less poignant.

"Follow me, Princess Wren. I will take you to your horse. Your sword, cloak, and clothes have been packed into a saddle bag and are with your horse. There is no need to return to the room in which you slept. Princess Lorenda said you may keep the dress. She said she has more dresses than she could ever need."

I followed Travin down the hall, through the enormous receiving room at the front of the castle where I had waited to speak to the king, and through the front door. The sun shone bright and warm outside and I smiled in spite of my circumstances. I couldn't help but feel joyful when the warmth of the summer sun permeated deep into my bones.

Travin walked to a stable just a stone's throw away from the castle, where my horse stood strong and sturdy in the third stall from the door. He was shiny from a thorough brushing earlier that morning and he whinnied when he saw me approach.

"Flynn," I whispered, as I caressed the horse's face. I was relieved to be reunited with my horse. He was one step closer to my freedom.

"You will meet your escort outside the stables." Travin smiled at me. He seemed genuinely pleased to see my joy at being with my horse.

I gave a gentle tug on the reins and the horse followed me out of the stable. Travin walked ahead of me into the bright light of the day outside. I was tempted to hop on my horse and gallop past Travin, a fantasy of escape. Instead, I followed him outside and waited beside my horse. Travin walked a few yards to where another rider stood. I couldn't tell what the escort looked like. He wore a cloak with a hood which covered his face.

I frowned, wondering why the man wore a cloak in this heat. Travin walked back to me and instructed me to follow the man out of the gate.

"Why does he wear a cloak?"

"He's very sensitive to sun."

My eyebrows went up but I said nothing. I used the same excuse in the past when I wanted to escape my father's castle. It made me wonder who was under that cloak.

"Just follow the escort, Princess Wren. You will reach your destination in two days' time."

"Thank you, Travin, for being so kind to me."

Travin nodded. "You're a very brave lady and I respect that. Just be sure you defeat that dragon."

I nodded this time. "I will do it or die trying." I tried to smile but all that came to the surface were tears.

Travin took my hand and held it in both of his. "Don't cry, Princess Wren. I know the All-knowing One will protect and guide you. He was with you when you entered the contest and He will be with you when you face this dragon."

I wiped my hand across my wet cheeks and smiled. "I will trust what you say. I don't know this all-knowing one but if it is the one who gives the spiritual armor spoken of in the Bible, he will be able to carry me through this."

"That's the spirit!" Travin looked back at the cloaked escort and called him forward with a flick of the wrist.

I stepped into the stirrup and swung my leg over Flynn, revealing the pants I wore underneath the dress Lorenda had given me. I was not about to ride sidesaddle now that I knew what it was like to ride in pants.

The escort road ahead of me, summoning me to follow by waving his hand. I broke into a trot, following the cloaked figure in front of me.

"Goodbye, Travin." I waved and smiled down at him.

"Goodbye, Princess. Godspeed to you."

I directed my eyes forward and watched as my escort moved slowly down the street that cut through the little town that surrounded the castle. I followed, wondering how my guide could endure the dark heavy cloak in the heat of the bright morning sun.

We rode slowly to the castle gate. The guard at the gate opened it without question, yawning as I rode past him. I reasoned that he must know the escort fairly well. I expected there to be some sort of hassle like that with the guard at my father's castle gate, but things were different here. There was no conversation between the two of us until we reached the forest. That's when the guide took off his cloak revealing long, shiny red hair.

10 |

"Lorenda!" I couldn't believe what I was seeing. I rode up beside her and grinned. "How did you get past Travin? I saw him speaking to you."

"He was speaking to one of the castle guards who agreed, after I persuaded him with a few gold coins, to help me escape. He agreed to wear a cloak and as soon as Travin went back to talk to you, he left, and I climbed on the horse he was riding."

"That was risky. Travin could have seen you."

Lorenda's blue eyes sparkled in the sun cascading through the forest trees. "I couldn't let you do this on your own. You need a friend to help you face this beast, not a stranger who doesn't care."

I wanted to hug her. I had never had anyone risk so much on my behalf. I thought of King Olerion and frowned. "What about your father? He'll be looking for you!"

"No. He won't. He's banished me to my room for seven days. He's done this in the past and he won't speak to me until my sentence is up."

I considered this. "Won't the castle servants report that you are missing?"

Lorenda shook her head, her long crimson curls moving side to side. Raising her left hand, she rubbed her fingers together and exclaimed, "Everyone can be bought for a price. I paid the cook and some of the other servants to keep their mouths shut."

"You are very brave, Lorenda. It means a lot to me that you would go to such lengths to accompany me."

"It is my pleasure, Wren. I haven't had a friend for a very long time. Father chases them all away, feeling they will corrupt me. He doesn't realize that I'm the one doing the corrupting." She laughed at this.

I laughed along with her, smiling at the thought that Lorenda had called me a friend. I had never had another woman as a friend. I was friends with the cook at my father's castle but that wasn't the same. She was more like a mother figure to me than a friend. In spite of my dire circumstances, I was glad I had entered the sword fighting contest. If I hadn't, I probably would have never met Lorenda.

"There shouldn't be a problem with anyone discovering us. Most of the people in my father's kingdom avoid this part of the woods because of where it leads. No one wants to go near the dragon."

I shivered in spite of the warmth. I tried to imagine God's armor protecting me when I faced the beast, but I had trouble seeing myself wearing the armor. I wasn't even sure if God was with me.

I was so deep in thought about God that I didn't notice when the woods became dark and dense, the trees growing so close together that they nearly blocked out the sunlight. It was difficult to see the path in front of me.

"What do you think about God, Lorenda?" I wanted something to distract me from this terrible darkness so I figured I would talk to her about this mysterious God that occupied my mind.

Lorenda had been quiet for a long while and I worried she regretted coming along with me on this journey. "What do you mean, Wren?"

"I mean do you believe He exists?"

"Of course. How else would we be able to breathe and have life? It's only because of Him that we are alive."

"How do you know this? You seem so certain."

"I just know. I've done some tests to prove it."

I accidentally nudged the back of Lorenda's horse with my horse. "Oh! Sorry. I wasn't paying attention."

"Don't be concerned, Wren. We are friends, remember. Let's stop and make a fire so we can eat and find rest."

I realized I had never slept in the woods. I had no idea how to make a fire. I was suddenly very afraid.

We came to a small clearing and Lorenda slid off of her horse, tying it to a tree. I followed, tying Flynn to a tree next to Lorenda's horse. I could see the sky in the clearing turning a deep blue as evening swiftly approached. An owl hooted in the distance. There was little sound except for the cool breeze in the trees overhead.

Lorenda began gathering sticks and pieces of fallen branches from the trees. I followed suit, acting as if I knew what I was doing. I was amazed by Lorenda, who seemed perfectly at ease about spending the night in the woods.

"How do you know all of this?" I was overcome with curiosity about this girl. Travin had characterized her as shallow and weak but she was anything but this description.

"Know what?" she asked, dumping larger branches in a pile beside the smaller sticks she had gathered.

"How do you know how to make a fire and set up a camp for the night in the woods? It's as if you've done this before."

She looked at me and smiled. "I have done this before. My mother and I used to camp together in the woods all the time. My mother was a very different sort of queen. She could ride a horse as well as any man and taught me how to build a fire and how to survive on what the forest has to offer. She was wonderful."

I could hear a quiver in Lorenda's voice. It was obvious that she missed her mother deeply. I wondered what that would be like, to have a mother who meant so much. I loved my mother, but never felt close to her the way Lorenda did to hers.

Lorenda laid more branches and sticks on top of the piles at the center of the clearing. "My mother and I camped in this very spot many times. We would come to this part of the woods often. She loved the density of the trees and felt like she could hide from the rest of the world in this place. She never wanted to be queen. She just wanted to be like everyone else."

I added more branches to the pile and gently touched Lorenda's shoulder. "I'm sorry she's no longer here."

She nodded and grabbed an armload of smaller branches from the pile. She stacked them on the ground, crisscrossing them to allow air to move beneath the branches. She pulled up a clump of dry grass from the forest floor nearby and placed the grass in the middle of the sticks. Walking over to her horse, she retrieved what looked like two stones from her saddlebag and carried them back to the pile of sticks.

I watched in fascination as Lorenda struck the rocks together creating sparks. Suddenly, one of the sparks caught hold of the grass and ignited. A tiny flame shot upward. Lorenda cupped her hands around the grass and blew on the flame. It grew bigger, igniting more blades of grass. The twigs and sticks beneath the grass caught fire and the tiny flame grew into more flames, bigger and stronger. In a matter of minutes, the flames consumed the twigs and small branches and a small fire began to burn.

She selected some bigger branches and, after breaking them in half, laid them across the fire. The fire blazed higher, brighter and thicker.

I stood beside the fire, enjoying the intense heat that coaxed my tired muscles to relax. We had been riding most of the day and I was still tired from all of the sword fighting that I had done the day before. I couldn't believe I'd only known Lorenda for a day. It seemed like we had been friends all my life.

She went back to her horse and pulled out some bread wrapped in a white cloth along with two blocks of cheese. She also carried a wineskin with wine and two wooden cups. She set the items on the ground, went back to her horse and retrieved a blanket from a second saddle bag and spread it out on the ground in front of the fire. "Sit, Princess Wren," she commanded.

I sat down on one side of the blanket while Lorenda sat on the other side. Taking a knife from the holder strapped to her side, she unwrapped the bread and cheese and cut slices of both for herself and me. Handing a slice of bread and cheese to me, she opened the wineskin and poured the red wine into the wooden cups. I took the cup she handed to me and raised it into the air to make a toast.

"Here's to new friends."

Lorenda smiled and tapped her cup against mine. "To new friends."

We drank the wine and I was about to eat the bread and cheese when Lorenda stopped me. "Wait. Before we eat, let us give thanks to the Heavenly Father for keeping us safe and giving us food to eat."

I frowned and then bowed my head, following Lorenda's lead.

"Heavenly Father, Who sees all, thank You for Your protection and provision. And thank You for Wren, my new friend. Please watch over us as we sleep under your starry sky. Thank You for being with us. In Christ's holy name, amen."

I lifted my head and looked at her. "Do you pray to Him every day?"

"Of course. I can't imagine not talking to Him. He's everything to me."

"I didn't know you could talk to Him so freely. I've always thought you had to be a priest or monk to talk to Him like that."

Lorenda shook her head and took a bite of bread. Swallowing her bite, she spoke again. "The Christ made it possible for us to talk to God. He took away the veil between us and our Maker by washing away the sin that stood between us. He made it possible for us to have a relationship with the Creator of the universe." Lorenda ate some cheese and took a sip of the wine in her wooden cup.

I chewed my bread slowly and tried to understand what she was saying. I wondered if the blood of Christ could wash away the sin of causing my mother to disappear. That's what I longed for above all else.

"You don't know Jesus?" Lorenda stared at me, her eyes searching.

"I've read about Him in the Bible but I've never heard anyone talk about Him the way you do. I didn't know He made it possible for us to talk to God. I don't really understand it."

"Ask Him to show you who He is and He will help you understand."

"What do I say?" I felt a nervous fluttering in my stomach. I was a little excited and afraid at the same time.

"Ask Him to help you believe in Him and receive Him into your life."

"If I do that, what will happen?"

"He will come into your heart. He will forgive you for your sins if you ask for His forgiveness. You will be able to have a relationship with God."

I took a sip of the wine. There was a hint of lilac in the flavor. I could feel the warmth of the wine spread across my face. I felt my entire body relax and wondered if God was there with us as Lorenda had prayed.

"You will also have eternal life if you believe that the Messiah was and is who He says He is and you confess your sin to Him. There's no one else like Him in this world."

I trembled at the thought of confessing my sins. I never admitted to another person my fault in my mother's disappearance.

"It's not difficult to talk to Him, Wren. He already knows what you're thinking and feeling so there's no point in hiding anything. It's wonderful to be loved like that."

"Where did you learn all of this?"

"My mother taught me to seek God when I was very young. She taught me to search his word when I had questions. Above all that, she helped me to see that the Heavenly Father loves me deeply. He loves every person."

I shook my head. "My own father doesn't really love me. How am I supposed to believe the Creator God loves me?"

"What other reason would He have offered up His only son for us if it wasn't because He loves us?"

I took another sip of wine and shrugged. "I don't know."

Lorenda finished eating the bread and cheese she had cut for herself and walked back to her horse to retrieve more blankets from her saddlebags. She asked me if I wanted any more food and then wrapped the bread and cheese in the white cloth, placing the food back in the bag.

"Here's a blanket for you, Wren. You can use the blanket you're sitting on as your bed. Bunch up some of the blanket at one end for a pillow. It works well."

She moved a few feet from where I sat and spread her blanket in front of the fire. Gathering the blanket at one end, she lay down her head and covered herself with the remainder of the blanket in her hand.

I did as Lorenda said. The warmth of the fire and the wine quickly caused my eyes to grow heavy, and I vaguely remembered Lorenda saying goodnight when I drifted off to sleep.

When I awoke, it was still dark, and a full moon shone like a giant pearl in the black oyster of the sky. The fire had died down to an ember and I shivered in the cool night air seeping in through the blanket.

"Wren!" Lorenda's voice whispered at me from the darkness of the woods.

"Lorenda?" I looked over where she had been laying but couldn't tell if she was under the blanket piled on the ground. I couldn't see her fine, curly head, so I presumed she had gotten up.

I rose to my feet, the blanket that had been covering me draped over my shoulders and nightshirt.

"Wren," came the whisper again from the shadows of the woods that surrounded the clearing. I could see her dress shining in the light of the full moon but couldn't see her face as it was concealed in the darkness of the forest.

"Come, Wren." The dress disappeared into the woods and I followed, wondering why Lorenda wanted me to follow.

"Where are we going, Lorenda?" We had been walking for a while and I felt uneasy. I could hardly see my friend in front of me. The darkness was thick and heavy. The dense trees let in very little moonlight.

Lorenda did not answer but kept walking so I followed for a long while. Finally, I stopped, refusing to take another step. "Lorenda, I will not take another step unless you tell me where we are going."

She turned around to face me and started walking back toward me. My heart felt like it dropped into my stomach. This was not Lorenda! I had no idea who this woman was. The darkness made it difficult to see, but I could tell this wasn't my friend. The woman had a long, straight nose and prominent chin unlike Lorenda, whose nose was small and delicate and whose chin was rounded and small like the rest of her face.

I touched my side, expecting to find my sword there and then remembered I left the weapon back at the campsite. "Who are you?" I asked the stranger, filled with terror over being led astray by someone pretending to be Lorenda.

A small shaft of moonlight lit up a tree near the woman. The shadowy figure moved into the light and I could now see her eyes. They were dark, almost black, much different from Lorenda's. Her skin was pale as the moon and her red hair hung in waves about her face. She had an otherworldly appearance as if she was something from the spirit world.

"Who are you?" I whispered, afraid to hear the answer to the question. Perhaps the woman was sent from King

Olerion to kill me for luring his beloved daughter away from the protection of his castle. She didn't look like a killer. She was actually quite beautiful, which made her even more terrifying.

"Who I am does not matter, child." the woman spoke slowly, her voice a raspy whisper, very different than the voice she had used to summon me. That was Lorenda's voice. The woman had been able to imitate the voice of the king's daughter perfectly. Or, maybe that was my dream talking.

"I am here as a warning. You are on your way to slay the dragon. If you are successful, you will never find true love. You will be cursed for all your days, living as a lonely spinster."

"What!?" I was bewildered. "Who sent you? How did you know I was sent to slay the dragon? Are you here to trick me?"

"If you do not heed my warning, you will be sorry. Mark my words." The woman walked out of the shaft of moonlight and back into the darkness of the forest. I stared after her but couldn't see anything in the darkness. The woman was gone, vanished from sight.

I walked into the forest a little farther, searching for the woman. I didn't really want to find her but wasn't sure how to get back to the camp.

Fear gripped me as I tried to discern which way to go. I had to get back to the place where the shaft of moonlight sliced through an opening in the trees, the place where the woman had stood before she disappeared into the woods. I turned this way and that, growing more confused every second. Everything looked the same no matter which direction I went. I started running, hoping I would see something that looked familiar. Nothing.

Tree branches grabbed at my arms and legs, causing small red scratches to rise to the surface of my skin. I kept running in spite of the pain as one branch after another clawed at my body.

Thud! I didn't see the large tree root protruding from the ground in front of me. I fell to the ground, tripping over the root. My head collided with another tree trunk and everything went black.

11 |

"**W**ren! Wren! Wake up!"

Something wet and cold came splashing down. I sat up, coughing and sputtering, wiping the icy cold water from my face. I opened my eyes to see Lorenda just inches away.

I screamed and shoved her away, scrambling to my feet. "Who are you?" I asked with my voice shaking.

"It's me. It's Lorenda!" She started to walk toward me, and I yelled once again.

"Stay back! How do I know you're Lorenda?!"

"What's going on?" Lorenda seemed as confused as I felt.

I looked down at my arms covered in tiny scratches. Looking back at Lorenda I accused, "You led me into the woods last night."

"When?"

"The fire had died down to embers and the moon shone bright and full. You called to me from the woods."

"Wren, I did not go into the woods last night." She defended herself in her confusion. "You were asleep when I awoke this morning so I left you alone while I went and gathered berries in the woods. When I came back, you were still asleep. I tried to wake you because we need to get moving so that we reach the trail to the dragon's home before nightfall. You would not stir. No matter how loudly I yelled, you would not awaken. That's why I poured water on your face. I didn't know what else to do."

I buried my face in my hands and started to cry. I could feel a large knot on one side of my forehead where I had run into a tree the night before. "I don't know what is going on."

Lorenda walked over to me and put her arms around me. "Tell me what happened."

"I don't know. I awoke last night and you were calling to me from the edge of the woods. I followed you deep into the woods. I did not realize I was following a total stranger until you turned around and stood in the shaft of moonlight shooting through the trees."

"What do you mean you were following a stranger?" She let go of me and put her hands over mine, pulling my hands away from my face.

I stared at Lorenda, my eyes now red and puffy. "The person I followed had long red hair like yours, but when she turned around, she didn't look like you. Her eyes were dark and foreboding and her skin was as pale as the moon." I shook all over thinking about the terror I felt the night before when I found myself alone in the woods.

"You were under an enchantment, Wren."

"What?" A deeply furrowed frown fixed itself upon my forehead.

"A witch must have put a spell on you. There are witches who live deep in these woods."

I continued to shake and shiver, wishing once again that I was in the safety of my father's castle. Sure, I was being stifled to death, but at least things made sense and I knew how to handle life there. I couldn't understand why a witch would want to cast a spell on me and lead me deep into the woods only to warn me not to kill a dragon that would, more than likely, kill her.

"Did she say anything to you?"

I rubbed my forehead and winced as my fingers brushed the large bump on the right side.

"You're hurt!" Lorenda grabbed my hand and pulled it away from my forehead. She could see the swollen, purple bump. "Sit back down on the blanket, Wren."

She grabbed the cloth the bread had been wrapped in, soaked it with icy cold water from the water pouch at her side, and gently pressed the cool rag against my head. She sat beside me on the blanket and asked again, "Did she say anything to you?"

"Yes. She told me if I slay the dragon I will never find true love. I will live out my days as a lonely spinster."

Lorenda frowned. "How strange. You would think the witch would want you to kill the awful dragon. I don't know of anyone who doesn't wish the dragon was dead. The beast torments all human beings, consuming their young and destroying anything in its path. Surely this is some sort of vision sent forth by the dragon itself to frighten and disturb you. I've heard they can possess such powers."

I took the cool cloth from Lorenda and continued to press it against my head. "I can't do this Lorenda. I can't slay the dragon. Who am I fooling?"

"This is exactly what the dragon would have you believe. It must know that you are a serious threat."

"I have no idea how I'm supposed to slay something that is ten times bigger than me and breathes fire."

"I don't know, either. The same way you fought ten different swordsmen and defeated every one of them. If anyone can accomplish this task, it's you."

I shook my head. "Maybe I just got lucky, Lorenda." I stood and nearly fell back to the ground, the sudden movement making me dizzy.

"Sit down and rest for a while, Wren. You've hurt your head and you need to take it easy."

"Yet another reason I can't do this. I should just turn myself into your father and offer to serve my time in prison."

"No! You will do no such thing. You must quit telling yourself you can't do this. You'll die in my father's dungeon, if not physically, for certain spiritually. You must fight your fear and conquer it. We will pray, and the Heavenly Father will be with you."

"I don't know about that, Lorenda. You talk about God as if you know him personally. I don't feel the same way. I don't really know him."

Lorenda leaned back on her hands and looked out across the open glen. Sunlight reflected off the dew on the grass and trees, turning the scene into a dazzling picture. "You don't know Him because you need to know the Savior first. That is the only way to know the Father. You must go through the Savior. He is the door."

I glanced at Lorenda and let my eyes follow her gaze into the open field. "How can I know the savior? How do I go through him to know God?"

"You ask Him to take over your life and you confess your sin to Him."

I nodded, but still didn't truly understand. Everything was so confusing after what happened last night.

"What sin?" I wondered whether she also believed my mother had disappeared because of me.

Lorenda rose to her feet and extended a hand to me. "Come on, Wren. We need to be going so we can reach our next camping spot before nightfall."

I rose to my feet more slowly this time and didn't feel quite as dizzy. I was getting better.

Lorenda folded the blanket we had been sitting on and walked over to where the horses stood, still tied to a tree.

She stuffed the blanket into one of the saddlebags and opened the other, retrieving two apples.

I stood next to my horse, brushing Flynn's coat. Lorenda handed me an apple and then mounted her horse. I followed suit and soon we were off, munching the apples as we rode through the forest.

I couldn't get Lorenda's words out of my mind. "You ask Him to take over your life and you confess your sin to Him." I wondered if I had to say all of that out loud. Or, could I think it and it would still count? I didn't want to ask Lorenda, fearing she would think I was even more cowardly than I already appeared to be. I wasn't ready to disclose my many faults to her.

I decided to privately give it a try. Within the confines of my mind, I prayed, "Heavenly Father, if you see me and care even a little, please hear my prayer. Please tell Jesus, the Savior, that I want Him to take over my life. I believe in Him and who he claimed to be. I want to belong to Him the way Lorenda belongs to Him. I've sinned, oh, God. I caused my mother to disappear. Perhaps if I had been a good daughter, my mother would still be here. Perhaps she would love me. Please forgive me for this sin and forgive me for lying to King Olerion. From me, Wren. Amen."

I could feel the warm sun on my face as I rode, and something felt different inside. I was lighter. I felt free. It made me smile. Maybe I was truly forgiven. Maybe God would be close to me now like he was with Lorenda.

I looked around and noticed that the forest had changed. The trees weren't as close together and giant rocks sprung up from the ground here and there. The dirt had a reddish hue, unlike anything I had ever seen. We came to a stream that tumbled and bubbled over smooth and jagged rocks.

"Let's water the horses by this stream and refresh ourselves with a noonday meal." Lorenda stopped her horse in front of the stream and dismounted. I followed her lead, walking my horse over to the stream.

Lorenda sat on a large, flat rock. I sat down beside her. I took the slice of bread and cheese Lorenda offered and began to eat.

"You seem to be in better spirits than you were this morning."

I nodded. "I am feeling better. Last night's nightmare seems like a long time ago."

"Good. How is your head?"

I had forgotten about my injury. I reached up to touch the knot on my forehead and winced a little as my fingers found the tender spot. "It's still sore, but better."

Lorenda ate in silence. I had to ask her what I had been wondering about earlier.

"Lorenda, do you think the Heavenly Father can hear your thoughts?"

Lorenda smiled. "The Heavenly Father knows all. He knows your every thought. Sometimes I wish He didn't." She laughed and took another bite of bread.

I thought about that. Maybe He had heard my confession and He forgave me and that was why I felt so much lighter. The thought was almost too much to comprehend. I wanted to rise to my feet and dance. "I think He forgave me and now I've asked Jesus to take charge of my life." The words were out before I could stop them.

"You talked to God and asked His son to forgive you and be Lord of your life?" Lorenda stared at me.

My face grew warm. It felt like such a private thing but I couldn't keep it inside. "Yes. I talked to Him in my head while we were riding."

Lorenda grabbed my free hand and squeezed. "That's wonderful, Wren! That means your new life has begun!"

I looked away, staring at my horse still drinking water from the stream. "I feel different; lighter and freer somehow.

I don't completely understand all of this. I just know I wanted Him to forgive me and lead me."

"That's what He wants from you, your whole life. He wants you to seek Him in everything."

I looked at Lorenda, who was smiling at me. I wanted her to focus on something else. I needed time to let all this sink in.

"We need to start riding again. Once we reach the trailhead to the dragon's cave, you'll have to finish the journey without me."

"What!?" I frowned now, glaring at Lorenda.

"I made a promise to my father that I would never set foot on that trail again. I can't break my promise. When I give my word, I keep it, for the most part."

"How will I know how to find the cave?" I couldn't believe Lorenda would come this far, only to abandon me at the very end of the journey.

"It's easy. The trail ends at the mouth of the cave. You won't have any trouble finding it. Don't worry, Wren. Remember, you won't be alone. God will be with you."

I was too angry to hear her. I thought it was completely unfair of her to expect me to be okay with this arrangement. Everything had changed now that I had discovered Lorenda's friendship. It felt like I was only strong because she lent me her confidence. My own confidence seemed to be leaking away. It was bad enough that I had to face a dragon. Now, I would be all alone doing it. I started to wish that Lorenda had never come with me.

I rose slowly to my feet and walked over to my horse. I climbed into the saddle and waited begrudgingly for Lorenda to lead the way. I didn't feel strong or wise. I felt like an idiot.

We rode in complete silence. I noticed the landscape changing more and more. The trail grew steeper and there were more rocks now than trees. We stopped at what looked to be the last grouping of trees on the side of the mountain. Lorenda tied her horse to one of the few surrounding trees and walked back down the trail, toward the forest, to gather firewood. I did as she did, gathering an armload of fallen twigs and branches, depositing them in a pile in the center of three rocks that formed a semicircle.

"We need to water the horses before lighting the fire." I untied Flynn and followed Lorenda further up the trail, around a bend that led to a waterfall cascading into a pool of clear water. The horses bent to drink.

"The trail that will take you to the dragon's cave is on the far side of the pool." Lorenda pointed to a footpath leading away from the waterfall. It went almost straight up the side of the mountain and looked to be quite treacherous.

I stared at the path and felt beads of sweat trickle down my face, wondering if this was the path that would lead to my death. I wished that I could just grab my horse and flee, finding my own way back to my father's castle. I would never leave the castle grounds again. All I wanted was to crawl beneath the covers of my own bed and awake to the smell of fresh bread baking in the oven. Home seemed so far away.

I was silent as I stood beside Lorenda, staring at the horses and then at the path I would take to the dragon's cave. The mountainside was covered in sharp, jagged rocks. A cold breeze, as cold as winter stone, blew down the mountainside. I shivered. Walking to where Flynn stood drinking water from the crystal-clear pool, I pulled my cloak from the saddle bag and wrapped myself in its warmth. I hadn't needed the cloak until now. The air here on the face of the mountain was much cooler than it was in the valley below.

Lorenda shivered as well. "It's always cold up here. That's why the dragon lives in this area. It prefers the cold."

"You seem to know a lot about the dragon." I wondered why Lorenda was so knowledgeable about this horrible beast.

"After my mother died, I wanted to know everything I could about the monstrous thing that had killed her. I planned on finding a way to kill it."

"Why didn't you?" I challenged. Lorenda had been telling me to be brave and trust God to be with me. If she was so sure of God, why hadn't she done the job herself?

"My father forbade me to step foot on that trail leading to the dragon's lair. He said in no uncertain terms that I was not to ever walk the trail again. He made me promise."

I nodded, still suspicious of Lorenda's reason, or more like her excuse, to abandon me. Seeing that Flynn had finished drinking, I grabbed his reins and led him to the trail, where I climbed into the saddle. Lorenda led her horse close to where I waited and mounted it, leading us back to camp.

Soon a fire blazed in the middle of the semicircle of rocks. I sat close, warming my hands near the flames. I still didn't utter a word to Lorenda, my anger simmering closely below the surface.

"I'm not abandoning you, Wren. I will be here at the camp when you return tomorrow evening."

"How do you know I will return?"

"Because you belong to Him, now, and the Heavenly Father will watch out for you." She looked at me sideways, then rose and hugged me for a long time.

"Perhaps my sin is too great. Maybe He can't forgive me for what I've done."

"The Heavenly Father can forgive anything."

My back stiffened. I felt more angered by her speaking with such confidence.

"You will see, Wren."

"What about the woman who told me I will never find true love if I slay the dragon?"

Lorenda was silent as she poked the fire, causing the red-hot embers to glow again. "I believe that was a witch and witches do not follow God's ways."

I sat back and leaned against a rock. I was too tired to think about any of this any longer. I yawned.

Lorenda walked over to her horse, pulling out the blankets for the evening. She handed two to me and then spread one out on the ground where she planned on sleeping for the night. I spread one of the blankets on the ground and was about to lie down and cover myself when Lorenda walked over to me and sat beside me on the blanket.

"I want to pray for you, Wren. You must rise early and begin walking to the trail to the dragon's cave at dawn. You will most likely reach the cave when the sun is directly overhead. Once you complete your task you must hurry back to our camp. You don't want to be on the path in the dark. It's treacherous and at some spots you need the light to guide you."

I sighed. I didn't know how I was going to do this. I fingered the sword that lay beside me on the ground and wondered if I even remembered how to fight. I felt so afraid. It was as if all of my training had been drained from my memory.

Lorenda held one of my hands with both of hers and bowed her head. "Dear Heavenly Father, you say in your holy book that wherever two are gathered in Your name, there You are in the midst of them. We welcome You here with us, oh, God. We ask You to make us aware of your mighty presence. We ask You to guide our thoughts and our words. Father God, my dear sister must face a great demon tomorrow. There is fear of the unknown inside her. She isn't sure how she's going to carry out this task, which seems so impossible."

I nodded, my eyes shut and my head bowed. I felt as if I was sitting on holy ground. No one had ever prayed over me like this.

"Oh Savior, You know how to get this done. You know how to slay this devil. We thank you for this. We thank You for equipping Wren to fight. We thank You for the armor you've already given us -- the helmet of salvation, the breastplate of righteousness, the shield of faith and the sword of the spirit. Clothe her in these things even as we speak, O mighty God. Bless her with a calm spirit, a good night's sleep and courage for the task ahead. We thank you for these things. Amen."

I opened my eyes and quickly wiped away the tears that ran down my cheeks. I knew at that moment that Lorenda really cared for me, that she wasn't abandoning me the way everyone else had in my life. She was a true friend.

"You will be fine, Lady Wren. Remember who you are." She hugged me again, her own cheeks shining with tears.

I smiled and suddenly felt at ease. Perhaps things really would be okay. Maybe I would truly live through this ordeal. I had a glimmer of hope, unlike the way I had been feeling the last couple of days.

The words the witch had spoken to me still bothered me. Why had she said those things to me?

"The witch does not seek the Heavenly Father, Wren." It was as if Lorenda could read my thoughts. "The witch thinks she knows the future, but she only knows the lies her dark magic tells her. Do not give her another thought."

Was it only a couple of days ago that I had felt such strength and determination that I had won a sword fighting contest before an arena of onlookers?

I nodded, staring at my hands folded in my lap. I tried to put the witch out of my mind, but kept hearing her words,

"If you slay the dragon, you will never find true love." This was all so confusing. Lorenda was so certain of the Heavenly Father and I was just getting to know Him. Who was I supposed to trust?

"We should get some sleep, Wren. You will have to get an early start if you're going to get back to camp before nightfall." Lorenda rose from my blanket and walked over to her blanket, covering herself with the second blanket when she laid down on the first one.

I laid down and pulled the other blanket around me. The ground was much harder on this mountainside and I had a difficult time finding a comfortable position. Rolling onto my side, I lay facing the fire. Its warmth soon lulled me into a drowsy state that quickly turned to sleep.

A dream soon followed. In the dream, I was wearing no clothes. I stood in the dark and a glowing, brilliant white light floated overhead. It moved through the air, entering my head and my throat, then coursing through my shoulders and chest as it made its way down my arms. The light continued to travel through my stomach, into my upper thighs and finally, to my calves and feet.

Filled with the light, I walked through the darkness into a sunlit beach with a dark, gray sky as the backdrop. My bare feet sank ever-so-slightly into the fine, white sand. I walked across the sand to a pair of two tables covered in shiny objects. A white cushioned seat sat between the two tables. The first table I approached held a set of garments; white silk pants, a white silk shirt and a silk jacket with diamond buttons that fastened on one side and flared out at the waist. A pair of sky blue boots lay on the table next to the jacket. I pulled on the pants and shirt and then tucked the shirt inside the pants. A belt covered in diamonds glistened in the sun on the table next to where the pants had lain. I pulled the belt through the loops on the white pants. It fit my waist perfectly. I slipped the jacket over the white silk shirt and buttoned the diamond buttons on the left side of the jacket.

Sitting down on the white cushioned seat that was positioned in between the tables, I grabbed the blue boots. I slipped them over each foot and fastened the diamonds that ran down the inside and outside of the boots to loops that held them closed. Soft, white fur covered the inside of the boots. I had never felt anything so warm on my feet in all my life. Across the top of the toe of the boots and spilling onto each side was a pattern of diamonds in the shape of a dove.

Looking down once more, I saw a breastplate. Diamonds made into a cross were in the center of the breastplate. I fastened the silver chain connected to the top of the breastplate around my neck. Then, I fastened the bottom chain around my waist, which held the breastplate snugly to my body.

Farther down the table, I found a shield encrusted in diamonds in the shape of a lion. Beside it was a sword like none other I had ever seen. Tiny diamonds were inlaid in the shaft of the sword. The handle was solid gold, with more diamonds embedded in the gold.

I held the shield in my left hand and the sword in my right. I turned away from the tables and looked out over the ocean waves that rolled into and out of the beach where I stood. I bent down on one knee and bowed my head. I began to pray.

"Jesus, you are the only Lord and King, and you are my Lord and King. Thank you for the belt of truth, the boots of the gospel of peace, the helmet of salvation, the breastplate of righteousness, the shield of faith and the sword of the spirit. I am your servant and I am here to do as you wish."

I felt a warm breeze blow across my body. I knew I was in the presence of God Almighty. I found myself holding my breath, hoping to hear whatever God might have to say to me. He spoke.

CHARMAYNE HAFEN

"You will know when the time is right to use the sword. You must learn a difficult lesson first and then the time will come."

I opened my eyes. I could see the ocean waves rolling over my boots and my knee that was bent to the ground. My clothes were getting wet and I felt cold. I shivered.

"Wren, wake up!" Lorenda stood over me, water dripping from the cloth that covered her thick, red hair.

I sat up. Cold raindrops were beginning to soak through the blanket that covered me. Rain poured from the sky. I ran with Lorenda to some nearby trees that provided meager shelter from the storm.

"I have an extra cloak. I want you to take it and wear it on your journey." Lorenda handed me a dry, dark blue cloak. I put it on and covered my head with the hood.

The darkness was turning a pale grey, as the morning was swiftly approaching. The sun was hidden behind a layer of thick, grey clouds. I wished more than ever that I was in my bed safely inside my father's castle.

"You need to go, Wren. It's time." Lorenda looked at me with a somber face. I nodded and ran to the blanket to retrieve my sword, which lay glistening under a sheet of raindrops.

Seeing the sword brought the dream of the beach and the armor to the forefront of my mind. I wondered if I'd actually heard the voice of God, or if that had been an illusion. What did it mean? "You will know when the time is right to use the sword. You must learn a very difficult lesson first and then the time will come."

Oh, how I wished I had time to tell Lorenda about the dream! I stared down at the sword in my hand and thought about the dream.

"Wren!"

I swung around to face Lorenda, who still stood under one of the trees. "How are you doing? Your mind seems to be far away. You must focus now!"

"I'm just thinking about what lies ahead."

"Oh, of course." She sighed deeply and then continued. "I am trusting that the Heavenly Father is with you and you will wear His armor."

I smiled. The dream was confirmation that I was not alone. My fears began to fade.

"I will ride with you to the trailhead and then bring your horse back to our camp. We will wait for your return. I will bring the horses back to the waterfall before the sun sets so that we can ride back to camp together. Hopefully, the sun will appear and dry out the ground and our blankets."

I climbed on Flynn as Lorenda made her way to her horse. We rode through the rain to the waterfall. At the waterfall, Lorenda and I dismounted.

She walked over to where I stood next to my horse, put her hands on my shoulders and looked me in the eye.

"Be brave and trust the Heavenly Father. He will deliver you."

I nodded, feeling a lump of tears swell in my throat. Lorenda hugged me. She took Flynn's reins and climbed back into her saddle.

"I will aim to be back close to twilight. Please pray for me," I asked.

I waved. Without looking back, I made my way around the pool to the trailhead that led to the dragon's cave.

12 |

The rain continued its gentle rhythm as I climbed up the trail. The path was steep and littered with rocks, which had grown slippery in the rain. I felt like I was climbing straight up the mountainside.

I crawled on my hands and knees for some time because, at one point, the trail grew so steep that I was afraid to remain upright. Scrambling across jagged rocks, I cried out time and time again as my knee or hand scraped against them.

Finally, I reached a level area of the path. I could feel the warm sun on my back. I climbed high enough to ascend through the low clouds that hung over the forest. From this vantage point, all that I could see below was a thick mass of clouds.

I sat down to rest for a moment and let the sun warm my cold, wet body. Looking at my dress, I could see blood stains midway down it. I lifted the dress, exposing the pants I wore underneath, and saw that I had torn two holes in the knees of the pants. Bright red blood oozed to the surface of both my knees.

"So much for God's armor," I said sarcastically, looking at the blood. My knees stung and I was thoroughly miserable. I dismissed the thought that felt more real than my new faith, not wanting to be negative at this crucial point in my journey. I had to keep a positive outlook if I was ever going to make it through what lay ahead.

The path before me was dry. I attempted to be thankful. The air was cool and a strong wind blew. I was physically dry in a short time. But, my soul felt as shattered and dried as a long-dead garden flower left standing unobserved. The path was covered with loose rocks and I was grateful that I was able to walk upright instead of crawling on my hands and knees. My knees stung and my hands were raw from crawling on the ground.

The sun rose higher in the sky. The trail continued to rise along the mountain, winding back and forth. A large rock protruded out onto the path, and I reached a corner I could not see around.

The wind blew. I could smell the dragon's cave before I even reached the entrance, which was on the other side of the large rock. The stench of rotting flesh assaulted my nose with a vengeance. My eyes stung and watered, and I gagged involuntarily. Drawing my cloak up over my nose, I took a few steps forward and stopped, peering around the rock.

About thirty paces from the rock was a dark opening to a cave. On the threshold of the cave were bones that held the decaying hides of cows. Strewn alongside the cows were smaller skeletons of dogs and chickens. A human skull lay on one side of the opening. I could feel my heart begin to race inside my chest. How would I ever find the courage to enter the cave? I felt like my feet had become one with the rock beside me and I couldn't move.

The air was completely silent, except for the howling wind and a low rumbling coming from the mouth of the cave. The noise grew more rhythmic as I walked toward the cave, trembling with each step. I put my hand on the sword that hung by my side to make certain it was still there. I recognized the rhythmic noise as I drew closer to the opening of the cave. It was the sound of heavy breathing, of something large breathing in and out.

I had the hopeful thought that perhaps the dragon would be asleep. I could sneak in and stab the beast in the heart before it had a chance to assault me. I continued to walk into the cave, not allowing myself to think for fear I would turn around and run down the mountain without confronting my nemesis.

The cave grew darker the farther I went. I could hear dry bones crunching beneath my feet. The stench of blood and rotting flesh became stronger. I wished I had a torch so that I could better see what was  around me, and not risk my life with my clumsiness.

My wish for a light source was fulfilled as I arrived at a larger space within the cave. The rock walls to my right and left fell away, and I entered a large cavern, where pieces of wood smoldered in one corner. I picked up a piece of wood that wasn't on fire. I lifted my dress and grabbed some of the fabric that was ripped at the knees of my pants. I ripped the fabric down to the bottom of the pant leg. Wrapping the fabric around the end of the piece of wood, I placed it on the burning wood and made a torch for myself.

I knew I had to move quickly. The wood would catch fire and I would have to discard the entire torch. I could see that the pile of wood had once been a wagon, or a cart, most likely pulled by an ox. Some of the wooden pieces were still intact, forming one of the wheels of the cart.

The cavern was immense. Water trickled down one of the walls, forming a deep pool on one side of the room. I searched frantically for the dragon but could not see anything that looked alive in the voluminous space. My boots crackled as I walked over more bones and broken pieces of wood, searching the black space for the beast.

Just when I thought that perhaps the rhythmic breathing sound I heard was the wind moving in and out of the cave, I felt something warm and wet splash on top of my head and my hand. Moving my hand into the light from the torch, I could see a large red spot covering the top of my hand. I moved my hand back and forth and the red liquid ran down the side. I brought my hand closer to my face. I finally realized that what I was looking at was blood!

I jerked my head upwards. Above me, suspended from the ceiling of the cave, was a large, bat-winged creature. I dropped the torch and covered my hand with my mouth to keep from screaming. The torch went out and I was surrounded by cold blackness. I pulled my sword from its sheath at my side and moved it back and forth in front of me.

The heavy, rhythmic breathing continued. I tried to stop my body from shaking as I stepped quietly toward the faint glow of one of the fires in the corner of the cold, damp expanse. I had to get another piece of wood, wrap it in cloth, and carefully make my way out of the cave without waking the dreaded monster.

I was nearly close enough to the fire to reach out and grab a piece of wood when suddenly, my sword slipped from my hand, clattering to the ground! I froze, holding my breath, hoping that the noise had gone unnoticed by the beast. Cold air suddenly crept across my shoulders and I heard a heavy thud behind me. I didn't have to turn around. I knew the dragon was right behind me.

Retrieving my sword from the dirt, I ran as hard and as fast as I could toward the dim light at the opening to the cave. Bones clattered and shattered beneath my pounding feet. My heart was pounding as fast as my feet. I fell twice, losing my footing on the debris that littered the cave.

Just as I reached the opening, I felt a moist, heavy claw on my back, knocking my face into the dirt. Two razor-sharp talons pinched my shoulder, picking me up off the ground and tossing me into the blinding daylight.

I landed on the ground on my stomach. I couldn't breathe for a moment, as the breath was knocked out of me. Scrambling to my feet, I caught my breath and turned around. In the daylight, I could see the dragon clearly. Its black talons were covered in thick, red blood from a recent kill. A small amount of blood formed a streak down the right side of its immense mouth.

The beast's eyes glowed a deep yellow-orange and had a black slit for a pupil in the center. Its eyes reminded me of a cat's eyes, except they were twenty times as large. Sharp, ebony horns, one on each side of the dragon's head, curled into the air.

The giant, ugly beast was so much worse than I had ever imagined. So much worse that I couldn't breathe. I could hear my heart pounding.

Shifting my gaze from the dragon's eyes to its mouth, I could see raw flesh caught in between razor sharp teeth. Above the upper line of teeth was a large snout, coal black with two glistening nostrils. Fire blazed in and out from the nostrils each time the dragon breathed.

Sweat poured from my skin and evaporated like steam.

Below the dragon's mouth was a snaking neck covered in shiny moss-colored scales. The neck connected to an enormous, muscular body. Two legs as large as tree trunks stood upright on the ground. One giant, sharp talon extended from the backside of each clawed foot.

Standing upright, the dragon was as tall as the wall that surrounded my father's castle. I felt like a mouse standing in front of the formidable creature. I shook violently. My shoulder ached from where the dragon's talons had pierced my flesh. Blood seeped into my dress at the shoulder.

"Why have you disturbed my slumber?" The voice, deep and heavy, shook the ground. I stared at the beast. Had it just spoken to me? I wasn't sure. The cat-like eyes stared back at me expectantly.

"Answer me, child!"

I saw the huge mouth move. Indeed, it was the dragon speaking to me. I was dumbstruck for a moment. I had no idea dragons could speak so that humans could understand. I hadn't even been sure they existed until now.

Fire shot from the dragon's nose, singeing the end of my dress.

"I said answer me!"

The vow I'd made to King Olerion, my last arrogant feeling of power and might, dissolved. I forgot that Lorenda was waiting confidently for me. I forgot that my new God was upholding me. I held my hands in front of my face and begged, "Please, don't burn me alive. Please! I came to make peace between you and the people of King Olerion's kingdom."

"And how do you propose to do that?"

I said a quick, silent prayer, not sure what to say next. "Heavenly Father, please help me know what to say."

"Well?" Again, fire shot forward from the dragon, narrowly missing my arm.

"What do you want from the people? What can they give you to keep you from wreaking havoc on their farms and homes?"

The dragon laughed a cold, heartless chuckle. "Isn't it obvious? What do you see lying around my home?"

I glanced at the bones that littered the entrance to the cave and the rotting carcass that sat to the right of the doorway. "Death. I see death." I looked back at the dragon, fear seeping into every corner of my being.

"Not death, child. This is my food. I want food. It's a good thing I just feasted or I would have had you as a meal rather than for curious entertainment."

I stood still, staring at the beast. I felt something rise within me. I knew it was disgust. I had felt this towards King Olerion when he had trapped me into this. Now, I forced myself to look away, thinking about what to say next.

"If you bring me a cow or two pigs or ten chickens every other day, I will no longer torment the townspeople. I will not steal their livestock or burn their homes or eat their horrific children. If you will swear to bring these to me, I will leave the people alone."

I wondered how I would get a cow or chickens or pigs. I thought, given the circumstances, I would figure that part out later on. I had to find a way to get out now.

"I will do as you say. However, I will not be able to get to your home every other day because it takes two days to get here from the nearest town."

The dragon wrapped its tail to one side and sat on its haunches. "This is true." It moved its talons up and down as if the movement helped it to concentrate.

"I have it! Stay where you are, child. I will be back in a moment. Don't forget that I can fly. If you try to run, I will hunt you down and eat you for dessert."

I nodded, gulping at the thought of being eaten alive. The dragon walked to the entrance of the cave and went inside. When it returned, the beast carried something green and shiny in its talons. As it came to stand in front of me once again, it tossed the object on the ground at my feet.

I reached down and picked it up. It was a gold necklace with a finely appointed pendant of jade attached.

"This necklace will allow me to see where you are at all times. You will not need to come to my lair. I will come to you every other day for the food you've promised. If you fail to provide me with what I require, I will kill you then and there."

I stared at the necklace. It was so delicate and pretty, yet it seemed like an iron ball and chain to me. It was a harness to keep me under control. I wanted to cry as I slipped the necklace over my head.

The dragon chuckled the same cold, heartless laugh. "You now belong to me, child. Don't ever forget it."

I looked at the ground, not wanting to see the satisfaction and glee in the dragon's face. I was ready to flee, but now I was weighed down by a magical ball and chain.

"I will give you three days from now to find my first meal. I have enough scraps to last me for another two days." The beast waved its talons around, indicating the rotting carcass that sat at the entrance to the cave.

"Be aware, child. I will be very hungry at that time and will be fiercely angry if there is no food."

"I un-un-understand," I acknowledged. "I wi-will have your food in three days." I was willing to say anything to get away from this horrible creature.

"Then be off. You have three days from this exact moment. When the sun is directly overhead on the third day, you had better have my meal."

The dragon blew another gust of fire from its nose and walked over to the entrance of the cave. Turning its head, it glared at me. "Don't ever awaken me again. If you do, I will surely kill you."

I nodded. The dragon disappeared into the cavern and I ran down the path leading away from the lair and back to the pool. I kept looking behind me, checking to see if the dragon was following. Once I realized I was not being followed, I stopped running and walked slowly down the path. My legs wobbled, and I fell down repeatedly.

The dragon's necklace hung heavily around my neck. I felt it against my chest as I walked, a constant reminder of my obligation to the beast. Still, I was amazed and relieved to be alive. This was a miracle.

"Heavenly Father, thank you," I said aloud. "Thank you for saving me. Thank you for clothing me in your armor." A warm breeze blew across my body, reminding me of the dream I'd had the night before. I knew God was with me.

I finally came to the place on the trail where I had to crawl on my hands and knees. Sitting, I slowly slid down the path until I reached a level area. Standing, I continued on, feeling lighter and lighter as I descended. I couldn't believe the worst part of my journey was over.

The clouds continued to cover the sun as I traveled lower. It had stopped raining and a warm breeze dried the rain-soaked ground. I reached the waterfall and pool just as the gray light began to fade.

Lorenda waited by the pool with her horse. She smiled a large, welcoming smile and slid from her horse. Running to me, she embraced me and kissed my cheek. "I knew you would make it!"

She stood, holding both of my hands. I looked at her and smiled weakly. The buoyant feeling I'd had while traveling down the mountainside was replaced by a feeling of heaviness and dread. The dragon's words echoed in my head, "You belong to me now." The jade pendant was a crushing weight against my chest.

"What's wrong, Wren?" Lorenda frowned. She stared at my downturned head and then noticed the blood smeared shoulder of my dress where the dragon had picked me up with its talons. "What happened up there?" She tightened her grip on my hands.

I started to cry. The reality of what had happened settled in and it was as if I was living the horror all over again.

"Sit down right here." Lorenda led me to a large rock that stood beside the pool. Its flat surface made a perfect place to sit. I sat on the rock and Lorenda sat down beside me.

Wiping the tears from my eyes, I tried to calm my trembling body. I wrapped my arms around my chest and rocked back and forth.

"Take your time, Wren."

After a few moments I stopped crying and shaking. "I didn't kill the dragon, Lorenda. I didn't even come close."

She nodded. Tears clouded her eyes. "What happened?"

"I made a deal with the beast in exchange for my life." I held up the necklace the dragon had given me.

"You see this necklace? With it, the dragon can track me wherever I am. In three days I have to provide the dragon with either a cow, two pigs, or ten chickens. If I don't, it will kill me. Afterward, I must provide the dragon with food every other day. It has promised to stop tormenting the people of your father's kingdom as long as I continue to bring it food."

Lorenda looked out over the pool of water, tears trickling down her face, deep in thought. "We must talk to my father about this."

"We can't! He will put me in his dungeon for certain. I did not fulfill the task he sent me to do."

"He will understand. He will know what to do."

"No!" I yelled, surprising both Lorenda and myself. "We cannot tell your father. You must keep this secret, Lorenda. I know you think he will understand, but look at how he acted when he discovered us talking together. He is a harsh, unrelenting man like my father. He will not understand."

Lorenda shook her head. "He is not like your father." Her eyes were dark and her voice was thick. She was obviously offended by what I had said.

"I'm sorry, Lorenda. You're right. He's not like my father. My father could care less if I exist and yours wants to know where you are every moment of the day."

Lorenda's face softened and a small smile crept across her mouth. "You're right about that."

"We just can't tell him. I have to find a way to keep the dragon fed without your father knowing it. If I don't, he will imprison me."

Lorenda looked at me. "We'll figure something out. Don't worry."

The light was fading quickly. It was time to get back to camp before night fell. We rode in silence. Once we reached the clearing we dismounted, tying our horses to a tree. On the ground by the fire pit were two piles of pine needles.

"I made two beds for us. This will keep us off the damp ground. We won't be able to make a fire because the wood is too wet."

Lorenda walked over to a rock in the clearing where our blankets lay. "The blankets are almost dry. This warm breeze has dried them." She grabbed the blankets and handed me two. My face remained strangely hot. I wondered if the dragon had burned it too.

Piling her two blankets on the pine needles, Lorenda went back to her horse to get food and wine. She brought back another small loaf of bread and a mound of yellow cheese. In the leather pouch was red wine. She set these things on the ground and spread the other blanket over the pine needles.

Both of us sat on our beds as day turned into night in what seemed like an instant. Lorenda handed me a cup of wine, tore off some bread and cheese and handed these to me as well.

My friend kept glancing over at me and smiling. "Why are you smiling?" I questioned.

"I am just so grateful you're here. I thought you would make it but I wasn't always certain, and that made me feel anxious."

"I, too, am grateful. I can't believe I'm here!"

I ate hungrily. I hadn't eaten all day. Now that my confrontation with the dragon was over, I realized just how hungry I was. The bread and cheese tasted like the most extraordinary meal I had ever eaten. The wine slid down my throat, smooth as silk. In no time I was drowsy, ready to fall asleep.

"I felt the Heavenly Father's presence when I was on the path to the dragon's lair."

"Tell me," Lorenda answered.

"I had just come up the steepest part of the trail. I was finally above the clouds and the sun shone down upon me. A warm breeze blew. I could sense that God was reminding me of the dream I had about wearing His armor. In my dream the sun was shining down on me and a warm breeze blew. I was at the ocean, or at least what I imagine when reading about it, kneeling before Him on the sand. He reminded me that He was with me."

Lorenda nodded. "He will do that when you are uncertain."

I took another bite of bread and cheese and washed it down with another sip of wine. Talking about my experience made me remember that God was there. He would help me figure out what to do about feeding the dragon. I wondered if He was displeased with me for taking the necklace from the beast. I didn't want to belong to anyone but God. I was almost certain that He knew this, but still felt a little worried that He was disappointed in me.

"Do you think the Heavenly Father is angry because I took the necklace?"

"He knows your heart. He sees that you were afraid for your life. He also knows the way out of this difficult circumstance. You must trust Him and look to Him for answers. He knows that you belong to Him."

I nodded, my throat swelling with the emotion that Lorenda's reassuring words provoked. I needed to know that God understood and forgave.

"Let's get some sleep, Wren. We have a long journey tomorrow."

I swallowed the rest of my wine, pulled the blanket over me and lay down on the bed of pine needles. I was surprised by how comfortable it felt. The clean fragrance of pine rose through the blanket, calming my frazzled nerves.

Maybe it was the exhaustion, or maybe it was the kindness and safety of a friend, but I fell asleep almost certain that everything would be right in the morning.

13 |

Morning appeared without any vivid dreams or visitations from a witch. I folded the blankets Lorenda carried in her saddlebags and ate the apple she offered me. In no time we were back in the saddle, retracing our steps to King Olerion's castle.

At midday, while giving our horses a drink at a stream that ran near the path, Lorenda said. "I have an idea about how you can get food to appease the dragon."

I brushed Flynn's side as he drank and looked at Lorenda, wondering what she was going to say. Flynn seemed skittish to me today, turning away from my touch.

"My father is always looking for entertainers in his court. As the champion of the sword fighting contest, perhaps you could offer to fight anyone daring to challenge you. You could ask for a certain wage and use the money to purchase the food you need every other day."

I continued brushing Flynn and thought about the proposal. It sounded like an unlikely plan, but perhaps it was worth trying. I didn't have any better ideas. Perhaps God had given this idea to Lorenda.

The forest was drier the further we went on the trail. By the time we stopped to camp, we were able to find dry wood to burn for a fire. I helped gather the wood and then settled in on my blanket in front of the orange and yellow blaze. Lorenda brought out more bread, cheese and wine and we ate in silence, staring at the fire.

"Tomorrow we will reach my father's castle," Lorenda finally spoke after the long silence. "When we enter the castle gate, you must address me as Sir John, my father's servant. I will wear the cloak and sneak into my room. You will have to appear before my father and tell him the dragon will no longer be a problem for his people. If you tell him that, you will not be lying and you will still honor the Heavenly Father's command to tell the truth."

I hadn't thought about what I was going to tell the king. I didn't want to lie but I also did not want to be thrown into prison.

"What if he asks if I killed the dragon as I said I would?"

"Tell him you worked out an arrangement to keep the dragon from tormenting the people. Since that is his main concern, he will be satisfied with that."

"What if he isn't?" I looked at Lorenda, who continued to stare at the fire.

"Don't be afraid, Wren. God will give you the words to speak. You may have to suggest our plan to him. Just be honest."

I shook my head. This was all too much. How was I supposed to tell the truth and risk losing my freedom? It seemed like the Heavenly Father wanted too much from me.

We sat gazing at the fire for a while longer and then Lorenda spoke. "God is teaching you how to trust him, Wren."

"I just wish I'd never entered that contest. My entire life has changed with one bad decision. I could be home right now, reading books in my bed, without any of these worries or troubles."

Lorenda directed her attention to me. "But you probably wouldn't know the Savior if you had never entered the contest. God sometimes uses difficult things to draw us to Him."

I looked away, anger spreading across my chest, hardening my heart. Lorenda just did not understand. She did not have to feed an angry dragon for the rest of her life or appease an angry king. She had no worries.

Silence hung heavy in the cool night air. I knew it was better that I remained quiet instead of trying to talk to Lorenda to get her to understand how I felt. I had a temper like my mother, or what I could remember of my mother. Because I remembered the way I felt when my mother was angry most of the time, I was determined to refrain from any angry outbursts.

Lorenda put the wine cups back into her saddlebag. As if sensing that I was angry and finished talking, she laid down on her blanket and pulled the second blanket over her body. "Goodnight, Wren."

"Good night." I laid down as well and bunched some of the blanket on the ground into a pillow of sorts. I spread the second blanket over my body and laid, wide awake and staring at the fire, for quite some time. Finally, sleep overcame my weary mind and I was blessed with a night of seemingly dreamless rest.

I awoke before Lorenda. I poked at the fire with a stick the way I had seen Lorenda do, and added another couple of branches to the glowing embers. I blew on the coals until they glowed and caught the branches on fire. In no time, a small fire blazed against the dark blue sky, which was swiftly turning to a royal blue with dawn's light.

Lorenda continued to breathe heavily in slumber as I warmed my hands by the fire. I looked around me at the edge of the forest that was still dark. I shivered as I remembered the witch who had disguised herself as Lorenda on my first night of camping in the woods.

Was the witch here now, watching me? What did she mean that I would grow old alone and unloved if I were to slay the dragon? Why would slaying the dragon cause me such misfortune? None of it made sense. I wanted to wake Lorenda. I needed someone to talk to. I looked up into the sky and prayed.

"Heavenly Father, I don't understand what is happening. I need your help. I'm in a terrible mess and I don't know how to get out. Please help me know what to do."

The fear that I had felt creeping up the center of my back faded. A calm, peaceful feeling overcame me and I knew I'd been heard. I couldn't believe I could talk to God at any time and He would listen. This was more amazing than learning how to sword fight or ride a horse. This was the greatest gift I had ever been given.

"Good morning, Wren." Lorenda sat up, rubbing her eyes. She smiled and sighed. "I had the most glorious sleep. How about you?"

I returned her smile. "I slept well, thank you."

"I'm sorry that I made you angry last night."

"That's okay. I was just feeling sorry for myself, not sure of what to do."

"You seem to feel better this morning."

"I prayed, and God heard me. It's so amazing."

"I know." Her grin woke her sleepy face. "I'm very pleased that you have discovered the truth about the Heavenly Father's presence. It will give you peace like no other." Lorenda walked over to her saddlebag and retrieved two apples.

"We will arrive at my father's castle in time for the midday meal. Once he has eaten he will want to see you. You need to take charge and immediately let him know that you have resolved the problem with the dragon. Perhaps he will not ask if the dragon is slain. No matter what, you must tell the truth, Wren."

I nodded. "Just like the servants who are covering for you are telling the truth."

Lorenda sat back down beside me. "You're right. I'm not following my own instruction. It's just that my father would have never let me go with you if he knew what I was doing. I'm kind of like Rahab and the Israelite spies." Lorenda grinned.

I frowned. "What are you talking about?"

"In the Bible, the Old Testament mentions a woman named Rahab, a prostitute, who hides the Israelites spies from their enemies. God blesses her and protects her and her family when Israel attacks the city. She lies to the soldiers who are looking for the spies. She tells them that the spies are not in her house, when they actually are hiding in her home. She lies and God still blesses her."

"So you think that God will bless this situation, even though you lied to your father?" I stared at her.

"I could have let you travel with one of my father's guards," she said simply.

I took a large bite of my apple and chewed slowly, swallowing after chewing for some time. "I am grateful to you Lorenda, I truly am. I'm sorry for judging you. I still believe a lie is a lie but God is your judge, not me. You have helped me more than anyone ever has, and I owe you a great deal of gratitude."

Lorenda put her arm around me. "We are friends, Wren. We will have disagreements. Don't worry, things will be okay."

I realized I had never had a friend like Lorenda. Aleric was my friend but he didn't understand what it was like to be a woman in a world that put many restrictions on females. Lorenda knew what this was like.

We finished our apples and then mounted the horses for the half day's journey to the castle. With each step that the horses took, I could feel my stomach tighten in a knot.

Before we came to the edge of the forest, Lorenda pulled the cloak from her saddlebag and wrapped it around her shoulders, pulling the hood over her head.

"It's so hot, Lorenda. I'm sorry you have to wear that."

"I don't have to wear it for very long. So, I just think about the coolness of my room in the castle and it helps me to endure."

"You've taken a great risk on my behalf and I truly appreciate it. You are a true friend."

Lorenda patted my shoulder as she rode her horse past me to take the lead on the trail. "You're a true friend, too. I've never met anyone as courageous and honest as you."

I felt a flash of warm pride spread across my cheeks. I had heard so few compliments in my life that when I received one, I almost couldn't bear it. The pure joy it brought was overwhelming.

Lorenda pulled the cloak tightly around her face to ensure she was not recognized. She couldn't afford to be seen. Her father would banish her to some high tower in the castle for life.

We rode in silence, traveling as quietly as possible through the towns surrounding King Olerion's castle. People threw glances our way now and then but otherwise paid little attention to the cloaked figure and young lady on horseback.

I was relieved. The fewer people that noticed us the better. We had to make it back within the castle walls before Lorenda was seen. I couldn't bear to be the cause of trouble between her and her father. I knew how it was to be at odds with my father and I didn't want this for Lorenda. I was weary with causing trouble. I just wanted to be at peace.

Down the hill through the town we rode, until we came to the giant wooden castle gates. A watchman stood in the lookout on the right side of the gate and stared down at us as we rode up. The cloak Lorenda wore bore her father's crest, the bear and the deer. From viewing the crest, the watchman could assume Lorenda was one of the castle guards.

"A cloak seems an odd sight on a hot day like today." The watchman made no move to open the gate.

"My skin is quite pale," Lorenda replied, disguising her voice and speaking as deeply as she possibly could. She wasn't lying. Her skin was whiter than mine. With her red hair, Lorenda naturally had pale skin.

"Who are you?" The watchman was not going to let us pass by easily.

"I am one of the king's loyal subjects," Lorenda answered, still trying not to lie.

"You are being vague and odd and..."

"Watchman! Open the gate!"

I recognized the voice on the other side of the castle wall. It was Travin.

"Open the gate, man!" Travin sounded angry.

"There's an intruder outside the gate, Travin," the watchman replied, exasperation in his voice.

"That's no intruder. That's the king's second-in-command escorting Princess Wren on her journey to slay the dragon that torments this land."

I wondered how he knew it was us. I then realized that no one else would be wearing a cloak on such an extremely warm summer day.

"You are new to your post, William. I realize you are just trying to fulfill your duty. However, if the king knew you were delaying the arrival of Princess Wren, he would be infuriated."

The gate slowly creaked open as William turned the wheel.

Lorenda kept her head down until we were in the stables. Travin followed us.

"It's so good to see you, Princess Wren," Travin said, staring at me with a wide smile on his face.

I climbed off of Flynn and led him into an empty stable. Lorenda did the same and joined me where I now stood in front of Travin.

"It's good to see you, Travin."

"And you as well, Princess. I heard you had followed Princess Wren. I was, at first, angry. But then I was grateful that you were with her. Thank you for taking such good care of her."

I could see genuine appreciation on Travin's handsome dark face. His dark brown eyes seemed softer than the way I remembered them. He seemed to be very pleased to see me. I was puzzled by his reaction.

"Your father is already eating his noonday meal. He told me to inform him whenever Princess Wren arrived; if she arrived."

"I will go to my room and take my meal in there. Report to me as soon as you can and tell me how my father received Wren. I will be anxious to know," Lorenda said.

"Of course. I will report to you as soon as I am able."

Lorenda turned to me and grabbed both of my hands. "It will all be okay. Just be honest and take charge like I told you."

"I will." I swallowed the huge lump in my throat. I wasn't sure when I would see Lorenda again. We had to be careful not to be seen together, or risk incurring the wrath of King Olerion.

Lorenda walked out of the stable without looking back and snuck into the castle, making haste to her room before being seen.

I stood next to Travin, looking at the ground. I found it difficult to look him in the eye. It made me feel restless inside.

"We had better go see the king, Princess. He expects me to escort you to him. He would be angry if he found out you were in the castle and had not gone in to see him as soon as you arrived."

I nodded, with my head still down, staring at the ground. Warm fingers lifted my chin as Travin gently tilted my head upward so that he could look into my eyes.

"You will always be friends with Princess Lorenda. Once you are her friend, you're a friend for life. Don't worry. You will have more time to spend with her. She will find a way."

We walked out of the stable into the warm sunlight and made our way into the castle. It felt cool inside, and I was grateful for the shadowed air against my hot skin. I sat on one of the red leather chairs positioned on top of the bear skin rug by the hearth which was, thankfully, not lit. Travin went to tell the king of my arrival.

The soft leather felt like the soft underbelly of a dog compared to the hard ground I had been sitting and laying on the last five days. It felt so good that I closed my eyes. In spite of my nerves, I started to fall asleep when I heard Travin calling my name. He stood in front of me with an odd look on his face. I thought I saw him smile but the smile quickly faded when I stared at him.

"The king will see you now, Princess Wren," Travin said, clearing his throat before he spoke.

I rose reluctantly from my chair and followed him out of the room. He walked so quickly that I nearly had to run after him. I wondered why he was walking so fast. The king must be angry. I had the urge to run the other way, but kept following him down the hall.

Travin knocked on the door of the king's dining chambers.

"Yes, you may enter," the king answered.

Travin held up his index finger to me, motioning for me to wait there. He opened the door and went inside.

"Princess Wren is here to see you, O King." I trembled at the thought of facing him. My mouth went dry and I couldn't seem to calm my rapidly beating heart. This was almost worse than facing the dragon.

"You may enter, Princess," the king called out.

I stepped through the doorway. There at the table next to the unlit fireplace sat the king, wearing a forest green robe. His plate of pheasant and potatoes sat untouched. It didn't look like he had taken one bite.

"I was wondering if I would see you today, Princess Wren, my treasured dragon slayer."

I nodded. "I took care of the dragon."

"I have to say, I'm surprised to see that you made it. I didn't think you'd be able to survive. I hoped you would, but I didn't think it was possible."

I looked down at my hands wanting to speak but thinking better of it. I knew my anger would cause the words to shoot out like venom. I couldn't afford to make the king angry once again. Still, how dare he send me on a mission that would most likely kill me? He was a cruel, ruthless man.

"You seem upset, Princess. Is there something wrong?"

I looked at him. I did not see any concern in his dark eyes. He was being facetious. I trembled once again, this time in anger.

"No, King. Believe me when I tell you, the terrible sight of that beast, the stench, the heat that burned my clothes and face, and the blood and the bones were too awful to ever talk about again. Now that I've made it back here safely, I'm trying to find the right words to say to you about an idea I have."

"Just say it, Princess. Do you think I would bite my dragon slayer?"

I took a deep breath. "I do not wish to return to my home. My father and best friend are gone. I don't know when I will ever see them again. I need to find a way to live without my father's help. I would like to propose a way for me to stay in your kingdom and earn a wage."

The king dropped his fork and stared at me. "What makes you think I want you in my kingdom?"

I hadn't anticipated this response. I wasn't sure what to say.

"I realize you don't want me around your daughter. I will keep my distance if you will allow me to stay in one of your servant's quarters or guest rooms."

"And how would you earn a wage?" The king stabbed his fork into the pheasant lying plucked and roasted on his plate. He carved a piece off with his knife and began to chew.

"I would like to provide entertainment to your kingdom by allowing swordsmen from far and wide to challenge me to a sword fight. If I win, I get paid a wage. If I lose, the entertainment is over and I leave and return to my father's kingdom."

King Olerion took another bite, chewed it slowly and swallowed, washing it down with a cup of wine. He looked at the unlit fireplace and then back at me.

"You are a very lonely young lady, aren't you?" He stared at me once again, as if peering into my soul. It made me shift nervously. "You must be extremely lonely to agree to trade the comfort of your home for servant's quarters and sword fighting every, what, week? Are you willing to fight every week? Can you take it? You looked ruined to me."

I nodded. My body and soul felt ruined. Yet, I needed enough money to buy ten chickens or a cow or two pigs every other day. I would have to do this. I would need three or four pieces of gold each week.

"I will pay you five pieces of gold a week if you will perform. If you lose, you will have to serve time in my dungeon to satisfy the people's sense of justice for humiliating my honor and then I will send you back to your father's kingdom. If I catch you talking to Lorenda, you will be escorted out immediately. You must stay away from her. She doesn't need someone like you in her life."

I nodded in agreement. I could feel tears begging to spring from my eyes. I hoped the king couldn't see them and that he didn't notice how shiny my eyes had become. He couldn't know how much Lorenda meant to me, that she was the first female friend I had ever had. The loneliness I'd been trying to ignore spread its cold fingers like tethers across my chest.

"You will begin tomorrow evening. I will make an announcement in the towns nearby. You may stay in the same guest room you stayed in four nights ago. Travin will see to your comfort."

"Thank you." I wasn't sure how to ask for this, but knew my very life depended on my courage to pose the question. "You have been very generous. I appreciate you giving me this opportunity. I need to purchase some things for myself and wondered if I could have my first payment before the sword fight in order to care for my needs?" I held my breath and stared at the king, hoping I hadn't completely overstepped my bounds.

I learned in an instant the effect of someone holding a grudge. It mattered not to the king that he believed I had slain his dragon. He was still going to punish me for insulting his authority and the rules to his sword fighting game before the public.

He waved his hand at me and took another bite of pheasant. Chewing vigorously, he stared at me. Having swallowed his food, he said rather loudly, "Travin, my courtier, will give you the payment. Now, be gone with you!"

14

Travin gently took my elbow as I walked out of the room and steered me down the hallway. He didn't say a word until we arrived at the door leading into the guest bedroom.

"Are you all right, Princess Wren?" His eyes held a thousand concerns as his hands gripped my shoulders in the softest way.

I sniffed and dragged the sleeve of my dress across my wet face. "Oh Travin, I'm just tired." I looked down at my clothes which were torn and filthy. I longed for a bath.

As if reading my mind, Travin spoke. "I will have the servants bring up buckets of hot water for a bath. You'll feel better once you get the dust from the road off of you."

"Thank you." I entered the room, immediately removing my shoes and collapsing on the bed. He disappeared, shutting the door behind him.

Moments later a knock came at the door. I had fallen asleep on the bed and almost didn't hear it. When I opened the door, ten servants, all carrying two buckets of water, walked through the door one at a time filling the tub in no time. They left without saying a word.

"Thank you!" I called after them.

The water was very hot and I had to wait for it to cool down. After testing the temperature a few times, I unbuttoned the top of my dress and slipped it down over my waist and hips. I carefully removed the torn pants. Blood had dried between my knees and the fabric, and I almost ripped the scabs right off. It wasn't until that moment that I realized how sore my body was. My right shoulder ached and burned where the dragon had grabbed me with its talons. My arms and legs were bloodied and bruised. I had been so worried about what I would say to the king that I hadn't realized I was hurting.

I put one foot into the water and then placed the other beside it so I was standing in the middle of the tub. Holding onto the sides of the tub with both hands, I eased myself into the hot liquid. Sharp needles stung my knees at first. I wanted to jump out, but forced myself to sit in the water. Eventually, the throbbing pain subsided. My shoulder continued to throb at the site where the dragon's talons had broken the skin. I gently rubbed the wounds on the front of my shoulder and on the back, feeling the thick scab that had formed over the puncture marks. Dried blood that had been smeared across my shoulder washed away into the water.

I thought of the dragon, and then glanced down at the necklace that weighed so heavily against my chest. Even in the safe warmth of the bath water, I felt exposed and in danger, not to mention the shame I carried for cowering to the beast.

Shaking, I cupped both hands and dipped them in the water. I brought two handfuls of refreshing water to my face. The water dripped down my face and neck, washing away the dirt and grime from the road that I'd traveled the last five days. I tried to focus on how wonderful the warm water felt on my skin.

Finally, I leaned my head back against the tub and let every muscle relax in the warmth that surrounded my body. In spite of my throbbing wounds, I could feel my eyes grow heavy. Within moments I was asleep.

Bam! Bam! Bam! I should have heard the pounding on the door but my exhaustion had over taken me. I remained asleep.

"Princess Wren! Princess Wren!" I didn't hear my name being called louder and louder until it was too late. Suddenly the door opened and Travin stood in the doorway staring at me.

"I'm so sorry, Princess! You wouldn't answer and I thought you had escaped." He shut the door as fast as he had opened it. I quickly stepped out of the tub and wrapped myself in the towel that lay beside the tub on the floor. The door began to open once again, allowing just enough of an opening for his arm to pass through the door. In his hand he held a royal blue dress.

I walked to the door and took the dress from his hand. "Thank you." I smiled as I returned to where I had been standing in front of the hearth. A small fire blazed at its center, warming my partially naked, bruised and battered body.

"Princess, I will return with food in a few moments," Travin called through the small opening in the door. "Do you require anything more?"

"No, thank you." I waited until I heard the door shut and then dried myself in front of the fire.

Walking over to the bed where I had laid the dress that Travin had delivered, I picked it up once again and admired the shine of the royal blue silk. Slipping the dress over my head, I let the smooth fabric cascade down to the floor, hugging my slender frame just so.

The sleeves of the dress fell below the shoulder. I was thankful to have my wounded shoulder free from the rub of fabric. I walked over to the table that held a mirror. Looking at my reflection was a shock. While my hair and face looked the same, my body from the neck down was bruised and wounded. I had no idea just how deeply the dragon's talons had dug into my skin, creating one deep hole in the front of my shoulder and two holes in the back. The skin around the puncture marks was red and inflamed. I gently touched it and winced.

I tried not to focus on the wounds and, instead, stared at my short, blonde hair. It had grown a bit since the sword fighting contest, but not a lot. I was anxious for it to grow long again.

I was glad it was my left shoulder that was injured. If it had been my right shoulder, I would not be able to hold my sword for my first sword fight tomorrow.

A gentle knock at the door drew my attention away from the mirror. I walked toward the door as it opened. Travin carried a tray containing pheasant, cheese, bread and wine. He smiled at me as he walked through the door, but his smile quickly faded as his eyes traveled downward from my face to my left shoulder.

"Princess Wren! You are injured." Travin set the meal tray down on the small table that stood next to the fire and rushed to my side. Taking my right hand, he drew me to the table where the firelight cast a warm, golden glow. He carefully placed his hand on my arm and used his other hand to tilt my head to one side to get a better look.

"This looks bad, Princess. It is red and I'd wager it feels hot." He took his hand away from my chin. He ran his fingers over one side of the inflamed skin surrounding the wound. "It is hot. I will get you a cooling salve from the medicine woman to draw out the poison in the blood."

I stared. I hadn't realized how handsome Travin was. His sun-darkened face was outlined by his dark brown hair. Large, dark eyes were encircled by thick, black lashes and framed by dark eyebrows that were neither too thick or too thin. Pale white teeth hid behind thin lips. His features were rugged and chiseled, softened by his kind eyes. I wanted to reach out and touch the smooth skin of his cheek.

"I will return with the salve shortly. Please sit and eat while I run and get it."

I looked at the food sitting on the table and felt my stomach respond to the sight with a growl. Travin pulled out one of the heavy wooden chairs for me. I collapsed onto the seat he offered me and picked up a chunk of cheese from the tray, taking a large bite of it. I ate on instinct, ripping off a piece of bread and washing it all down with a gulp of wine. I hardly noticed Travin leaving. When he returned, half of the food was gone.

He held a clay jar in his hand and removed the lid, as he walked across the room to where I was sitting. The smell that arose from the jar made my eyes water. A pungent scent of mint and pepper filled the room and I could almost taste the heat of the pepper and the coolness of the mint.

Travin set the lid and jar on the table. Reaching into the jar, he swiped a small amount of the clear, green salve on three of his fingers.

"Is it okay if I apply some to your wounds?" His eyes held concern and apprehension.

"Of course." I smiled, trying to put him at ease.

"This may sting for a moment." I nodded and closed my eyes. Travin dabbed the deep puncture on the front of my shoulder and then touched the two wounds on the back of my shoulder blade.

I held my breath as the salve melted into the wounds. What started out as a sting turned into an intense burning. I gripped the arms of the chair and clenched my teeth.

"I'm so sorry, Princess. The burning will cease and then it will grow cool."

As he spoke, the heat subsided, and a cool, tingling sensation spread across the front and back of my shoulder. It was as if the skin around the wounds had gone numb. The pain in my shoulder subsided and the throbbing ceased.

I opened my eyes to see Travin kneeling down in front of me. His face was pinched in anguish. It immediately began to relax when he saw me release my grip on the chair.

"That is amazing medicine! The pain is gone." I wanted to get up and twirl around the room. I couldn't believe how good my shoulder felt.

"I'm so glad to see you feeling better." Travin grinned and rose to his feet. "I should let you get some sleep. I know the night is still young, but I saw how tired you looked when I returned with the salve."

I yawned. I hadn't thought about how tired I was. I had been focused on the pain in my shoulder.

Travin began to walk toward the door. "Wait! Travin, can you get a message from me to Princess Lorenda?"

Travin turned around and looked at me. "I can give her a message." He seemed uncomfortable as he said it, looking down at the floor. I could tell he was concerned about my request.

"I just need her to know that the king agreed to let me sword fight for a wage."

Travin frowned. "What?" he looked up at me.

"I offered to sword fight anyone who wants to challenge the victor of the recent sword fighting contest to provide entertainment to the king and his people."

Travin continued to frown. "But why? You are a princess. Why would you need to earn a wage?"

Oh, how I wished I could tell him the truth: that I had to have money to buy food for the dragon to keep myself alive and out of the king's dungeon. I didn't know Travin well enough to discern if I could trust him or not. "I don't want to go back to my father's castle. There is no one there for me. My friend is gone and my father only spends a few nights out of the year at home. I want to stay here. In order to do that, I must earn a wage so that I might pay my way. As long as I am the victor each time I fight, I will get a wage."

"And if you lose?" Travin raised his eyebrows.

"I will be sent home. But, I won't lose."

Travin stopped frowning and nodded. "I didn't know you were so lonely, Princess. It must be a deep loneliness to want to stay somewhere with which you are hardly familiar and under such difficult conditions."

I looked away. Was it that obvious? I tried to keep my loneliness to myself, but Travin could see it even in the midst of my lies. It was true that I couldn't go home because I had to have a way to keep the greedy beast satiated. It was also true that I didn't want to face the loneliness that awaited me at home. Just a few days ago I wished I could crawl into my bed in my room at my father's castle. I was frightened and road weary. Now that I was back in a comfortable room with plenty of food, I remembered the loneliness of home. Travin had seen more deeply than I wished.

"Thank you for the salve and for making sure Princess Lorenda gets my message."

Travin bowed. "You're welcome, Princess. I will return tomorrow with your morning meal." Without looking at me, he turned around and walked out the door.

I felt sorry for the way I had so abruptly dismissed Travin. He had been so kind to me. I just couldn't have anyone meddling with my heart at this time. I had too many other worries.

Very tired, but too excited to sleep, I sat by the fire until it died down to just the coals, glowing in the dark room. I wished that I could talk to Lorenda. I held the finely cut, jade pendant in my hand and thought about the dragon.

When would it come to me and where? I couldn't afford to have the king see me handing over cattle to the demon. Surely, the dragon would be discreet when it came.

I had to find two pigs or a cow or ten chickens tomorrow and hopefully, find a secret place to conduct the exchange with my nemesis. Suddenly, a loud tap came at my bedroom window. Another tap followed. I rose from the high backed chair I had been sitting in and hurried to the window. When a third tap sounded, I realized it was a small rock hitting the wooden shutters of the window.

Pushing open the shutters, a small rock flew by my head, just missing my face. I looked down at the ground below. I could see Lorenda standing in the garden, wearing a long, golden gown. She waved and then moved her hand in a "come follow me" gesture.

I nodded, quickly pulled the shutters closed and slipped on my shoes. Then, I crept out the door, making certain there was no one lurking in the hall leading to my room. It was empty. I almost expected to see Travin standing guard by my door and then remembered I was no longer a prisoner. I was here at my own request.

Tiptoeing down the hall, I descended the stairs that led to the door that would take me to the garden. The castle was quiet. It seemed like everyone was already in heavy slumber. I stepped through the door. A cool breeze blew through the lilac bushes that lined the footpath in the garden, their sweet scent calming my racing heart. I saw Lorenda's shadow in the bushes. She was beckoning me to follow.

Stepping between two of the lilac bushes, I carefully made my way to the other side of the hedge and to the open field. It was the same field that Lorenda and I had stood in while gazing at the full moon on the first night I met her.

Lorenda sat on a blanket spread out near some of the lilac bushes. She patted the empty portion of the blanket and I sat down next to her.

"Aren't you afraid your father will find out we've seen each other?" I looked at Lorenda, waiting for an answer to placate this fear.

"Don't worry, Wren. My father goes to bed before dark. No one can see us if we stay close to the lilac bushes, and I'll only meet you at night when he's asleep."

"I suppose you know better than I." I looked up at the sky, a dark satin carpet sprinkled with diamond flakes. I stared at the display for a long time, appreciating the fact that I was able to enjoy the night sky, unlike the way it was when I still lived at home. I was forbidden to leave the castle at night and, therefore, never got the opportunity to openly enjoy the evening sky.

"I didn't think I would ever get you to open the shutters of your bedroom window. I threw several rocks before you opened them."

I looked back at Lorenda and could see her golden gown sparkling in the moonlight. I wondered why she was dressed so formally for taking a walk in the garden. I decided to ask.

"Why are you wearing such a beautiful gown just to take a walk in the garden?"

Lorenda smiled. "I haven't been able to dress up these last five days. I like to wear my most beautiful gown after I am subjected to deprivation."

I had forgotten this side of Lorenda. She could act like a man when wandering through the forest and then turn back into a woman when at home in her father's castle. I liked that about her, admired it even.

"I'm glad I finally got your attention. I wanted to talk to you about how things went with my father. Travin told me you had worked out a deal with him to earn a wage for sword fighting, but that was all he said. He seemed upset when he spoke to me about it. His face held a frown that didn't leave the entire time we spoke."

"He acted strangely when I told him I would be sword fighting. It was as if he was an angry husband and his wife had agreed to do such a thing."

Lorenda's laugh rolled easily. "Perhaps Travin has developed an affection for you, Wren."

It was my turn to frown. "How is that possible? He's only been in my presence on three separate occasions; the day your father discovered that I had disguised myself as a man, the following day when he escorted me out of the castle grounds and yesterday when we arrived. That is not nearly enough time to develop an affection, as you say."

"You would be surprised my dear, naive friend."

I was annoyed by Lorenda's maternal, wise tone. I could tell we were close to the same age and I didn't like someone so close in age acting as if they knew more than me.

She tapped my hand. "I haven't always followed the ways of the Heavenly Father, Wren. I used to flirt and chase after men and then push them away when they got too close. It was all a game to me. I know how quickly a man can acquire feelings for a maiden. I saw it happen again and again."

I glanced at Lorenda, who was now staring out across the open field. It was obvious that she had a difficult time admitting this. She never ceased to amaze me. She seemed to have so many layers to her personality, and she was honest about them. It made me want to be more like her and open up, be more honest.

"What made you stop?" I asked. Lorenda said she used to flirt. I wondered what made her stop behaving that way.

"A man who still lives here in my father's kingdom nearly violated me. Luckily, my father walked into the room or I believe he would have had his way, though mine was opposed." Lorenda looked at me, her eyes shining with emotion.

I grabbed her hand and squeezed. "I'm so sorry, Lorenda."

"That's okay. It taught me a difficult lesson. I came to realize I had no right to go around teasing and tormenting men the way I was doing. I had no right to pretend, one moment, that they could have their way with me and then shun them in the next when they tried to make advances."

I nodded. "I see what you're saying. That's still awful. Were you terribly frightened?"

"Yes, more than I've ever been." She caught her breath. "He had me pinned against the wall in my father's dining quarters. My father had forgotten a letter he had been reading while taking his evening meal. He came back to retrieve it, and this vile man jumped away from me when the door opened. I thanked the Heavenly Father for watching over me."

"You never told your father about it?"

"He would have wanted to know what caused the man to make these advances and I would have had to defend my own behavior. He would have had the man beheaded and that seemed too harsh of a punishment. I didn't think the man deserved to die. I didn't want to be the cause of his death. You actually fought against him in the sword fighting contest."

"I did?"

"He was wearing my father's crest on his breastplate and had a reddish-brown beard."

I could envision the man leering down at me as I bathed in the pool halfway between my father's castle & King Olerion's. "You should have had him beheaded."

"Why do you say such a thing, Wren?"

"He nearly assaulted me long before I ever came to your kingdom. I was bathing at the green pool between my father's castle and yours. He rode by and saw me in the pool and came directly to me instead of respecting my privacy. He was ready to get in the pool with me and he left only when I told him there were soldiers nearby that I could call to help me. I believe he would have done harm if he'd been given the chance."

"I'm sorry that happened. He is a devious man, looking for an opportunity to take advantage. Still, he's one of my father's best soldiers. My father would probably have a hard time believing anything dark spoken against him. I guess we both barely escaped something terrible."

"Yes, we did."

"I threw rocks at your window because I wanted to talk to you about...." Lorenda paused as she noticed my bare shoulder. "I didn't know you were that badly injured! Is that what the dragon did to you?"

I nodded and gently touched the injured area. I had almost forgotten about my wounds. The salve took all the pain from them.

"I'm afraid for you, Wren. Making a deal with this beast could get you killed. We need to find another solution. This is too dangerous."

"There's nothing I can do about it. The dragon would have killed me on the spot if I hadn't agreed to this deal."

Lorenda shook her head, picked up a small pebble that lay in the grass beside the blanket, and threw it into the open field. "I can't believe my father would send you to kill the dragon. He had to know this was an impossible task. Did he ask you anything about how you killed the beast?"

"I didn't give him time to investigate. I took charge just like you said to do. I told him I had taken care of the demon and that I had a proposition for him."

"You must have done a great job with that. I'm proud of you. I'm just worried that this is going to backfire. Don't you have gold at your father's castle that you could use to buy food for the dragon?"

"My father has never seen fit to grant me permission to use his wealth. I have never paid for anything in my life. The servants have always provided me with food and clothing. I wouldn't know how to get to my father's treasure."

"That's another way our fathers are different. My father gives me an allowance every month. Wait! I know what we can do!" Lorenda grabbed my arm and squeezed. "We can use my allowance to buy the food and then you won't have to sword fight."

"No, Lorenda. I won't allow that." I scowled at the idea. "I can pay my own way. I'm very good with the sword and can put it to good use."

"Wren, this is no time to be stubborn."

"I said 'no,' Lorenda. Please try to understand. I can't take anything else from you. Besides, if your father found out you were using your money to help me, he would banish me forever and be furious with you. I can't be the cause of you hiding something else from your father."

"But what if you lose, Wren? Travin told me father said he would pay you a wage as long as you were the victor."

"I'm not going to lose, Lorenda. You saw how I defeated every swordsman I came up against in the contest. There's only one person I've ever lost to and he's away at war. I won't lose."

Lorenda sighed. "Okay, Wren. I can see I will not be able to change your mind. I will just pray that the Heavenly Father will protect you."

"Thank you."

We sat in silence for a time, staring up at the milky white moon dancing against millions of stars. A warm breeze continued to blow and I closed my eyes, feeling more relaxed than I had all day. Having a friend like Lorenda who really cared for me was a deep security I had never known. It made me feel like I was home.

"We'd better go in, Wren. The guards will do a sweep of the castle grounds very soon and I don't want them to discover us out here and then report back to my father about their findings."

I stood after Lorenda rose to her feet and the two of us carried the blanket back to the entrance of the castle. I handed the other end of the blanket to Lorenda and opened the door. We could hear footsteps coming down the stairs.

"Quick!" Lorenda whispered. "Follow me."

She and I ran back outside and headed to the right of the door. A small house stood off in the distance from the garden grounds. It was made from the same stone as the castle. Lorenda rushed behind the house and I followed.

We could hear the castle door open and close. Voices carried on the breeze.

"There will be new entertainment in the castle tomorrow. Some foolish woman thinks she can sword fight any man and beat him."

"I heard she beat every man in the contest King Olerion had six days ago."

"She didn't fight me. I would have taught her a lesson."

"I'm sure you would have, Galahad," the guard replied, laughing.

Their voices grew distant and Lorenda grabbed my hand. "They're gone. This is our chance."

We ran back to the door and went inside.

"Sleep well, Wren."

"You too, Lorenda."

"I will be praying for you tomorrow. I will be in the crowd watching you fight, cheering you on."

"Thank you. You are my dear, sweet friend."

"And you are mine."

At the top of the stairs I went down the hall to the guest room while Lorenda turned right and went down another hall to her room.

Sleep came easily, as soon as my head touched the pillow. I was completely exhausted both mentally and physically and it took very little time before I wandered into the world of dreams.

I was back in King Olerion's arena, a crowd of countless numbers surrounding me. I stood in the center of the arena, my richly ornamented sword in hand. This time I wore a long, forest green gown tied at the waist with a thin, golden rope that matched the golden roses embroidered around the neckline of the dress. It was the same dress I had worn the day my mother disappeared, except this version was larger and longer to fit my grown body.

My hair was the length it had been before I cut it for the contest. I moved my sword back and forth, slicing through the empty space in front of me. The crowd both cheered and jeered. The mocking voices were deep and masculine.

From one side of the arena came a knight in full armor. His face was covered by his helmet's face shield. I couldn't see who he was and was disappointed to see that his breastplate had no crest. I didn't even know what kingdom he was from.

The man withdrew his sword from his shield and dealt a heavy blow to my sword, nearly knocking it from my hands. I was in shock, not expecting the man to advance so quickly. We exchanged several blows back and forth for what seemed like an eternity. At one point, I thrust my sword at the man's side. In an instant the man raised his sword overhead and brought it down on mine, knocking my weapon to the ground. In another instant, his sword was drawn overhead again and came crashing down on my left shoulder.

Fiery hot pain shot through my entire shoulder. I cried out, holding my shoulder as I fell to the ground.

Laying on my side, I gazed up and watched as the man pulled the helmet from his head. Shining sable hair spilled forward. Brushing the locks from his face, I saw familiar gray eyes peering down at me.

"Aleric?" I couldn't believe it was really him. I hadn't seen him in so long.

"You shouldn't be here, Princess. You should be back where you belong, at your father's castle."

"I don't belong there any longer," I cried out. My shoulder was throbbing. I tried to push myself up from the ground but couldn't find the strength to do so. The pain was immobilizing.

"If you don't leave, you will surely die." Aleric raised the sword once again over his head. I could see it glisten in the sun. The sword grew dark then and became a large black wing. Another wing appeared beside it. The wings moved against the bright sun.

In the glare of the great orb, Aleric's face was transformed into that of the dragon's. The beast now stood where Aleric had been standing. It opened its large, vicious mouth and spoke. "Where is my meal, child?"

I shook my head. "I don't have it yet. You aren't supposed to be here until tomorrow."

The beast laughed. "How dare you tell me when or where I am supposed to be! You are not my master. I am yours."

I started to cry and shake. I was totally helpless and unsure of what to do next.

"You did not keep your word, Princess. I told you I would be coming, and you did not listen. You shall surely die for disobeying me."

The dragon lifted its right talon. I screamed as the demon brought it down toward my face.

15 |

"**P**rincess Wren! Princess Wren!" Travin reached across the bed to shake me. I sat straight up and stared at him.

My hair clung to the sides of my face, which was moist with sweat. I was panting as if I had been running from someone chasing me. My fear of the dragon had caused my heart to race.

"My lady, are you feeling poorly?" Travin stood watching me, his eyes full of deep concern.

I used both of my hands to sweep the hair away from the sides of my face. I tried to smile but my bottom lip quivered, so I stopped trying to appear calm. "I had a frightening dream. I'm okay." My voice shook almost as much as my lip.

"You are not okay. I will fetch you some chamomile tea. That will help calm you."

"Thank you, Travin." I was grateful that he would leave and give me a moment to compose myself.

He turned and slipped out the door as quickly as he had entered it. I pushed the bedding off my legs and stood, nearly falling as my legs shook beneath me. The dream had been so real. I felt like I had barely escaped death.

Walking over to the hearth, I poked the coals inside. Nothing. No spark or red ember. I decided to dress quickly before Travin returned. I did not fancy him seeing me in a sleeping gown. On the bed lay a fresh purple gown, compliments of Lorenda, I guessed. I felt like a beggar wearing her beautiful clothes, but was grateful to have something to wear.

The gown was a rich, deep purple, similar to the color of the king's crest. On the bodice were two embroidered deer drinking by a stream of bright blue water. I pulled the gown over my head and then smoothed it down in the front. It fit perfectly. I went to the mirror and ran my fingers through my hair, which curled ever-so-slightly from being dampened by my sweat.

I stared at my pale face and wondered if I was actually seeing a ghost. My dreams had drained me of all energy. Still, the royal purple against the paleness of my skin looked quite fetching.

A knock came at the door and I tore my gaze from the mirror to walk to the door to answer it. Travin stood in the hall with a tray of tea, bread and some fresh plums.

My stomach growled as I realized how hungry I was. The dream had stolen my appetite and I had forgotten that the last time food had been offered to me was in the early evening yesterday.

"You look to be at peace now, Princess."

"Yes, except for my rabid hunger!" I walked over to the table that sat near the hearth and Travin followed, setting the tray on the table.

I motioned for him to sit in the chair across from me. "Please sit with me, Travin. I do not wish to dine alone." I stared at him until he had fully reclined in the chair.

"What were you dreaming when I came into your room? You seemed absolutely terrified."

I sipped my tea and then broke off a piece of bread from the warm loaf in front of me. Creamy butter sat on a plate, waiting to be spread on the bread. Two different kinds of jams were sitting next to it; cherry and blackberry. I took my time placing butter and jam just so on my bite, taking my time before answering Travin.

"I dreamt I lost a sword fight."

Travin's brow furrowed into confused creases. "That's what made you cry out? You were screaming, Princess, as if something or someone was about to kill you."

I grabbed a plum and took a large bite. The juice ran down my hand and chin. A white muslin napkin lay beside the bread. I grabbed it and wiped my face and hands.

"I can't bear to lose, Travin. It devastates me."

He leaned back away from the table and folded his arms across his chest. "I must tell you, Princess, I don't believe it's fitting for a lady such as yourself to be fighting with a sword."

"And what sort of lady do you think I am? Am I a helpless damsel in distress? Am I weak and fragile?"

"You are anything but weak, Princess. I am speaking of your royalty, your position in this world. You are a princess, not a soldier. You should not have to earn a wage. Someone of royal blood does not do such a thing."

I slammed the plum down on my plate, scattering juice everywhere. How dare this man who hardly knew me make a judgment about my life. "You do not know me or where I come from, Travin! You speak foolish, empty words. I may come from royal blood but my life has not been one of a princess as you have defined such a thing. I am not Lorenda. Sword fighting is what I know and it is all I have."

Travin dropped his arms and placed his hands on the table. "I am sorry, Princess Wren. I overstepped my position. Who am I to tell you how to behave? It will not happen again."

I could feel the anger and indignation drain from my body. I knew I needed Travin. I had to get the food I had promised the dragon and I needed his help to do this. I couldn't afford to stay angry with him.

I placed my soiled napkin on top of my plate, my hunger satiated. Travin stood and reached for the tray, prepared to take it back to the kitchen.

I grabbed his hand. "I need your help Travin," I said, releasing my grip on his hand.

He sat back down and nodded. "Tell me what I can do."

"I need the five pieces of gold promised to me by King Olerion for the evening's sword fight. He said I could get that from you."

"I will see to it that you receive your payment."

I noticed Travin's formal tone. Something had shifted. The warmth that had been there yesterday was somehow snuffed out by a new attitude. I pressed on. "I also need you to help me buy a cow or ten chickens."

Travin frowned at me. "You wish to purchase a cow or chickens?"

"Or two pigs."

"Why would you want to buy farm animals?"

"That is my business." I adopted the same formal tone. I, too, could be distant and cool.

"I know someone in the village that will sell you a pig."

"I'll need two pigs."

"It can be arranged." Travin stood once again, holding the tray in his hand. "I will return soon with the gold and take you to Mrs. Craddenbrook."

"Very good."

Travin paused. His face softened, the hard lines that had settled there somehow falling away. "I am sorry for neglecting to ask how your wounds are today. Are they feeling better or do you need more salve?"

I looked at my shoulder and then back at Travin. The pain that had been there when I awoke had subsided. "It feels much better today, thank you. If it's not too much trouble, I would like more salve if there is pain once again."

Travin bowed and turned to go. "I will make haste."

I nodded and watched him as he made his way through the door.

As soon as the door was shut, I could feel the necklace that hung from my neck begin to vibrate. The finely chiseled jade pendant grew warm and then hot to the touch. I wanted to rip the chain from my neck but remembered that the dragon had said I must never remove it.

"I will come to you tonight child."

The voice rang more in my head than in my ears. It was the low rumbling voice of the beast. I knew it well. I could never forget the sound of it, the way it made my heart pound and my mind race.

"You will meet me at the far end of the field beyond the castle garden tonight. I will summon you when I have arrived."

I was struck with terror, my arms and legs frozen in the chair where I still sat after breakfast.

"Do you understand, Princess Wren?"

"Yes," I whispered.

The pendant stopped vibrating and felt cool once more against my skin. I started to cry, the shock of the moment wearing off. My entire body shook uncontrollably. I stared vacantly into the space in front of me, thoughts erupting and disappearing like a mist. "How could I bear to face this beast once again? What if I lost the sword fight this evening? How long would it be before the dragon came for me?" There was no conclusion, no answer to these questions that piled up on top of each other. I was stuck.

Thankfully, a knock came at the door. Travin walked in carrying a purple velvet pouch. He walked over to the table and set the bag on top of it. Looking at my pale, drawn face, he asked, "Princess Wren, what's wrong?"

I rubbed my face with my thin, ice cold hands. "I'm just tired, Travin. My dreams have exhausted me."

"Perhaps you should lie down. You will need your strength for this evening's contest." Travin's face grew hard and distant at the mention of the sword fighting event. I wondered why this upset him so much. I didn't understand it.

Pushing my chair back, I stood to my feet and nearly collapsed as my legs began to shake beneath me.

Travin rushed around the table and caught me by the waist. He picked me up in his arms and carried me to the bed. Laying me down as gently as a baby, he spoke with tenderness. "Please forgive me for acting without permission, Princess. You looked so pale that I thought you would faint. I should not have carried you without asking first."

I produced a weak smile and shook my head. "You do not need to apologize, Travin. You were helping me. I took no offense."

Travin's face brightened and relaxed. He looked relieved to know that I was not offended.

"Thank you for bringing the gold." I looked over at the purple bag that sat on the table.

"You're welcome." Travin bowed low. "I am at your service, Princess."

"I feel better now." It was true. I felt my strength returning. Talking to the dragon had drained me of all energy and now I felt more stable. Warmth was returning to my hands and feet.

"I'm not sure how you're going to be strong enough for this sword fight tonight." Travin was frowning once again. "What about your wounded shoulder?"

"Luckily it's my left shoulder and I fight with my right hand." I grinned and sat up. Swinging my legs over the side of the bed, I stood.

Travin reached out to steady me and I grabbed his hands to stop him. "I truly am well now. Please don't worry."

A deep crimson color spread across his face and he looked down as if he were unable to look me in the eye. "Again, I apologize."

"No need," I said, patting his arm. "You just need to trust that I'm telling the truth."

"I'm glad you are better now."

"Thank you." I walked across the room feeling much stronger and picked up the bag sitting on the table. "I need you to help me buy a couple of pigs or some chickens."

Travin looked at me with curiosity and then nodded. "Follow me."

I followed him out the door. We walked without talking into the bright sun that hung high overhead. We continued to walk past the barn and into the village. I trailed close behind Travin.

We walked past a bakery and blacksmith and went inside a third building, which belonged to the butcher. The outside of the shop was made of stone like the other two businesses. Inside were three tables arranged in a row. The table closest to the far wall was red and wet with blood. The second table held pieces of white cloth. A chicken, plucked and cut into pieces, lay on one of the strips of cloth. A short, stocky woman with long, graying yellow hair stood wrapping the meat in the cloth. When she finished, she tied the bundle with twine and set it on the third table closest to the door and front window of the store.

The woman finally looked up, her light blue eyes dancing with merriment at the site of Travin standing in front of her. "Well, hello there, Travin. What brings you to my shop on such a fine day?"

Travin nodded at Wren. "This fine lady beside me is why I'm here, Mrs. Craddenbrook."

I gave her a quick glance and smile and then looked at the ground, feeling shy all of a sudden.

Mrs. Craddenbrook smiled a semi-toothless grin. "And what is your name, fair lady?"

"Wren."

"Princess Wren," Travin corrected.

Mrs. Craddenbrook frowned. "What is a princess doing in the village butcher shop?"

I blushed and wanted to crawl under one of the tables. I felt exposed and out of place.

"Never you mind, dear. That was a rude question." She wiped her hands with a clean white cloth and continued. "How can I help you, Princess?"

I looked at the chicken that lay bundled up in cloth. "Do you have any of those, but still alive?" I pointed at the tidy bundle.

The woman frowned again and looked where I was pointing. "Oh, you mean you want a live chicken."

"Or two pigs or a cow," I blurted out.

"Well, I have all of those animals. What would you like?"

I thought about the dragon's dietary preferences. I'd decided that pigs would be the least conspicuous breed to take to the field behind the garden that evening. "Two pigs will do nicely," I answered.

Travin said nothing. I knew he wanted to know why I needed two pigs. How could I tell him I had to satisfy the appetite of the local dragon? I wished that I could explain. I'd never felt more alone than at that moment.

"The price for two pigs is one gold piece."

I reached into my pouch and retrieved one of the gold pieces given to me by the king. I felt the weight of the gold in my hand and wished I could keep the coin and buy a new dress for Lorenda. I owed her so much.

Mrs. Craddenbrook took the coin and slipped it into a pouch that hung around her broad waist. She disappeared through a door that stood behind the row of tables.

"I will bring the pigs around to the front of the shop."

In a short time, through the front window, I could see her and the two pigs.

Ropes were tied around the pigs' necks and she led them to the front door. "Princess Wren and Travin, please take these filthy beasts away." She laughed and handed the ropes to Travin as we walked over to the pigs.

I had never been around pigs, and was surprised to discover how bad they smelled. Keeping the dragon fed was not going to be an easy task. Not only would it require me to fight in a contest every week, but it would force me to do things with animals that I was not accustomed to doing. Once again, I wished that I could go home.

Travin clicked his tongue and led the pigs away after shaking Mrs. Craddenbrook's hand. I smiled and took the old woman's plump hand. "Thank you for helping me." The old woman had no idea how she had helped me.

"You are no problem to me, child."

She reminded me of Aleric's mother, Mrs. Pendelin. This made my heart ache. I longed for home. I wondered if Mrs. Pendelin thought of me. I was sure my father did not.

Travin walked ahead with the pigs. He looked like a jester on his way to perform a show dressed in brown pants, white socks and a purple shirt that was embroidered with the king's crest. It was the standard uniform for all of the castle servants but, paired with two pigs, it became a jester's garb.

My chuckle carried on the warm breeze to Travin's ears. He stopped and looked behind him. "What amuses you, Princess?"

"Why you do! You look like a jester hauling around those two pigs."

"I'm glad I can provide you with entertainment."

I noted slight irritation in his voice. He was most likely growing weary of my ruse.

"I need those pigs to pay a debt I owe," I said, walking up beside him.

Travin nodded, looking at me with a stern expression. His face was blank and I could not read it. "Your affairs are yours to reveal or conceal, Princess Wren. I do not expect you to tell me something when it is obviously a private matter."

I looked at him and tried to read the message between the words he spoke. In a strange way, I wanted him to be pleased with me. He was the only other friend I had here besides Lorenda, and I could only risk talking to her in the cover of darkness.

Travin continued walking and I followed. My shoulder ached a little as I walked and I wondered how I was going to perform that evening. "It doesn't matter if you're in pain," I thought. "You have to fight to stay alive."

"Where do you want to keep these animals?" Travin stopped in front of the barn where the horses were housed.

I shrugged. "I don't know where to keep them. I hadn't thought of where I would house them." I looked at Travin, my eyes pleading. "I only need to keep them for a short while."

Travin walked behind the barn. "Follow me." We came to a fenced-in pen where other pigs stood eating what looked like garbage from a trough. Travin yelled at them as he opened the gate and led my two pigs inside. He took two red pieces of yarn from his pocket and tied them around one ear of each pig. "This will be the way you will know which of the pigs belongs to you," he said, untying the rope from the pigs' necks.

"Thank you, Travin." I marveled at the fact that he had thought through the details regarding how I would store my livestock. I hadn't anticipated what I would need to do to take care of the animals I purchased. "I am grateful to you for helping me the way you have. My very life depends on this and I couldn't do what I must do without you."

Travin nodded. "It disturbs me that your life depends on my assistance. I hope I never let you down." He walked out of the pen and closed the gate. "You should not have to worry about your life depending upon the help of someone else."

He walked past me, around the barn, and toward the castle. "I will escort you back to your room now, Princess."

I followed once again, feeling the great distance between us.

Travin opened the door to my room when we arrived, but did not enter. "I will bring you your evening meal before the sun sets." Without waiting for me to respond, he turned on his heel and walked down the hall.

I closed the door and sighed. I wished that I had someone to talk to. I had never felt this lonely at home. But, home was where I belonged, so of course being somewhere in which I was only a guest felt different.

My shoulder ached. I went over to the little table near the hearth to get more salve to put on my wounds. When Travin brought the king's gold, he had also brought more salve in a small clay bowl. Carrying the bowl over to the mirror, I stared at my reflection. I unbuttoned my dress, exposing my shoulder and chest to the soft afternoon light streaming through the open windows.

Dipping my hand into the bowl, I scooped out a small amount of salve and spread the thick brown concoction over the wounds on the front and back of my left shoulder. Very quickly the wounds grew hot and burned as if on fire. Shortly after this, they tingled as if they had fallen asleep.

I kept my dress off of my shoulder to give the salve time to dry. I glanced at my sword leaning up against the wall to the left of the door. I knew I needed to practice but felt weary from the pain initially produced by the salve. I chose to lie down on the bed instead.

I didn't awaken until I heard someone tapping at the door. Pulling my dress over my shoulder, I quickly buttoned it and ran to the door. Travin stood outside with a tray full of food.

He walked over to the table without speaking and laid the food tray down on top of it. Still silent, he walked back to the door and was about to leave when I cried out, "Wait!"

Travin stopped in his tracks and turned around, waiting for me to speak.

"Please stay with me, Travin, while I eat. I hate eating alone. I did plenty of that while living at my father's castle."

"As you wish, Princess." Travin walked back over to the table and sat in the chair opposite me. He looked around the room and out the window. The room was growing dark with the setting sun. He went over to the hearth and lit a fire and then carried a small torch to various candles around the room.

Soon, the soft glow of candlelight filled the room as the warmth of the fire spread across my cool skin. I nibbled on a piece of cheese and took a sip of wine as Travin repositioned himself at the table. This time he stared at the food.

"Would you like something to eat?" I was hungry for conversation. The sharp tang of cheese and the sweetness of the wine went unnoticed as I focused on the man sitting across from me, willing him to speak.

"I have already eaten, Princess Wren." Travin gave me a stoic look and then directed his eyes back down to the table.

"I don't know why you are angry with me." I was exasperated. "Why are you so upset that I am performing for the king?"

"A lady of your stature should not be performing or fighting with a sword. I don't understand why a princess must do such things."

I chewed slowly and swallowed, trying to figure out what to say. "I have my reasons, Travin." I took a sip of wine as if to seal the statement, showing this information was too private to be disclosed.

"I understand, and I also understand that you could get hurt."

I watched his eyes grow soft once again, at least for a moment, and then return to their dark, far-away stare. I realized at that moment that he cared for me. He was worried that I would be injured.

"I thank you for caring and for thinking of my safety. I have not known you very long and, yet, you are more concerned for me than my father. You are a good friend, Travin. I need your help to be strong through this. I need you to believe I am able to fulfill my obligation. Your downcast face causes me to question myself."

I took another sip of wine and followed it with another bite of cheese and bread. Travin sighed. "I must apologize, Princess. I have been sour in my mood and approach, feeling frustrated and angry that such a noble young woman would subject herself to the savagery of sword fighting. I have overstepped my bounds. I will not discourage you one moment longer. Please forgive me."

"I do. I want you to know I am not alone in this fight. The Heavenly Father is with me. He was with me when I faced the dragon and He will be with me tonight when I face my first opponent."

Travin nodded. "I will trust what you say."

I took a bite of plum and then nibbled on the chicken breast on my plate. I didn't want to eat too much because I needed to be alert for the evening combat.

I pushed myself away from the table and walked over to my sword. I picked it up and felt the weight of it pull at my arm and shoulder. I lifted it and grabbed the handle with both hands. My left shoulder hurt a little, but still felt numb from the salve, so there was not much pain to contend with.

In the golden glow of the candlelight, I moved forward and back, slicing the air with fluid movements of the sword. The ache in my shoulder left me as I moved faster and faster, my body responding from memory of the hours spent in practice. My cool arms and legs grew warm and then glistened with a thin layer of sweat.

I wasn't sure how long I had been moving. When I stopped, my hair was damp with sweat. Travin stared at me. I set the sword by the door and then sat back down at the little table where he was sitting.

"That was amazing, Princess Wren." Travin had a different look on his face. His eyes spoke of awe and wonder. "I had no idea. I was not at the sword fighting competition the day your true identity was discovered. I did not know you were so skilled."

I smiled and wiped my moist brow with the back of my hand. "I've practiced for many years. My body just knows what to do when I hold a sword."

"Indeed it does." Travin nodded. "You will do well tonight. I have complete faith." He smiled and winked. I felt something warm and tingly all over my body. I hadn't felt this alive in a long while.

"It will soon be time to escort you to the great hall for the show this evening. Perhaps you should sit and rest and I will return shortly to take you to the place where the battle will be." Travin stood and picked up the tray of food with a question on his face.

"Yes, that would be fine." I watched his lean, muscular frame walk to the door.

"I will return shortly, then," he said, waving at me as he opened the door.

I waved back. As soon as the door shut, I could feel my stomach twist into a tight knot. The competition was about to begin. I wondered if Travin was right, that I would do fine. The ache in my left shoulder had intensified. The salve still sat on the table. I decided to put more of it on my shoulder.

Staring at myself in the mirror, I pushed the shoulder of my dress down to expose the wound and rub the salve as gently as I could over the puncture marks. My shoulder burned and throbbed. My face was pale and drawn. "Who are you fooling?" I thought. There was no way I could fight in this condition.

I looked up at the stone ceiling above me. "Heavenly Father, please help me. I don't know what to do. I have to fight but I don't feel like I'm able. I'm in pain and I need to be strong. Please show me what to do." I had felt so strong when I practiced earlier. As soon as I stopped, the pain began and now it was worse than ever. "Please help me. Give me your peace and your strength. Protect me the way you did when I faced the dragon."

A knock at the door told me Travin had arrived to escort me to the Great Hall. I quickly wiped the tears from my cheeks, pulled the shoulder of my dress back into place and then ran to open the door.

"Are you ready?" Travin stood at the door with his arm extended for me to grasp as we walked to the hall.

"Yes." I tried to sound confident and sure. I grabbed my sword, took Travin's arm with my left hand and walked down the hall to the stairs leading to the first floor of the castle.

16

I could hear the noise of a crowd nearby. We walked past the king's dining quarters and traveled through the grand entrance of the castle to another room just off the entrance.

I was shocked by the number of people gathered in the room. Travin guided me through the crowd to the far end of the room, where a wooden stage stood three feet off the floor.

I looked out over the crowd. The ladies wore colorful summer gowns and beaded hair ornaments. The men were dressed in richly embroidered jackets and velvet trousers that gathered at the knee. These were the wealthy townspeople who could afford to wager on the fight they were about to witness.

The king walked onto the stage, his royal purple robe flowing behind him as he made his way to the center of the wide platform. A large candelabra that hung from the ceiling illuminated the room. Gold candelabras stood at different intervals around the room, brightening dark corners. Two tables heaped with an assortment of breads, cheeses, fruits and meats stood near the doorway I had entered.

The king cleared his throat and began to speak. "Ladies and gentlemen. Tonight we will see if Princess Wren, champion of the sword fighting contest, will, once again, be victorious in her duel against Lord Maverick. Lord Maverick has been in my service for many years as one of my finest swordsmen. He has volunteered to be the first to steal away the victory from the hand of the fair princess.

"If he succeeds, Princess Wren will relinquish her title. If she is able to defeat Lord Maverick, she will dual once again in another seven nights against the next person willing to take her on."

"I'll take her on in my chamber," someone in the crowd yelled.

"So will I!" another man yelled.

"Silence!" The king's dark eyes held the menacing weather of a storm. "I will not have this become some sort of mockery. The princess may not be a man, but she can fight as well as any man I have encountered."

I looked at Travin, who still stood beside me with his arm extended. I held onto him, an anchor in the swirling crowd. He smiled at me and winked. The gesture made the same rush of warmth flow through me that I had experienced back in my room.

I smiled, realizing the king had just paid me a compliment. Previously, I didn't think this would have been possible with King Olerion. He didn't dislike me as much as I thought.

The king continued, "The rules of the duel are the same as those of the sword fighting contest. Whichever swordsman is able to knock the sword from his or her opponent's hand is the victor. You may place your wager now. If you bet on the victor, you will be paid double the gold you put up for the contest. Are there any questions?"

The crowd was silent. No one dared to speak for fear of provoking the king's anger.

"Then, without further ado, let the duel begin. Princess Wren and Lord Maverick, please join me on the stage."

Travin patted my hand and then dropped the arm he had extended for me. As I let go, I felt like a dandelion floating on a mighty wind, no longer tethered to anything safe and secure. Legs trembling and heart pounding, I walked up the steps on the side of the stage while Lord Maverick walked up the steps on the other side. I carefully centered my entire being and raised my sword.

I surveyed the giant man before me. He was much taller than me and his arms were almost as thick as my waist. "The king hates me after all," I thought. He had made certain I would fight someone nearly impossible to beat. After going up against the dragon and nearly losing my life, my confidence was dwindling.

The man had hair the color of the blackest of nights and his eyes were pale blue. He was strikingly handsome with a stern nose and chin and dark brows that made his eyes seem to glow. I wondered if Princess Lorenda had ever fancied him. He was unusually good looking.

"Pay attention, Wren," I murmured under my breath. I had to visualize the moves I would make instead of thinking about Lord Maverick's striking appearance. There was no way I could afford to lose this duel.

The king walked past me and went down the same steps I had just walked up. He stood at the front of the crowd and announced, "You may begin when I clap my hands."

I searched the crowd and caught sight of a red dress. The red hair of its owner, piled high on top of her head, belonged to none other than Princess Lorenda. I smiled, and she returned the gesture.

Clap, clap! The king signaled for the duel to begin.

Lord Maverick brought his helmet down, turned to his side, his right foot in front of his left, and raised his sword. I took a similar but opposing stance. We moved toward each other, our swords crashing together as we advanced and then retreated.

We moved in a circle for some time, exchanging blow for blow. I was aware of the throbbing pain in my shoulder and tried to ignore it. "Oh, Heavenly Father, please give me the strength to endure this pain," I prayed, as one of Lord Maverick's blows nearly knocked the sword from my shaking hands.

I tried to imagine I was back at home in the barn once again. I could see Aleric in the face of Lord Maverick. The candlelight in the room reminded me of the dimly-lit barn. I wished I could close my eyes, even for a moment, and go there in my mind.

Lord Maverick began swinging his sword from side to side in rapid succession, causing me to take several steps backward, nearly knocking me off the stage. I met each blow but barely recovered before the next one came at me. I jumped to one side and Lord Maverick's sword sliced through thin air. This gave me time to gather myself and deliver more offensive moves that caused my opponent to retreat.

I performed this maneuver several times, hopping from side to side so that Lord Maverick could not anticipate where to place his next strike. I could tell he was uncertain and frustrated. My smaller size in comparison to his large frame was an advantage. It took him longer to get his body moving in a different direction. I gained the upper hand.

Out of the corner of my eye, I could see Travin smiling at me from where he stood in the crowd. I watched as he mouthed the words, "Finish him." Heat surged through my entire body at that moment and I delivered one blow after another until Lord Maverick nearly fell from the stage. As he lunged forward to keep from falling backward, I raised my sword high above my head. With my left shoulder still burning and throbbing, I smashed my sword down on top of his, knocking the weapon from his hand.

Lord Maverick and I both stared at the sword now laying on the stage floor. I looked at the sword still in my hand to confirm that the weapon on the stage floor was not mine, and then stared at Lord Maverick. He looked at me with an expression of shock and bewilderment. Then, he bowed low before me, paying tribute to my victory.

King Olerion walked up on the stage and raised my arm in the air with his hand. "We have our victor! Princess Wren remains our sword fighting champion."

I blushed and gave the crowd a shaky smile. Some of the men and women smiled back while others glared at me. My eyes quickly found Travin's. He had his arm in the air, shaking it back and forth, a look of pride and admiration on his handsome face.

"We will return to this very stage seven nights from today and watch as the sword fighting princess take on another opponent. Who will be next? Who will dare to swallow their pride and fight against a woman? Come see if Princess Wren can maintain her champion status."

The king released my arm. "You are dismissed, Princess," he whispered in my ear. I made my way down the stage steps.

Travin rushed to the stage and extended his arm to escort me out of the crowded room. He folded my arm underneath his own and steered me to safety through the crowd, past the tables of food and out the door.

I carried my sword in my left hand. Travin stopped in the entryway and reached across me, pulling the sword from my hand. "You must be very tired. Let me carry this."

I nodded. "I am very tired."

"You'd better rest up because you will meet your match next week." A voice from behind us echoed across the room causing us to turn around. A man a little taller than me with an ordinary face stood behind us.

"Who are you?" I could hear the anger in Travin's voice.

"That does not matter. I have come to warn the princess that she will no longer be champion the next time she fights."

"We shall see about that." Travin tightened his grip on my arm and clutched the sword in his right hand.

"Yes, you shall," the man said. With that, he spun around on his heel and walked out the front door of the castle, his long black cloak trailing behind him.

I thought the voice sounded somewhat familiar but couldn't place where I'd heard it before.

"Do you know that man?" Travin asked.

"It seems like I've heard his voice before, but I don't know where, so I'm not sure if I know him." I shrugged and then followed Travin down the hall that led away from the room with the large hearth. He continued to keep my arm neatly tucked beneath his as if he were protecting a delicate bird.

I paused at the door to my room and looked up into Travin's kind brown eyes that remained soft and welcoming. "Thank you for protecting me tonight."

Travin smiled, fairly neat rows of teeth gleaming in the dim light of the hall torches. "I don't think you really need protecting. You could fight your way out of any situation with no assistance from me."

"It was good to have you near me." I gave him a demure smile and felt that same heat rush through my entire body once again. "I need a friend."

"I am your friend."

I turned the knob on the door and opened it. Before stepping inside I asked, "Could you please help me with something?"

"But of course. Anything, Princess."

"Would you bring me some rope?"

Travin frowned. "I do not understand what you could possibly need with rope but I will bring you some."

"Thank you." I rushed into my room and shut the door, not giving him a chance to ask any additional questions.

I needed the rope for securing the pigs so that I could walk them to the garden where I would meet the dragon very soon. I wished that I had already fed the dragon and that I could just go to bed. A feeling of dread came over me as I fingered the piece of jade at my throat.

Travin was back with a long length of rope before I had more time to worry. He handed the rope to me and I took it, yawning as if I was extremely tired. The truth was, my heart was pounding at the thought of facing the beast once again, but I needed Travin to leave to get this most undesirable task accomplished.

"You seem very tired, Princess. I will go now and return with your breakfast early tomorrow morning."

"That will be very good, Travin. Thank you again for being with me this evening."

"You're welcome." Taking my hand very gently, he kissed the top of it and left.

I shut the door, clutching the rope to my chest, and thought about the way his warm lips felt on my hand. I wondered for a moment what it would be like to feel his lips on my own. The thought made me dizzy, causing my hands and feet to tingle. I shook my head. These thoughts had to be put away for another time. I needed to focus.

I stood looking out the window of my room. I could see into the garden below. Suddenly, the necklace began to shake and grow warm.

"Princess Wren," came the haunting voice. "I am waiting for you in the garden. I hope, for your sake, that you have my food."

"I do. I have pigs. I will get them now and bring them to you."

"Hurry, or I shall become angry."

My hands trembled as I grabbed the rope and headed out the door. There was no one in the hall or on the stairs and I was able to make it to the barn without being seen. I grabbed the lit torch that hung on the outside wall of the barn. I went behind it to the pen where my pigs were confined. A hole in the top of the fence of the pigsty created a perfect holder for the torch. I opened the gate and shut it behind me, searching for the two pigs with red yarn tied around their ears.

The longer it took to find the pigs, the more my hands shook. All I could think of was the dragon grabbing me with its sharp, black talons and carrying me off for its next meal.

The pigs snorted, squealed and scurried. I didn't know pigs could move so fast. Finally, I caught a glimpse of one with red yarn around its ear. After almost falling twice, I somehow got the rope around the pig's neck.

Holding onto the rope, I spotted the second pig wedged in between two black and white spotted pigs. It was bigger than the first pig and seemed determined to remain free, running from me as soon as I reached down to tie the other end of the rope around its neck.

With only the dim light of the torch to guide me, I dragged the first pig after the second pig and lost my footing in a mud puddle.

While sitting in the middle of the mud puddle, covered in mud, I could hear laughter coming from the gate. I could see the shadow of a figure smaller than myself. "Lorenda?"

"Yes, it's me."

"How did you know I was here?"

"I followed you. I saw you going down the stairs and wanted to know where you were going, so I followed you."

"I have to hurry. The dragon is waiting for me in the castle garden. The beast wants its food, hence the reason I'm in this pigsty trying to retrieve the two pigs I bought today."

Lorenda's eyes enlarged and she gasped. I could see fear spreading across her face. She slowly opened the gate and went into the sty as well.

"I have one of the pigs tied with this rope. I need the second pig wearing a piece of red yarn around its ear tied to the other end of the rope."

The pig with the rope around its neck was squealing and snorting, trying to break free as if it knew it was about to die. Lorenda walked over to me and offered me her hand. I took hold of it and stood up, walking out of the mud puddle. The beautiful dress Lorenda had given me to wear was covered in a thick brown layer of muck.

Lorenda stared at the rope in my hands and frowned. "Where's the noose to put around the pig's neck? You have to have a noose to make it tight enough so the pig won't escape."

I stared back at her, shrugging my shoulders.

She took the rope from me and made a noose in what seemed like seconds.

"How did you know how to do that?" I was always amazed by the skills Lorenda possessed.

"My father taught me how to tie many different kinds of knots. I think he really wished he had a daughter and a son, but that was not to be. Since mother was unable to bear children after I was born, father taught me things he normally would teach a son."

She handed me the rope with the perfect noose at the end. Holding the rope in my left hand, I retrieved the torch and searched the cluster of pigs that now stood in a tight circle near the fence. The pig closest to the fence had red yarn on its left ear. Handing the torch to Lorenda, I pressed against the other pigs to part the squealing sea, and I was able to reach the little pig before it could run.

Grabbing the other end of the rope, I quickly had it around the pig's neck. The animal squealed in terror. I was afraid that all the noise the pigs were making would cause someone to investigate the cause of all the commotion. For a moment, I listened, but I didn't hear any footsteps approaching.

Securing the rope around the second pig, I pulled both pigs toward the gate. Lorenda followed. The pigs squealed and snorted the entire way to the castle.

"How can I get to the garden from here?" I stood at the front of the castle and Lorenda came up beside me.

"Follow me." She walked down a path that led from the front door of the fortress all the way around the far side of the structure. I could see Lorenda shaking with each step she took. I was almost comforted by her reaction to seeing the dragon. At least I wasn't the only one who was terrified.

Lorenda looked both ways before stepping out into the garden behind the castle. She took the rope of one of the pigs and we dragged both of them to the lilac bushes and beyond to the open field. I stepped into the field, pulling the pig after me. Lorenda followed.

"Wait!" I turned around to face Lorenda and put my hand out. "I don't think you should go with me. I don't think the dragon would be very pleased if you were with me."

"I will wait for you here in the bushes." She retreated into the shadow of the bushes while I continued to walk to the center of the field. I stopped in the open and waited.

The sound of heavy wings beating against the air caused me to turn around and look behind me. From out of the night sky, a large shadow swooped to the earth below and in two breaths, the dragon in before me. Its pointed teeth gleamed in the moonlight as it snarled at me.

"Where is the food you brought me?" the beast demanded.

I stepped aside, showing the dragon the two pigs that stood behind me. Their light pink bodies seemed to glow in the moonlight. They squealed and snorted and looked pathetic, with no defense against the demon that stood before them.

In one fell swoop, the dragon grabbed one of them with its razor-sharp talons. The pig screamed as the dragon lifted it through the air, its short legs flailing.

Crunch. I only thought to turn away after I saw the monster's teeth sink into the fat little pig. Blood oozed down the sides of the beast's mouth and dripped to the ground. I felt my own food from earlier that evening rise in my throat. I dropped the rope and turned away, running toward the lilac bushes.

The horrible sound of the pigs' screaming and squealing lasted for only a moment, but as I hid among the trees, I wept as if someone dear to me had just died. It wasn't that I was attached to the pigs. It was the pure violence of the scene and the fact that I was responsible for making other living creatures die a horrible death that made me weep.

"Wren." Lorenda moved through the shadows to where I stood. She put her hand on my arm and pulled me out of the bushes to the other side, where the garden was. Walking past the planter of purple and black flowers, we made our way to a bench that sat next to an apple tree to the left of the back door of the castle. The shadows cast by the tree helped hide us beneath the bright moonlit night.

"Are you all right?" Lorenda sat down next to me on the bench and folded her hands in her lap.

I wiped the tears from my cheeks and nodded. "I guess I was not prepared for what it would be like to feed that horrible creature. I didn't imagine it would feast in front of me."

"The beast has no manners," Lorenda stated in a solemn tone. "It does not care who it offends and is not polite in any way. It is a savage creature, intent on satisfying its own cravings. It has no concern for any other living creature."

I laughed. "I don't know what I expected."

"My mother died at the hands of that vile serpent. I feel nothing but contempt for it and I know its true nature. You can never trust it, nor let your guard down when you are around the beast."

I ran my fingers through my hair, which was starting to grow out. It had been nearly three weeks since I had cut it. I couldn't believe how my life had changed since I decided to enter the sword fighting contest. "My life will never be the same, Lorenda. I don't know how I will ever be able to go back home."

"You can always stay with me. We are friends for life now."

I knew that what she was saying was true. This was comforting but didn't quite take away the longing I felt for something familiar, for the smell of warm bread rising from the kitchen in the morning or Aleric's bright blue eyes in the soft light of the barn. I even missed my mother, although I had never been very close to her. In the midst of this longing for home I felt a never-ending ache to undo the terrible bond I shared with the dragon.

I shivered. I felt a little damp and looked down at my dress, which I hadn't noticed was covered in blood. The blood from the pigs had dripped onto the dress while the dragon was eating. "Oh my! I'm so sorry, Lorenda. I ruined your dress!"

"It's okay, Wren. I have plenty. Burn it in your hearth. Let's go in so you can change and we can get to sleep."

I nodded and followed her into the castle. I was exhausted and needed to rest. The jade pendant bounced against my chest as I walked. It took every ounce of reason to keep me from yanking it off. How I hated this connection with that demon!

As soon as I closed the door to my room, I stood in front of the hearth and peeled the blood-stained dress from my body. Naked, I reached for a cloth and dipped in repeatedly in the basin of water that was sitting by my bed. Then, I rinsed myself off as best I could. The water in the basin turned red from the blood washed off of my skin. I dabbed myself dry and then walked to the hearth, stoking the glowing embers that remained from the fire at dinner. Grabbing the soiled dress from the floor, I threw it into the fire and stood watching it burn for quite some time feeling that nothing would ever feel fresh or pure again.

With my eyes heavy and my body aching from the evening's ordeal, I pulled the sleeping gown over my head and crawled into bed. My mind, however, kept returning to the screaming pigs and the blood spilling onto the ground. Looking up at the ceiling, I prayed. "Heavenly Father, please take these vile images out of my mind. Grant me your peace and some sleep. Guard my thoughts and my dreams."

In little time, I was fast asleep, dreaming of riding my horse along the path that led to the pool where I loved to swim. I could feel myself in the cool water, a warm breeze blowing across my bare skin. I smiled as I slept, peace finally enveloping me.

17 |

Bright sunlight was streaming through the window when I heard the knock at my door. I rose, grabbed the robe - another gift from Lorenda - from where it lay at the end of my bed, and rushed to the door.

Travin stood at the door with a tray of bread and fruit. He smiled at my disheveled hair. "You're a late sleeper. It's fast approaching the noon hour and you're still in your bedclothes."

I blushed. "I didn't get to bed until late in the evening. It was too hard to sleep after my dual." I hated to lie to Travin, but I couldn't tell him I had to feed a hungry dragon before retiring for the evening.

"You don't have to explain. You can do as you please. You are a princess, remember?" Travin walked to the table and set the food down.

I clutched the pendant that hung cold and heavy against my chest. I wished his words were true, that I could do as I pleased. As it was, I had to find another meal for the dragon before tomorrow evening. I had no idea how I would explain this to Travin.

Without saying another word, I sat down at the table and grabbed a piece of fruit. Travin sat across from me, watching me intently.

"Did I say something that upset you, Princess Wren? Your mood seems to have shifted."

I took a bite of the plum, the juice spilling over onto my hand, and chewed as I shook my head back and forth. "No," I answered after swallowing the bite. "I was just thinking."

"About what, if I may ask?" Travin leaned forward on his elbows, face in his hands, his dark eyes stared at me.

"I was thinking about buying more farm animals. Perhaps with the money I make from the sword fighting, I can start a farm with cows, chickens, and pigs."

Travin raised an eyebrow in surprise. I hoped he wouldn't ask too many questions. "You never cease to puzzle me, my dear Princess. I will take you to Mrs. Craddenbrook again if you wish."

"I do. I would like to buy a cow." I hoped a cow would create less of a commotion than pigs. I needed to fulfill my obligation without drawing attention to myself.

"When would you like to buy this cow?"

"Today would be lovely."

"I had a feeling you would say that. You waste no time pursuing what you want."

"I've never been one to sit still and wait."

"I can see that. You are unlike other maidens."

I ran my hands through my disheveled hair. I wasn't sure if Travin was paying me a compliment or remarking on some weakness.

"I find your persistence refreshing." A gradual smile spread across Travin's face. I could feel every inch of my skin tingle. I knew from the heat radiating from my face that I was blushing once again.

I had been hungry when I sat down, but now my appetite was gone. I had never felt this way before except for when Aleric held me in his arms prior to leaving with my father. It was exhilarating and so uncomfortable all at the same time.

"I will give you time to get yourself prepared for the day and then I shall return and take you to Mrs. Craddenbrook."

I smiled and nodded, still smoothing my hair. "I shall look forward to your return."

Travin rose and left the room, waving back at me as he walked through the door.

My heart fluttered at the sight of him walking out the door. I didn't want him to leave; I wished he could always stay.

With him gone from the room, I felt a renewed sense of hunger. I broke off another chunk of bread and spread jam across it. I ate in the silence, savoring the tart sweetness of the jam on my tongue. With a few more bites, I was full.

I walked to the window and opened it. I could see the king and Lorenda sitting on the planter wall in the center of the garden, arguing as usual. Their voices carried up to the window.

"I can't make that promise to you, father. Wren is my friend. I will not act as if this isn't so."

"You will, or I will banish her from my kingdom. I will not have you entertaining wild ideas of sword fighting or roaming about the countryside on your own because of spending time with her."

"I am not so easily influenced. Please don't banish her. She has nowhere to go. Her father has forgotten she exists and her dear friend has left her to go to war. We are her family now."

"Princess Wren is not your family, nor are you her friend. I will not have this in my home. You will obey me or I will banish her."

I could see Lorenda nod. "I will do as you wish," she said, her voice sad and small. I turned away from the window and walked over to the bed. I sat down and felt tears sting my eyes. What did this mean? If Lorenda agreed with her father not to be my friend, would this mean we could no longer meet in the garden? I couldn't imagine facing the dragon without Lorenda nearby.

"Oh, Heavenly Father, what am I to do? I feel like every friend I am given gets taken from me. I don't know what to do. Please help me."

It was at that moment a knock came at the door. I wiped the tears from my face, sniffed and walked to the door to let Travin into my chambers.

When I opened the door, King Olerion stood before me, his rich brocaded jacket gleaming in the light streaming in through the windows. He always wore purple and black and his dark eyes glistened with anger against his pale skin.

"I will have a word with you, Princess Wren." He pushed past me and walked into the room. I followed after him and stood like a frightened deer in the hunter's sight.

"You will not spend any time with Princess Lorenda. If I see you with her, I will immediately banish you from my kingdom. You will never be welcome here again."

"Yes, your majesty." I looked at the ground and wondered if someone had seen me and Lorenda in the field the previous evening.

"That is all I wish to say." With that, the king turned and walked out the door.

I was relieved as I watched him walk out the door. He frightened me with his complete disregard for who I was. He saw me as a threat as well as a source of entertainment. I wished once again for the one-hundredth time that I had never entered that sword fighting contest. I could be home right now within the safety of my father's castle, wasting away from boredom. That sounded better than wasting away from fear of dragon and foreign king.

Another knock came at my door. I was afraid to open it, afraid to see the king's angry eyes once again. I forced myself to walk to the door and open it. Travin stood outside, his arm extended for me to receive his escort to Mrs. Craddenbrook's.

"What's wrong, Princess? You look as if you've seen a goblin."

I walked out the door and took his arm. We went down the hall, down the stairs and out the front entrance of the castle toward the village. I was silent until we reached the village.

"The king came to my room," I said. "He warned me that he would banish me from his kingdom if he caught me visiting with Princess Lorenda."

"Hmm." Travin said nothing more than that.

"She's my friend, Travin. Without her I have no one."

Travin stopped in front of the blacksmith shop, two buildings up from Mrs. Craddenbrook's. "What am I to you, Princess Wren?"

I could see the hurt in his eyes and wished I could swallow the words I had just spoken before they left my mouth.

"You are my friend, Travin. I didn't mean to imply that you were not. I'm just so sad about Lorenda. She has become very dear to me."

"She will continue to find a way to see you. Princess Lorenda does not give up easily."

"But she told the king she would no longer be my friend."

"She has said many things to her father that she does not do."

"Travin, I'm so sorry. I didn't mean to imply that you are not my friend. You have helped me more than I could have ever asked. I can't thank you enough for what you have done."

"You can thank me by taking care of yourself. You seem to have yourself involved in dangerous activities."

I was silent. How could Travin know I was fighting for my very life? I was sure he knew nothing of me feeding the dragon but seemed to sense I was in danger. He was very perceptive.

We walked in silence the rest of the way up the dusty street to Mrs. Craddenbrook's butcher shop. When we walked through her front door, she quickly moved from behind the counter to greet us. She embraced both of us as if we had been on a long journey and then resumed her place at the counter.

I had never been treated so warmly. I had only met this woman once and yet there was a familiarity between us as if I had known her as a little girl.

"What can I do for you, my dear?"

I swallowed and mumbled, feeling ashamed by the reason I needed another animal. I couldn't bear the thought of sacrificing another innocent creature to the hellish beast, but didn't know what else to do.

"I couldn't hear you dear. Speak up a little. These ears are old and heavily-used."

"I need a cow."

"A whole cow?"

"Yes, ma'am. I would like to build a farm and I must acquire the animals slowly as I earn the money to buy them."

"I see." Mrs. Craddenbrook squinted up at me as if to question the truthfulness of my statement. I fidgeted and squirmed, feeling uncomfortable with the small but wide woman's gaze.

"Who's going to help you on this farm?"

"What do you mean?"

"You aren't married and some of the work on a farm only a man can do."

"I will help her Mrs. Craddenbrook." Travin stepped up to the counter and smiled at the suspicious shopkeeper.

"That's good. This one needs your help." She winked at me and smiled. I could see that a couple of her teeth had made their escape, leaving the woman with a semi-toothless grin. How different this woman's life was compared to my own! I felt a bit foolish for telling her I wished to build a farm. How ridiculous I must have looked to this villager who had known only hard work all of her life.

"I will get that cow for you, but it will cost you double what you paid for the pigs a couple of days ago."

I nodded. "I understand." I determined that this would be the last time I would buy a cow for the dragon. I had to make my money last until the next sword fight, which would not take place for six more days. I would have to feed the dragon three more times before I would receive any additional money. I would just buy chickens or pigs for the demon.

Mrs. Craddenbrook hurried out the door behind the counter and returned shortly to the front of the shop with a small brown and white cow. I stared at the animal's big brown eyes and wondered how I would hand this gentle creature over to the dragon to be eaten alive.

"My dear child, are you quite well?" I had been staring at the cow so that I didn't hear the shopkeeper ask me to step back into the shop to pay for the beast.

"Oh...yes...I'm fine. I was just thinking that the cow is a very sweet creature."

"Well, that may be true but if you milk her wrong, she'll nip at you."

"I'll be careful."

Travin stood outside and held on to the cow while I went back inside the shop to pay for it.

200

"That will be two gold shekels," Mrs. Craddenbrook said, reaching out her small, plump hand to me. I opened the mouth of my velvet pouch and deposited the gold coins into her hand.

She grabbed my hand with both of hers. "I can see the trouble in your eyes, child. You are heavy laden and need a hand to lift you out of the deep water in which you find yourself. The Heavenly Father can help you find your way. Ask Him and He will direct your steps."

I stared, frightened by her words as well as comforted. Had she figured out why I needed the animals? Did she somehow know that I was pacifying the dragon? I tried to appear calm, but I felt my throat begin to swell and tears well in my eyes.

"There, there, child." Mrs. Craddenbrook patted my hand. "Do as I tell you, and you will find the way out of this trouble."

I gave her a weak smile and gently removed my hand from her grasp. "Thank you," I whispered and hurried out the door.

Travin saw me wipe the tears from my cheeks as I walked toward him. "What happened, Princess?"

I wished I could tell him the truth, but I knew this was impossible. "Nothing. Mrs. Craddenbrook just reminds me just how much I need a real mother. I haven't seen my own since I was twelve, and being around the kind, old woman made me miss her." I wanted to get away from my companion and this uncomfortable conversation.

Travin nodded, grasping my arm and giving it a gentle squeeze. "You're looking fragile, may I help?"

"Yes, no, um, thank you. I will be fine."

We walked slowly to the barn, the cow trailing behind us. I made certain not to look at the animal with its sweet brown eyes. In a day I would have to hand the poor creature over to the beast.

Travin handed the rope tied around the cow's neck to me and opened the barn door. He walked back over to me to get the rope, and led the cow through the barn and out the other side, across the pig pen to the pasture land behind the barn. Taking some red yarn from his pocket, he tied a piece of it around the cow's ear. Leading the cow through the pasture gate, he untied the rope and set the animal free to roam and eat.

I watched the cow walk slowly across the grassy field and bend its head to pull up a chunk of grass in its mouth. I wished I hadn't bought the cow. It would make more of a bloody mess than the chickens. How would I bear the horror of the scene?

"Princess Wren! Princess Wren!" I jerked my head around to see Travin standing in the pig pen. He been trying to find my pigs and could not locate them.

"Your pigs are not here. Do you know where they are?"

"What?! They should be there!" I felt the heat of shame as soon as the lie left my lips. I didn't know how to answer him.

"I will find out what has happened. I told the castle butcher that the pigs with the red yarn did not belong to the king. He must have used them for the feast during the sword fighting contest. He will have to pay you, Princess. I will see to it."

"No! No! I'm sure the pigs just got out somewhere. Please don't make a fuss with him. I'm sure he's just letting them wander."

Travin walked out of the pig pen to where I stood. "You are gracious and kind, my lady. I am amazed by your goodwill."

I felt like a pile of cow dung. I had just told Travin a lie and now he was complimenting me on my gracious spirit. If only he knew the real reason the pigs were gone, he would probably never speak to me again.

202

"Let us do something out of the ordinary today, Princess." Travin smiled at me as he extended his arm to escort me back through the barn, his eyes dancing with mischief.

"What do you propose?" I felt myself tremble with excitement, in spite of the shame I still carried over the lie.

"You shall see. It will be a surprise for you."

"No one has ever given me a surprise. I cannot wait to see what you are talking about."

"We shall be riding horses. You may want to wear some different shoes."

"I'm fine. I do not have any other shoes to wear. I have ridden horses ever since I was twelve. I have no trouble."

Travin smiled. "I should have known you were an experienced equestrian."

We stopped in front of my horse. I hadn't checked on Flynn for two days. He whinnied at the sight of me.

"Hey there, boy. You look good." I rubbed his neck. His proud coat shone with care. I was pleased with the job the stableman was doing caring for my friend.

Travin brought my saddle to the stall and placed it on the horse's back. I tightened the saddle against the horse's side while Travin put a saddle on a horse in the stall next to mine.

Leading the horses out of the stable, we mounted them and rode to the castle gate.

"Good afternoon." Travin waved at the guard. He yawned and turned the wheel that opened the gate. We made our way through it and were soon on the winding road leading out of the valley.

"Thank you for doing this for me, Travin." I was relieved to be away from King Olerion's domain. I felt like a weight had lifted from my spirit.

"You seemed to be a caged bird in that castle. I wanted to help set you free."

We rode into the woods, heading in the direction of my home. The woods were shaded and gave a cool reprieve from the hot afternoon sun. I wondered where Travin was headed. I felt a little uncomfortable not knowing where I was going. The last time I had been unaware of what my destination would be like, I had to face a terrible monster.

We soon came to my waterfall, the same pool I had often bathed in before living at King Olerion's castle.

Travin turned off the path and walked his horse over to the waterfall, several stones' throw away from the path. He paused at the pool and dismounted. "We have arrived at your surprise."

I tried to smile but all I could think of was the man with the dark red beard. The last time I had been to the waterfall was the day I had encountered this awful man for the first time.

"Is something wrong?" Travin asked, his forehead creased in concern.

"No! This is wonderful, Travin. I was just remembering something that troubled me, but I'm fine. Thank you for bringing me to this beautiful place." I dismounted and walked to where he stood. I put my hand on his arm as if to reassure him.

"I'm glad you approve." Travin smiled a wide, broad smile. I didn't have the heart to tell him that this used to be my secret bathing spot, so I just smiled back.

"Let's put our feet in the water."

I laughed, thinking about all the times I had taken off all my clothes at this very spot.

"What makes you laugh?" he asked, taking my hand and leading me to a rock which sat next to the pool.

"I'm not used to taking off any garments around a gentleman."

"Just your shoes is all I ask for." I sat down on the rock while Travin bent down in front of me, slipping off my shoes one by one.

After removing my shoes, he sat down beside me and took off his boots. I stared at his long feet and toes. I hadn't noticed until now what a big man he was. No wonder I felt safe with him.

He stood and then offered me his hand, helping me up from the rock. Still holding my hand, he led me to the water's edge. The bottom of my dress floated on top of the water as I moved my feet through it along the shoreline.

My foot slipped on a rock and Travin grabbed me before I fell into the water. Holding me tight around the waist, he lifted me from the water and drew me toward him.

With one arm around my waist, he placed his other hand behind my head and held it there as he moved his face close to mine. My arms seemed to move of their own accord, wrapping around his neck as his warm lips brushed against my own, once, twice and then a little more forceful lingering.

I felt my body grow limp as my head spun around and around inside. The kiss came and went on a whisper.

Travin pulled away, staring at me with dark eyes still flickering from the fire between us. He cupped my face with both of his hands and gently kissed the tip of my nose. "You are very beautiful, Princess Wren." Travin's voice was thick and deep. He sounded like one entranced.

"Thank you," I whispered. I never had a man tell me I was beautiful. I wasn't sure what to say. Travin's words erupted inside me, like a cloud of fluttering butterflies.

I looked down and realized the bottom of my dress was soaked by the water. It had been floating on the water and slowly began to sink below the surface. I laughed. "So much for being presentable."

Travin bent down, grasping me beneath my knees and lifting me into the air. He carried my wet form away from the pool and over to the rock which sat in the warm sun. Water dripped down the sides of the rock as he placed me on its flat surface. He sat down beside me.

"I hope I didn't overstep my bounds with you, Princess. I was overcome."

I smiled as my cheeks grew a soft pink and not from the heat of the sun. "I'm certain you could see that I, too, was overcome. I believe I kissed you as much as you kissed me."

"Perhaps," he replied, bending his knees as he put his long toes and feet on top of the rock. He wrapped his arms around his knees and looked at me.

"I never knew women could be like you, Princess."

I frowned, picking up a small rock and tossing it into the pool to see the ripples it would make. "What do you mean?" I stared at him, overcome with curiosity and a tinge of concern.

"The women I have served in King Olerion's land have been dull and lifeless, only concerned with dancing and what they would wear to this or that occasion. You are the first woman I have ever known that wishes to sword fight and is also very good at it. You're the first person of royalty that I have ever known to try and build a farm. You are wild and primitive, fearless in every way."

I looked down at the dark red dress which had almost turned black because of being soaked with water. I couldn't look at Travin with the shame and guilt I felt bearing down upon my head. If only he knew what a coward I had been with the dragon and that the only reason I wanted farm animals was to keep myself alive, he wouldn't be so enamored.

"You have trouble hearing what I say. Why is that, Princess?"

I forced myself to look at him. "There are many things you do not know about me."

"And I would like to know, if you would only let me."

"That's impossible, Travin."

"Why? Is it because I do not come from royal lineage? I am a servant of sorts to King Olerion, but I am more than that."

I looked down at my dress again. I didn't know what to say. I couldn't tell him about the real reason I was unable to talk to him. I was too ashamed and I wasn't sure how he would feel about me, knowing I had deceived the king once again as well as him. He would no longer trust me.

"That is why you keep me at a distance; because I am not of royal blood. And yet, you let me kiss you. I do not understand you."

Travin stood and walked back to where the horses were tied to a tree near the waterfall. I ran after him. "It's not because you are not from royal blood. There are just some things of which I cannot speak."

Travin climbed up in the saddle of his horse and stared at me. "Maybe you will finally learn to trust me someday. At some point, you will have to trust someone."

I climbed on top of Flynn and held the reins, waiting for Travin to lead the way. I had nothing more to say. It was true that I trusted no one, not even Lorenda. I figured she had abandoned our friendship and Travin would too in due time. Everyone I ever cared for had left. I was not about to trust anyone again. It was too painful.

The ride back to the castle was filled with awkward silence. I was at a loss for words. I didn't know how to make Travin understand that my secrets had nothing to do with him. He was not the reason I would not talk to him or tell him the whole truth. My fear of losing his affection was what drove me to silence.

When he brought my evening meal to my room, Travin did not stay to eat with me. He claimed he had official business to attend for the king. I was sure it was because I had refused to talk to him about what troubled me.

Eating only a few bites of my dinner, I placed my tray with the food outside my door so I wouldn't have to see him again and crawled beneath the covers of the bed before the sun went down.

My eyes grew heavy as I drifted toward sleep. A small pebble hit against the glass in my bedroom window. I rose from the bed to see what it was. There stood Lorenda below my window, the way she had stood the two evenings before.

I slipped on my shoes and hurried from my room, down the stairs, and out the back door.

Lorenda was walking away from me toward the lilac bushes when I arrived at the square planter. "Lorenda, we shouldn't meet like this!" I whispered as I approached my friend. "I overheard you and your father talking in the garden today. I know he will banish me from his kingdom if he sees us together."

Still not turning around, Lorenda turned her head to the side and pressed her finger to her lips indicating that I should be silent. She then motioned for me to follow. I followed as she led us toward the lilac bushes. She stood next to one of them as I approached.

"I have to find a way to slay the dragon," I said, finally speaking the thoughts I had been thinking ever since buying the cow. Lorenda turned around very slowly to face me. Dark eyes as black as soot stared back at me, surrounded by a pale face that nearly glowed in the moonlight. The hair was red like Lorenda's but the face was one I had seen only one other time. I remembered those dark eyes that frightened me in the forest the first night Lorenda and I had camped on our way to the dragon. I was face-to-face once again with the witch.

"If you do any harm to the beast, you will never find true love. You will live out your days alone and desolate."

I took a second, long look at her, turned and ran. I ran as fast as I could away from the lilac bushes and down the garden path that bordered the square planter.

Wham! My foot slipped on a small rock that lay on the path. I stumbled and fell, face-first, slamming my head on the ground.

18

When I awoke, I was back in my room in the castle in my bed. My head throbbed and when I raised it from the pillow, the room spun around as if I had been twirling in a circle.

Putting my hand to my forehead, I could feel a large lump at the beginning of my hairline. I carefully stood from the bed and walked in a slow, deliberate manner to the mirror above the dressing table that sat next to the window. Examining my forehead in the mirror, I could see a giant knot had developed. I touched it and winced. It was sore and tender. Then, I recalled my fall from the previous evening.

The room began to spin again as I thought of the witch's black eyes, staring at me from among the bushes.

"If you do any harm to the beast, you shall never find true love." The witch's words rushed back to me. Though I thought I had followed Lorenda, it was the witch all along as it had been in the forest. How I yearned to talk with Lorenda. I needed someone to help me sort through this.

A knock came at my door. I opened it to find Travin carrying a tray which contained my morning meal.

"I thought you might be hungry. You hardly ate anything last night."

My hair had fallen into my eyes and as I brushed it away, Travin could see the red swell of the bump at my hairline.

"What happened to your head?"

I waved him into the room and then shut the door behind him.

"I tripped and fell last night before going to bed." This wasn't entirely a lie. I just bent the truth regarding when I tripped.

Travin shook his head as he set the tray on the table and then walked over to where I stood. He took my face in his hands in a gentle embrace and examined the knot, frowning as he stared at it.

"You are certainly prone to injury, Princess."

I could feel the tears well in my eyes and spill onto my cheeks before I could will them to remain below the surface. The thought of never finding true love, of losing Travin forever, was more than I could bear.

"Oh, Wren," Travin said, wrapping me in his arms. "I did not mean to make you cry."

I noticed that he called me by my first name instead of addressing me formally. This made me cry even harder.

"You didn't make me cry," I said, my voice muffled by his collar.

Travin lifted my face from where it was buried against his chest. Cupping my face with both his hands, he kissed my forehead, my nose, and then my mouth, first gently and then more forcefully, pulling me close to him.

I sank into his embrace, returning his kiss with the same intensity. We stood in that embrace for a long while. I did not want it to end.

Travin pulled away, reaching for my hands. He held them both in each of his, his hands covering mine. "You are what I've been waiting for," he said.

I looked away, feeling suddenly ashamed. If only I had met him under different circumstances. He had no idea what a wreck my life had become.

"Why do you shrink away when I say that you are what I want?" I looked at him and could see the hurt in his eyes once again. And once again I didn't know what to say.

"Travin, you do not know me. If you knew all about me, you probably wouldn't want me."

"I don't understand why you say that. I've seen and heard enough to know that I love you."

I dropped his hands and stared at him with cool, distant eyes. I knew I loved him too, but couldn't bring myself to say it. This was all happening faster than a fall off the side of a mountain.

"Please don't say such things. Everything is happening too quickly. I am overwhelmed."

He moved toward the door. "I must go, Princess. I do not understand you and need time to think about what you have said. Enjoy your breakfast." He closed the door and I felt lonely once again.

I walked over to the table and tried to eat one of the hard boiled eggs on the tray of food. I could only force down a few bites. I was too upset to eat.

The large Bible I had read before sat on the table to the right of the tray of food. I picked it up and carried it over to my bed. Sitting on the bed, I turned to the middle of the book and began to read. "The Lord is my strength and my refuge, an ever-present help in times of trouble."

I closed my eyes. "Heavenly Father, please be my strength and my refuge. I need to know you are with me."

A soft tapping sounded at the window of my bedroom. I rose and opened the window. A dove with soft, white feathers flew through the opening and landed on my bed.

I smiled and looked up. "Thank you, Heavenly Father." The dove perched on the edge of the bed and then flew out the window once again.

I sat back down on the bed, folded my legs underneath me and continued to read one passage after another in the Psalms. I marveled at King David's passion and depth of sorrow. I felt like he had peered into my soul and put words to my struggles. I was not alone.

I was shocked when a knock came at my door during the noon hour. Where had the time gone? I closed the large Bible and walked to the door. When I opened it, there stood Lorenda.

"Lorenda you shouldn't be here! If your father sees you, he'll banish me."

Lorenda walked into my room and closed the door behind her. "My father has taken his soldiers on a week-long journey to France. We can move about the castle in freedom."

I ran to Lorenda and embraced her. "It is so good to see you. I thought that perhaps I would not see you again after your talk with the king the other day."

"How do you know about that?" Lorenda took a step back, but continued to hold my hands.

"I could hear you through the window of my bedroom when the two of you were in the garden."

Lorenda frowned. "I am sorry you overheard that. I won't allow my father to banish you. I know I said I would do as he requested but I had no intention of keeping that promise."

I sighed. "I'm so glad to hear that."

Lorenda walked toward the door. "Come. Let us go to the orchard beyond the field past the garden and pick fresh peaches for our noonday meal."

I slipped into my shoes and followed her out the door. In no time we were walking across the field where I had last fed the dragon. The green grass was beginning to fade in the midsummer's heat. I tried to think of the juicy peaches waiting for me in the orchard instead of the smell of blood which seemed to tint the air as I reached the very spot where I had sacrificed the pigs.

Lorenda walked swiftly toward the group of trees at the far end of the field. She seemed to sense that I was troubled by the gruesome memories the field held. I ran after her, anxious to put some distance between my nightmares and the day at hand.

Lorenda slipped through the trees at the far end of the field. I hesitated. This had a similar feeling to the dream I had of the witch.

"Wren, are you coming?"

It was Lorenda's voice. I walked between two peach trees and closed my eyes, afraid I would see the witch when I opened them.

"Have a peach." Lorenda held out a plump, light-orange colored peach.

I opened my eyes and smiled, relieved to see Lorenda standing in front of me. Her hair looked like red velvet in the dappled sunlight dripping through the trees. It stood out against the royal blue dress, its bodice embroidered with red and yellow flowers. Her pale face was flushed pink from the heat and her blue eyes were a tranquil ocean in a pink sunset. I touched my own hair, which was still short from when I had cut it for the sword fighting contest. I wondered what Travin saw in me. Lorenda was so beautiful and I was so battered and torn.

Lorenda walked down the row of trees and plucked a second and then a third peach. I followed her lead, carrying four peaches at one point.

"Let's sit near the river and eat them," Lorenda called from a stone's throw ahead of me. I followed her to the end of the row of trees, down a grassy slope filled with wildflowers, to another grove of trees which sat near a slow-moving river that curved and meandered its way away from the orchard.

Lorenda sat on a fallen tree near the river's edge and I joined her. The shade and cool water gave sweet relief from the heat of the day.

Setting our peaches on the smooth log, we each took one peach and ate in the shade, juice running down our hands and arms. When we finished, we hopped off the tree and walked to the bank of the river, washing the peach juice from our skin.

Lorenda went back to the fallen tree trunk and sat down. I followed. "You must find a way to slay the dragon," she said unexpectedly. "I can see what it's doing to your spirit. It's a heavy weight threatening to crush you."

I looked out over the river, amazed by how perceptive Lorenda was. I knew she was right. It was killing me.

"I will help you, Wren. Perhaps I can distract the beast while you drive your sword into its belly."

I remembered my dream of the witch. I could see the witch's dark eyes and pale skin. The medium mouthed the words, "You will never find true love."

"I can't slay the dragon, Lorenda."

"Yes you can, Wren. Look at the story of David and Goliath in the holy book. The giant was much bigger and more powerful than David and yet he killed him. The Heavenly Father gave David victory. He will be with you as well, and so will I."

"I can't slay the demon or I will never find true love."

Lorenda frowned. "That isn't true."

"I dreamed about the witch I saw in the woods when we journeyed to the dragon's home. She appeared to me again last night. I thought it was you summoning me from the garden last night. It looked like you. I followed you to the edge of the lilac bushes. You turned around and it was the witch. She told me that if I slayed the dragon, I would never find true love."

Lorenda shook her head. "The witch has no power over you. You do not belong to her. It was just a dream."

"I thought it was just a dream but I fell when I was running away from her. Everything went black and when I awoke, I was in my own bed with a large lump on my head. It was real, Lorenda."

"You don't have to be afraid of her, Wren. She lies and deceives. You can't take her words to heart."

I was silent. I wished Lorenda understood how difficult this was. If she had heard the witch's words, seen her speak them aloud, she would know that there was some truth to them. I believed I would be under a curse.

"Just think about it, Wren. The Heavenly Father is above the witch. He is the authority over both you and her. He would not allow her to curse you for slaying a demon. She can try, but it won't have any effect. He does not wish for you to be in bondage to that creature."

I looked at her. What she said was stronger than the fear paralyzing my will to be free. I had not considered what the Heavenly Father would want for me. He was good and full of light. There was and is no darkness in Him. He would not desire that I be tormented.

"Yes, Lorenda. I will receive your help. I have to meet the beast tonight with the cow I purchased yesterday. I want you to help me slay the creature once and for all." I began to shake at the thought of such a confrontation. I didn't know if I could be brave enough to bring it to fruition.

"We can do this together, Wren." Lorenda grabbed my hand. "Try not to be afraid."

I gave a weak smile. Lorenda hopped off the tree trunk and walked toward the river. "Let's cool our feet in the water." I followed. We set our shoes by the river and, holding our dresses above the knees, waded into the rushing ice cold water. At first, I gasped from the shock of the cold, but in a short time I smiled as the water made my feet and ankles tingle. My spirit soared with the swiftness of the moving water and the thought of being free once again.

"I can see you're already lighter just thinking about being free from that awful creature." Lorenda smiled at me.

"Yes. I have hope that I can return home instead of being obligated to fight with my sword every week just to buy food for that beast."

Lorenda was silent. I wondered what she was thinking.

"So you would return home once the beast was slain?" Her expression seemed melancholy to me.

"Well, yes. Your father doesn't want me here. He's made that very clear. That doesn't mean we wouldn't see each other. We could meet at the pool with the waterfall."

"What about Travin?"

I just remembered that Travin usually comes to my room to bring me my noonday meal. "Oh no! Do you think he came to my room to bring me my food while we were in the orchard?"

"I told him we were going to the orchard."

"I don't know if he wants to be around me anymore." I thought of our conversation earlier that morning. He had been very upset when he left my room.

"He just doesn't understand why you won't tell him what is troubling you."

"He told you that?" I was bothered that Travin had confided in Lorenda about me.

"Don't become angry, Wren. He cares for you very much."

"I can't tell him about the dragon. He won't want me to continue what I'm doing."

"And you aren't, remember? We are going to set you free."

"I still can't tell him. I'm ashamed of sacrificing those animals."

"Don't worry about telling him anything. It will all be taken care of tonight."

We made our way back to the castle as the day grew cooler. I was not surprised when Travin brought my evening meal but did not stay. He was polite, but as distant as the moon. I busied myself by reading the holy book until I felt the pendant around my neck begin to vibrate.

"Child," came the unholy voice. "I am waiting in the field beyond the garden. Make haste because I am hungry."

I shivered and slipped into my shoes. Lorenda was supposed to have come to my room by now. I wondered where she was and hoped she would somehow know to meet me in the garden.

I ran down the hall and stairs. I noticed a couple of the king's guards standing at their posts. I thought Lorenda had said they were all away from the castle. I went out the front door and noticed more guards. My heart sank. The king had returned.

I scurried into the barn and found my cow standing in the stall ready to be milked early the next morning. I tied a rope around its neck and, as gently as I could, pulled the animal forward from the stall. It mooed in defiance and then lumbered forward.

"I'm so sorry, Mrs. Cow. I hate myself for what I'm about to do, but I don't know what else to do." I pulled the cow along a path that led me around the side of the castle and out of the direct gaze of the guards. The path went past the little house where all the gardening tools were kept and led me to the lilac bushes. I could feel my stomach tie in knots at the thought of facing the beast without Lorenda. I knew she would not come tonight with the king back at the castle. It was too risky.

My pendant vibrated as I stepped into the trees. The cow continued to moo, unhappy with being dragged through the trees away from the safe and secure barn.

"You're tarrying too long, child, and I am growing impatient. You had better be here with my food momentarily or I will find something or someone to eat here at the king's castle."

"I am here. I'm walking onto the field right now." There was not as much light tonight as the moon passed behind a cloud. I continued to pull the cow forward, stepping gingerly through the field.

Something dark and heavy moved in front of me. The

dragon's head appeared as if suspended in mid-air. Its black body blended with the darkness that surrounded me, only its glowing orange-red eyes showing up against the backdrop of nightfall.

"It is good you are here, child." The eerie voice hissed thick and cool in the air. "I was ready to go on a hunt. Your king would have known your big secret."

I felt molten anger rise through my entire body. I hated this creature for everything it represented and everything it did to make my life miserable. I wished so much that I had the courage and strength to plunge my sword into the monster's belly.

"You are quiet tonight, Wren. You must be troubled. After I eat, I will hear your troubles."

I dropped the cow's rope. I couldn't bear to watch the cow be eaten alive.

"I must go. Here is your meal." I turned around and began walking toward the lilac bushes.

Flames shot out to my left and then to the right of me. I stopped walking.

"You will leave when I say you can leave!" The dragon's hiss had become a roar. "You will show me respect, child."

I turned around and stared at the demon. I had never felt hatred until that moment.

The dragon grabbed the cow by the leg. The animal mooed and screeched in terror. I shut my eyes as the dragon's jaws closed down around the middle of the cow.

Crunch. I knew the dragon had bitten the cow in half.

"Please, may I go?" I begged.

I could smell the salty sour scent of blood in the air. I felt the bit of dinner I had eaten rise to the surface of my throat. There was more crunching and groaning from the dragon as it devoured the remainder of the cow. I turned around and vomited.

"Leave me," the beast hissed through clenched teeth. "You will provide my next meal in two days."

I ran as fast as I could through the field and then the lilac bushes. I made my way through the trees and was about to sprint toward the garden when someone came out of the trees in front of me, causing me to come to an abrupt halt at the edge of the garden.

"Arrgh!" I screamed as the figure grabbed hold of me and held my shoulders in a vice grip. It was Travin.

19

"Princess, shall I call the king's physician?" It was Travin. When I didn't answer, he continued. "I came to your room to check on you and discovered you were gone. I thought you might be in the garden visiting Princess Lorenda and wanted to warn you that the king had returned. As I walked toward the lilac grove, I could hear voices in the field. That's when I saw that horrible beast speaking to you."

I started to cry as I sank into Travin's embrace. "The cow is dead," I said between sobs. "I gave the beast my cow."

Travin held me away from him so he could look me in the eyes. "Why would you do that?"

I covered my face with my hands and shook my head. I dropped my hands and forced myself to look at him. "I didn't kill the dragon, Travin. What the king sent me to do I did not do. I failed."

He was silent and then reached down to my face and wiped the tear from my cheek.

"I made a pact with that horrible creature that I would give it food every other day as long as it didn't torment the people of King Olerion's land any longer. If I hadn't made the agreement, the dragon would have killed me." Fresh tears spilled down my cheeks.

Travin pulled me close. "There, there, Princess. We will figure out what to do about this. I will help you."

I pulled away from him so I could get a better look at his face. There was no disgust or disdain in his eyes. I saw a sympathy there and even a look of deep concern that looked very similar to love. "You aren't horrified by me?"

Travin's brow scrunched into deep furrows between his dark eyebrows. "Why would I be horrified?"

"Because I'm feeding innocent farm animals to a demon."

"Wren, I grew up on a farm. Animals were killed for food all the time. It's part of life. I'm horrified by the danger you're in every time you are around that vile creature."

I never had anyone be so concerned about my welfare. My father had banned me from the garden and from leaving the castle grounds, but that had felt more like punishment than concern.

"When do you have to feed it again?"

"The evening after tomorrow."

"I will be with you and I will slay the detestable creature."

I felt a weight lift from my shoulders. I was no longer in this alone.

"You felt the need to hide this from me and that saddens me, but I understand what you were afraid of. You do not horrify me, Wren. Anything but that."

I loved to hear my name pass across his lips. His voice was thick and full of emotion. It made me light and heady.

"We will find a way out of this mess." Travin smiled. He grasped hold of my hand and led me along the garden. We walked in the peaceful silence that comes when all secrets are laid to rest.

"I will see you in the morning." Travin kissed my forehead at the bedroom door and walked away.

I slept without any disturbing dreams. It was the best sleep I had had in a long while. Knowing I was not alone made all the difference. Now I wished I had told Travin a long time ago what I had tried so hard to keep hidden.

A knock came at my door as the sun began to pour through the windows. I sprang from the bed and grabbed my robe, sliding the light blue silk garment over my white sleeping gown. Travin was early this morning.

He stood at the door wearing a grave face. He walked through the door without saying a word. I stepped aside and then shut the door behind him.

"The king has summoned you to fight this evening."

"I'm not supposed to fight for another three days." I frowned, a question spread across my face.

"Someone from another kingdom has traveled here to challenge you."

"Who is it?"

Travin shook his head. "I have no idea. The king just told me this morning that you will be fighting tonight against this swordsman."

I shrugged. "I am not afraid."

"And I am. I know you fight as well as any man but I can hardly bear to watch you put yourself in harm's way. I fear that one day you will meet someone who proves to be your equal and you will be injured or worse yet...."

"Shhhh." I put my fingers to Travin's lips. "I will be fine. You don't have to watch if it bothers you."

"It would bother me more to not know how you're doing."

"This will be my last fight, Travin."

"I don't understand why you must do this at all. You don't have to earn a wage so you can buy food for the demon because we are going to slay the beast."

224

"I need the wage to buy the dragon's last meal. I was going to ask you to ask the king if I could have the gold early so I would have enough to buy more chickens. The fact that I will fight tonight instead of two nights from now is much better."

Travin shook his head. "I wish you would just listen to me, Wren. You are so stubborn." He smiled and I knew this was one of those qualities in me he both liked and could do without.

"Just knowing you will help me slay the beast has made all the difference. I have hope once again." I twirled around the room in my blue robe and laughed.

Travin caught me in mid twirl and drew me next to him.

"You really are beautiful, Princess," he said. He lowered his face to mine and kissed me. I clung to him with all my strength, kissing him back with equal force.

Travin pulled away. "I will go and get the morning meal and we shall eat. You'll need your strength for tonight." He winked at me as he walked away, leaving me giddy with joy.

I quickly dressed while he was away, selecting a pink gown, compliments of Lorenda, trimmed in white flowers. The pink brought out the color in my blue eyes.

I glanced in the mirror and stared at my flushed face framed by my short, wavy hair. Perhaps Travin was right. Maybe I really was beautiful.

After breakfast Travin left to attend to some business for the king. I decided to practice my sword fighting.

I slipped my shoes on and then took them off, deciding to practice in my bare feet. The stone floor of my castle room felt cool against my feet and I welcomed the sensation as the heat rose higher and higher outside.

The sword felt like an extension of my arm as I held it out in front of me. I moved it through the warm air to the right and then left, shuffling my feet forward and then backward. My dress rustled against the floor and I wished I was wearing something less restrictive for the practice session ahead.

Laying my sword on the bed, I went to the storage trunk and retrieved the pants and shirt I had arrived in on the first day in King Olerion's castle. The castle servants had washed and repaired the pants after my journey to meet the dragon for the first time. Unbuttoning the gown, I gently laid it across the bed.

In no time I was dressed and moving around the room, jabbing and slicing the air with my sword. As I practiced, I thought of Aleric and wondered what he would think of me now. It was because of what he had taught me that I was here today. I wondered where he was and what he was doing at that very moment. I wished I could talk to him and ask him how he was and learn what he had been doing since we parted.

Travin brought me my evening meal a little early because of the fight. He had not come by at noon but another attendant, one I had never met, brought me the light noon day meal.

"Travin is attending to official royal business," he had explained when I inquired about him. I didn't ask what business he was attending to. The man seemed annoyed that he even had to be there. I quickly dismissed him, setting the food aside so I could get back to practicing.

By the time Travin arrived with my evening meal, I was ravenous. I grabbed a chicken leg and began devouring it even before he sat down.

"Well, someone is hungry." Travin smiled, tossing a grape into his mouth and then cutting off a piece of breast from the bird.

"I didn't eat the noonday meal. I was too busy practicing and you weren't here to eat with me." I grinned at Travin and he took a sip of wine, smiling back at me.

"I was going over the details of the evening's fight with the king. It's because of this duel that the king came home early from his travels. He met a man who claimed he could defeat you. He didn't want to miss the fight."

I dropped the chicken leg, suddenly losing my appetite. "He came all the way back just to watch me fight?"

"Yes, Princess. He is amazed by your skill."

"He wants to see me fail." I wiped my hands and mouth with the napkin on my lap and scooted my chair away from the table.

"This is why I didn't want you to participate in this last fight. I don't feel good about it." Travin sighed and then stood, walking over to where I sat, putting his hands on my shoulders. He rubbed my back with his thumbs as he spoke. "You will be fine. You truly are the best I've ever seen. I know you can do this."

Travin moved from behind the chair and stood in front of me. "It's time to go. We must not keep the king waiting."

I took the hand Travin offered and walked across the room and out the door. I trembled as we made our way through the crowd of onlookers in the great room. Standing in front of the stage, I watched as King Olerion walked to the center of the structure.

"Lords and ladies," he said, raising his arms in greeting. He looked regal in his dark knickers and white shirt with the gilded vest that bore his crest. "We gather here today to witness, once again, the sword fighting skills of Princess Wren and to see if she is able to conquer her opponent. Princess Wren, please come up on the stage so you may meet your opponent."

I squeezed Travin's hand and then made my way to the stage where I carefully walked up the steps on the side.

I looked out over the crowd, trying to determine who might be willing to challenge me. I saw the red-bearded man standing near the stage and my heart skipped a beat. "Surely not him," I thought.

"Will the challenger please make his way to the stage?"

I looked feverishly out over the sea of people, hoping to catch a glimpse of my opponent to size him up and perhaps gain a wave of confidence. If I could only see what he looked like, I would feel more secure in a strategy to snatch away his weapon.

There was movement in the middle of the crowd. I could see a head of sun-bleached hair making its way to the stage. I frowned. The head somehow looked familiar. Where had I seen it before?

As the soldier drew closer, I could finally see his face. Pale eyes, the very eyes I had looked into at least a thousand times, stared back at me. He climbed the stairs on the stage and there, on the other side of King Olerion stood Aleric.

I tried not to stare but couldn't seem to help myself. In some ways he looked the same as he always had; his streaked golden hair fell to the left side of his face, his grey eyes seemed to glow against his browned skin. In other ways, he was so different. He was taller and had a neatly trimmed beard and mustache. He was now a man instead of the cook's boy standing in the shaft of morning light in the barn.

King Olerion's voice cut into my thoughts. "Lords and ladies, this is Lord Aleric. He claims that only he can defeat the princess."

The crowd clapped and cheered. I was crestfallen. The people wanted to see me lose. Why did it seem like everyone was against me? Even Aleric had come to prove his domination over me.

King Olerion turned to me. "Princess Wren, are you prepared to fight Lord Aleric?"

I stared, forgetting for the moment that I had the ability to speak. "Yes, yes," I said quickly, clutching the sword at my side.

"Lord Aleric, are you ready to take on this long-standing, sword fighting champion?"

"I am," came his deep voice. Even his voice had changed. It was deeper than it had been when we'd parted two years ago.

"Then without further ado, let this duel begin." King Olerion nodded at Aleric and then me and hurried off the stage in order to get out of our way.

I drew my sword and held it out in front of me. Aleric smiled and withdrew his sword. We continued to stare at one another until someone in the crowd yelled, "Start the duel already!"

Aleric swung his sword through the air and nearly knocked my sword from my hand. I stumbled and quickly regained my balance, pulling my sword back and then swinging it forward to clamor against his weapon. I quickly swung my sword to the other side and was able to cause Aleric to stumble. He backed away and I moved with the swiftness of a deer, slicing the air from side to side, forcing him on the defensive.

He finally regained control and began to move forward once again. I had forgotten how good he was. He moved faster and faster, his sword flashing in the lighted torch lights all around the room.

I glanced at Travin in the audience. His expression looked worried.

Wham! I felt Aleric's sword crash against my own. I watched in complete dismay as my sword clamored to the floor of the stage. Soldiering had left him without any sympathy. I was humiliated.

The audience erupted with applause and cheers. King Olerion made his way over to Aleric, walking past me where I stood beside my fallen sword.

Grasping Aleric's arm, King Olerion raised it in the air and proclaimed, "We finally have a worthy competitor who was able to defeat Princess Wren. You are the victor, Lord Aleric." The king lowered his arm to his side and, along with the audience, applauded Aleric.

I picked up my sword and ran off the stage. Travin made his way after me as I pushed my way through the crowd and into the great room.

"Wren, wait!" Travin ran up to me where I stood beside the great fireplace in the castle entryway.

He took me in his arms as I wept.

"Wren?" Aleric stopped a few yards from where Travin and I stood locked in an embrace.

I broke away from Travin. "Why did you come?" I shouted at Aleric, tears falling softly down my face.

"What do you mean? I came to take you home. Your father sent me to get you. What did you do to your hair?"

I was beside myself. "You have ruined me, Aleric! And, I am protecting this kingdom. You have no idea what you have just done!"

Aleric looked at me with a confused and bewildered face. "What are you talking about?"

"The dragon! The dragon will take my life and it's all because you had to win!"

Aleric walked toward me. "I don't know what you're talking about, Wren."

Travin stepped in between us. "Stay right where you are!" he commanded Aleric.

"Who are you?" Aleric was beside himself with emotion.

"It's okay, Travin. He used to be my friend."

Travin stepped aside. I wiped the tears from my face and gave Aleric a hard stare. "You left and never came back!"

"I was serving in your father's army!"

"You said you would come back but you never did. What did you expect me to do, waste away inside the castle walls?"

"No, but this is ridiculous, don't you think?"

"I'm not doing this because I want to, Aleric!"

"Then why are you here?"

"I have to feed the dragon. It will feed on the people here if I fail!"

"What are you talking about?" Aleric looked more confused as the conversation progressed.

"I have to have gold to buy food for a dragon that will kill me if I don't provide it with food. I made an agreement and if I don't provide the food, the dragon will kill me."

"Why don't you ask your father for the gold you need?"

I rolled my eyes. "You should know by now that my father would never give me gold. He doesn't even acknowledge that I exist."

"How did you get involved with a dragon?"

"It's a very long story. It doesn't really matter because you just took away my ability to buy food. King Olerion will banish me and the dragon will find me."

"I told you that we would take care of that." Travin finally spoke up. "You don't have to worry about the dragon any longer."

"You can't fight the dragon, Travin. You will surely die. I almost died when I tried to kill it a few weeks ago. It's impossible."

"Nothing is impossible, Wren." The voice came from behind Aleric. It was Lorenda.

"Lorenda, you shouldn't be here! Your father would be furious if he saw you."

Aleric turned around and stared at Lorenda. His eyes followed her as she walked toward me.

"My father is preoccupied with his guests. He has no idea I am out here." Lorenda stood in front of me and took one of my hands in both of hers. "You must stop worrying, my dear friend. The Heavenly Father is with you and you have friends who love and care about you. You are not alone."

I began to cry once again. "I just don't know what to do about the dragon. It will be here tomorrow evening expecting another meal."

"We will help you destroy it." Travin put his arm around my shoulders and pulled me in next to him.

"Yes, we will help you just like I said I would do the other day when we were eating peaches. I'm sorry I wasn't there last evening to help you. My father put a guard at my door after hearing rumors that I had visited you in the garden."

"I knew you had run into trouble." I gave her a weak smile. "You don't need to apologize."

"I will also help you, my friend." Aleric still stood behind Lorenda, watching and listening.

"I think you've done enough!" I was still furious with him. "King Olerion will banish me from his kingdom now because I lost the fight."

"Let him help, Wren." Lorenda turned around and smiled at this newcomer who had all but abandoned me. "You must be Aleric. Wren has told me about you."

Out of the corner of my eye, I could see Travin stiffen. He obviously didn't like it that I spent time talking about Aleric. My heart beat furiously.

I heard voices coming through the door into the front room of the castle where we stood. People were filing out of the great room where I had battled against my old friend.

"Quick! We must leave. Your father cannot see us together." I grabbed Lorenda's hand and began to run toward the hallway that led to the stairs that would take us up to our bedrooms. Aleric and Travin followed.

I could hear Travin's voice as they climbed the stairs. "You should not have come."

"Who are you to tell me what I should and should not be doing? I have known Wren much longer than you have."

"You can clearly see how much you have upset her," Travin continued.

"She doesn't like to lose. She's been that way ever since I first met her."

I turned around on the stairs and glared at both Travin and Aleric. Lorenda continued up the stairs ahead of me. "Will you two stop bickering?"

Travin just shook his head and Aleric smiled. "Things haven't changed in the last two years."

"What is that supposed to mean?" I questioned.

"You are the same as you have always been, even with your hair cut like a boy's."

I reached up and touched the hair that was just starting to cover the back of my neck. "I cut it for the contest."

"I know. The king told me about it. You should never have entered the contest. That's where this trouble began. You wouldn't be here right now worrying about a dragon if you hadn't entered the contest. That's what I'm assuming."

I turned around and continued to climb the stairs.

"Travin," came a voice from the bottom of the stairs. "The king has requested your presence in his dining quarters."

Travin gave Aleric a scowl as he began to descend the stairs he had just climbed. "I will come and visit you very soon, Wren," he called to me where I stood at the top of the stairs.

I waved and made my way down the hall to my living quarters. Aleric followed. When I reached my room, he was right beside me.

"How quickly you forget our friendship."

"And how quickly you forget." I opened the door and walked into my room with Aleric following close behind.

"You said you would wait for my return and yet you were nowhere to be found when I came home."

I spun around to face him, my eyes bright with anger.

"How was I to know when you would return? You left me, Aleric. What was I supposed to do?"

"Friends don't give up on each other. You gave up."

"You call yourself a friend? You just sealed my fate. The king will banish me very soon and the dragon will find me and burn me or devour me with its grotesque mouth."

Aleric shook his head. "What are you talking about, Wren? Why does this dragon want you dead?"

I sighed and ran my hands through my hair. "After I won the sword fighting contest, King Olerion was furious to discover that I was a girl. The reward for winning the contest was his daughter's hand in marriage. He was looking for an excellent protector for his daughter. He said that for my deception I could either spend ten years in his dungeon or slay the dragon that had killed the queen and was tormenting his kingdom."

"You chose to slay the dragon, of course."

I smiled. "Yes. I tried to kill the dragon but it got the upper hand before I could plunge my sword into its belly. The creature negotiated another deal with me that as long as I provided it with food every other day, it would not kill me.

"I knew my father would never give me money to purchase food for a dragon, so I asked if King Olerion would provide me with gold in exchange for the entertainment of a sword fighting contest once a week in which I would compete against whoever wanted to fight me. If I won, he would pay me. If I ever lost, he would banish me from his kingdom. Your appearance here has caused me to be banished. I am doomed."

"How was I to know that you would be banished? All I did was beat you fairly in a contest. You can't blame me for what you agreed to with King Olerion."

I felt anger simmering below the surface of my skin once again. How dare Aleric show up and then blame me for being banished when he clearly was the one who had made a mess of things!

"Just leave, Aleric. Go home. You have no idea what trouble I'm in or you wouldn't say such things."

"I will leave when you are ready to go. I promised your father that I would find you and bring you home."

"I will go when King Olerion orders me to leave. I will not go home because the dragon will follow me there."

"How do you know it will follow you? If you leave here it won't know where you are."

"It will know because of this." I held up the jade pendant that hung around my neck.

"What is that?"

"This necklace tells the dragon where I am."

"Then take it off."

"I can't. If I take it off, the beast will track me down and kill me. This town would be next."

Aleric shook his head. "I can't believe you are tangled up in this web."

"Just leave!" I shouted, pointing at the door.

The door opened at that moment.

"You heard the princess," Travin said, staring at Aleric. "King Olerion said you may stay in the guest chambers at the end of this hallway. You will be required to leave tomorrow."

Aleric stormed past Travin and paused at the door. "You will leave with me tomorrow, Princess Wren." He continued down the hall to his quarters for the evening.

"What can I do, Princess?" Travin walked over to where I stood crying in front of the hearth. He pulled me close and wrapped me in his arms.

"He was my mentor with the sword, my friend. Now he says it's my fault that I will be banished."

"Perhaps it is your fault, Wren. Perhaps not. You have been caught in a difficult place due to circumstances you could not have foreseen."

I felt the emotion drain out of me, knowing I was understood.

Travin rubbed my back and kissed the top of my head. "The king ordered me to tell you that you must leave at daybreak tomorrow morning."

I buried my face in Travin's chest, not wanting to face the future.

"I will go with you. Perhaps your father, King Belodawn, will grant me a place in his army."

I looked up at him and frowned. "You can't just leave your home, Travin. You have friends and family here."

"How do you know? I've never spoken to you about my family. I have no brother or sister and my parents both died when I was a young boy. Mrs. Craddenbrook took care of me."

"I had no idea, Travin. I've been so consumed with my own struggles that I never asked you about your family or your life. Forgive me."

Travin smiled down at me and kissed me softly. "You are forgiven," he whispered as his lips brushed my ear.

The sound of someone clearing their throat broke both the silence and the kiss. I pulled away from Travin and saw Lorenda standing just inside the door.

"You two aren't leaving without me, are you?" She shut the door and walked over to where Travin and I stood beside the hearth. Grabbing my hands in her own she continued.

"I will find a way to come with you, Wren. I told you I would help you defeat the dragon and I shall keep my word."

"Your father will lock you away if he discovers that you have run off to help me."

"That's a risk I'm willing to take." Lorenda squeezed my hand and then turned to go. "I will leave you alone and will see you both tomorrow morning." She left as quickly as she had come and I almost wondered if she had really been there at all.

Travin left shortly after Lorenda. It was late, and I was exhausted from all the emotion of the evening.

"I will escort you tomorrow, of course, and we will disguise Princess Lorenda the way we did when you went to slay the dragon."

"I'm afraid, Travin. I don't know how we are going to conquer the beast."

"We will figure that out tomorrow. Try and get some sleep." He kissed me gently and left. I put on my sleeping gown and crawled into bed.

20 |

Sleep came swiftly, a vapor that swept in like a thick fog. In my dream, I was riding Flynn on the trail home. The day was bright and cheery. Travin rode in front of me and Lorenda was behind me. We rode in a comfortable silence, enjoying the day.

A strong breeze began to blow. I looked from side to side, marveling at the movement of the trees. When I looked ahead of me once again, Travin was nowhere to be seen.

"Travin. Travin. Travin!" I began to panic. Maybe I went the wrong way. I wasn't paying attention and perhaps Travin had turned to the left or right and I had missed the turn.

"Lorenda, where is Travin?" I turned around in the saddle to see if Lorenda had been watching and discovered that she was gone as well.

"Travin! Lorenda!" I looked around me. I was no longer on the trail headed back to my father's kingdom but back in the same woods I went through on my way to slay the dragon.

I shivered. Darkness was descending quickly. I was cold and afraid. I had no idea how I got here.

A flash of red flickered at the corner of my eye. I saw Lorenda's red hair cascading down her back as she walked into the woods. I dismounted and followed.

"Lorenda! Lorenda!" The figure in front of me would not turn around. I went deeper and deeper into the woods trying to get her attention. The trees were thick and covered any light created by the moon.

I could barely see in front of me. The far-off figure carried a torch. That was the only light I could see and the only way I knew where Lorenda was.

The light from the torch went out. I could not see my hands when I held them up in front of me. I was in total darkness.

"Help! Help me!" I started to scream. I had no idea from which direction I had come or where my friend had gone.

"Shhhh." Someone nearby hushed me. A small flicker of light appeared to my right in front of me. A candle began to glow. The soft light illuminated red hair that fell long and full around a pale face with large, dark eyes that were almost black. I gasped. The witch.

"Don't be afraid, child. I'm not here to hurt you. I'm here to warn you of the grave danger that awaits you if you try to slay the dragon." She raised a long, pale finger which, to my surprise, was not bony but long and graceful.

"You will never find true love if you succeed in slaying the beast. If you try and are not successful, you will surely die. You must turn back from this plan and submit to your destiny of providing food for the creature for the rest of your life. You are not your own. You belong to the dragon."

I began to sob. I closed my eyes, trying to block out the horrible sorceress. I wept aloud. When I finally stopped, I opened my eyes to the cool gray of morning that seeped through the window of my room.

My pillow was wet with my tears. I sat up and then stood, still shaking from the horrible dream. Walking over to the table near the hearth, I stoked the coals of the fire lit by Travin the evening before and put a log on the red hot coals. I poked the coals again until the sparks caught the wood on fire.

Collapsing into the green velvet chair that sat to the right of the hearth, I began to pray.

"Heavenly Father, are these dreams from you? Are you trying to warn me not to kill the dragon? I am so confused. I know not which direction to turn. Please help me know what to do."

I saw the holy book sitting on the table nearby, so I picked it up and sat back down in the chair. Laying it on my lap, I opened the heavy cover, closed my eyes and turned thick handfuls of pages until I felt I should stop. I started reading the author, Matthew, at section 11:29.

"Come to me all you who are weary and burdened and I will give you rest. Take my yoke upon you and learn from me, for I am gentle and humble in heart, and you will find rest for your souls. For my yoke is easy and my burden is light."

I frowned. I wasn't sure what this meant. I closed my eyes again, turned more pages and came to Galatians 5:1: "It is for freedom that Christ has set us free. Stand firm, then, and do not let yourselves be burdened again by a yoke of slavery."

This made more sense. Christ wants me to be free. He does not want me enslaved to a dragon.

Travin knocked at my door as the sun warmed its way through the morning clouds.

He spoke as soon as I opened the door. "Princess Lorenda is going to meet us at the barn. I have brought the cloak we will use to cover her appearance."

Travin sat at the table while I quickly gathered my belongings. I trembled as I put the few clothes Lorenda had given me into a brown satchel. This was the last time I would see this castle and possibly the last time I would ever see Travin or Lorenda.

A knock sounded at the door. I jumped and then stared at Travin, who was frowning the way he did when there was something perplexing him. He walked to the door and opened it.

"Where's Wren?" It was Aleric. I would know his deep, earthy voice anywhere.

"I'm right here." I stood beside Travin at the door and stared up at Aleric.

He looked from me to Travin and then back to me. "What is going on here, Wren? It seems that the moment I left, you quickly found someone to replace me."

I put my hands on my hips and gave Aleric an angry look. "First of all, I didn't replace you. You're the one who left and didn't come back for two years. Would you have me wither away in my father's jail? You left me, Aleric. How dare you speak to me that way?"

"Oh yes, I forgot, my lady. You are a princess and I am a mere soldier. I am not fit to be in your presence." Aleric stepped back away from the door and bowed.

"That is enough!" The courtier stepped between me and Aleric. "I think you had better either decide to help Wren against the dragon or you'd better leave."

"That's fine with me. My time here has come to a close as with many things." Aleric looked around Travin as he said this in order to catch my eye.

"Just leave," Travin commanded.

Aleric turned around and walked away.

I felt myself clench and unclench my fists. For a moment, seeing my sword standing against the wall next to the door, I fought a dangerous urge to grab it and run for Aleric. I wanted to hurt him for hurting me. His words stung like the cuts and scratches that often come with sword fighting.

"Forget him. We have more important business to attend to." Travin grabbed the soldier's cloak he had brought for Lorenda off the table where he had laid it. Taking my hand, he led me out the door and to the barn where Lorenda stood next to a horse stall waiting patiently.

"What's wrong, my friend?" Lorenda frowned and moved toward me, putting her arm around my shoulders.

"I just lost the friend I have held dear since age twelve."

Lorenda squeezed my shoulders. "Now you have me and Travin."

I glanced at Travin who looked angry. He nodded just the same.

"Truly, we will always be as good of friends tomorrow as we are today, Wren," said Lorenda.

"Quickly now! We need to mount our horses before someone sees us." Travin handed the soldier's cloak to Lorenda. She pulled the purple garment on and then placed the hood over her head. Her face was nearly hidden by the depth of the hood.

Travin let Flynn out of the stall and gave the reins to me. I led the horse out of the barn and mounted it outside. Travin did the same for Lorenda.

When we were all on horseback, Travin led the way to the castle gate.

The gatekeeper was someone King Olerion's courtier didn't seem to recognize. Had the king appointed a new gatekeeper since our return from the dragon's lair?

He gazed down at us from his post on top of the stone pillars of the gate as we came to the required civil stop before the wooden wall not yet open to our passing.

"Awfully hot day to be wearing a cloak, isn't it, soldier?"

"He's one of those pale types and cannot expose any skin to the sun."

"Better him than me." The gatekeeper laughed, then he glared quietly at each of us. "All right then. King Olerion informed the commander of the guard that you would be escorting our unwanted guest back to where she belongs."

Travin nodded, although I could tell he was trembling with anger over the guard's unwanted guest comment.

A heavy burden lifted from my shoulders as I passed through the castle gate. I hadn't realized till then what a burden it could be to stay in a place where you were not wanted.

The three of us rode in silence through the streets lined with houses and farms. It wasn't until we had passed the edge of the forest that Lorenda took off the cloak.

"Oh my goodness," she exclaimed. "I thought I would surely die wearing that thing! Of course, when you're susceptible like I am..." Lorenda giggled as Travin rode past her and took the lead.

"I'm glad the guard didn't ask too many questions. I was going to tell him you are like a rabbit that has pink eyes and can't be exposed to the sun."

Lorenda laughed wholeheartedly.

I smiled, my mind miles away from the moment in front of me. I was already trying to figure out the weakness of the dragon in my mind in order to slay it once and for all.

"Where are you, Wren?" Lorenda asked.

"What do you mean? I'm right here."

Lorenda pulled her horse alongside me. "No, you are far, far away from here."

"I'm afraid. I don't know how we're going to do this."

"We will find a way. There are at least three, perhaps four, of us agreed on what needs to be done now."

Travin turned in his saddle to assess both of us. "You are both very brave, my ladies."

"How can you be so sure that we will find a way?"

Lorenda smiled. "I just know."

"What if the witch is right, Lorenda?" I whispered, not wanting to discuss what the witch said to me with Travin in our midst.

"She's not and she's not your friend. But you get to choose who you are going to believe."

I knew Lorenda was right. This made the irritation I felt by her comment feel even more intense. Her statement seemed so unfair. How could I be expected to just ignore what the witch said? I had seen her three times since deciding to slay the dragon. Each time she had said the same thing. I was terrified that what she said would come true. How could I risk losing Travin's love? I had already lost my friendship with Aleric, and that felt rough enough to unsteady all the years of confidence his care had built in me.

I knew the witch was not my ally. Just because she wasn't a friend didn't mean she wasn't telling the truth. Lorenda didn't give the witch much credit for being truthful, either. Maybe she was right. I was brutally exhausted from living in so much deception for so long. Yet, this was my reality.

I looked back at Lorenda. Now, being so perplexed by the situation, I also became furious at her simplicity.

"Sometimes you don't get to choose, Lorenda. Sometimes the truth is just the truth whether you want to believe it or not."

We continued to ride along in silence, not realizing we were being followed. From a distance, Aleric rode his horse as quietly as he could through the forest. He kept his eye on the three sojourners ahead of him while maintaining enough space to remain hidden. Unknown to Aleric, King Olerion had also followed shortly after him having discovered that his one and only daughter had escaped.

I struggled to keep my eyes on the path in front of me. I could feel something behind me, although every time I turned around in the saddle, all I saw was Lorenda sitting on her horse, frowning.

"What are you looking for, silly girl?"

"Nothing. I just want to make sure you're still with us." I didn't want to hear another lecture about how we weren't being followed and that I shouldn't be so worried about things all the time. I was sure this was what Lorenda would say to me if she knew I felt like we were being followed.

"I'm not going anywhere, dear Wren. You don't need to worry about me disappearing."

Suddenly, a sound like a twig snapping came from several yards behind Aleric. He turned to see what could have made the noise. He appeared to observe movement behind a tree in the distance when he motioned to warn us. He waited several moments before continuing down the trail. Another set of horses' hooves came from behind. Again, Aleric peered behind himself into the distance. He began to gallop and urged us to match his pace.

The three parties traveled along the forest trail all the way to King Belodawn's castle. As Travin approached the castle gate, Lorenda quickly pulled the cloak over her head. The castle guard saw me approach after Travin and instantly recognized me.

"Why, Princess Wren, you've returned! Your father will be so glad to see you!" Valderon seemed genuinely glad to see me.

"Is that so?" I had never known my father to be glad to see me. My heart beat wildly at the suggestion.

"But of course, Princess. You are his only child, the only heir to his throne. Why wouldn't he be pleased to see you?"

I was silent. I had no desire to debate my father's affections with Valderon.

"Who is this with you wearing a cloak in the heat of the day?"

I looked behind me and could no longer see Lorenda's face, now hidden by the cloak. I knew she was melting underneath the heavy fabric and hoped we could quickly escape the scrutiny of the watchful guard.

"That, my lord, is my friend who cannot bear exposure to the sun. Some have a rare condition which makes it impossible for them to withstand the sun on their skin."

"I see. I recall that your friend, Aleric, had such a friend. They must be more common than we realize." The guard winked at me and smiled.

I felt my skin grow warm. He remembered all the times I had snuck out of castle walls with Aleric. He had known the entire time that the friend in the cloak was actually the princess disobeying her father's orders.

Summoning my authority rather than inviting him into my duplicity, I ordered, "Allow us passage. Immediately! We have traveled far." I was more and more uncomfortable with being under the watchful eye of any trained guard.

"I am sorry, Princess." He bowed. "I forgot myself." The familiar guard finally opened the gate.

Travin, Lorenda and I passed through one at a time. Lifting his hat to the guard, Travin said, "We are most grateful."

I'd forgotten the condition of the castle grounds and had not considered the way the castle gardens would appear to strangers who would presume far better from a King. Weeds continued to grow en mass and tangles everywhere, and the stable looked as if it was about to collapse. My father had left everything in disarray for such a long time. It not only made me sad to see my home in such a state, I was also humiliated.

Travin dismounted and opened the stable doors, which were in desperate need of a coat of paint.

I led Lorenda into the stables. There were no other horses in the stalls. We had our choice regarding where to board our horses.

We walked our solid-hoofed steeds into the barn and each of us put buckets of grain and water with each horse in a stall. "I think we're being followed," Travin spoke his concern under his breath.

"Why do you say that?" My heart began to pound at the thought of Lorenda's angry father showing up at the castle gate.

"I saw the guard talking to someone at the gate."

I knew we were being followed. I wanted to tell Lorenda that I had every reason to worry when my instincts proved true.

"Hello, Travin." A voice from the stable door floated in on the soft breeze blowing through the door. I couldn't see his face with the bright sun behind him but knew the voice like I knew my own. Aleric walked his horse into one of the open stables and took off the beast's saddles and bit.

"What are you doing here?" I nearly shouted. I hadn't forgotten our last conversation when Aleric accused me of betraying him.

"I live here, remember?"

"Aren't you supposed to be fighting a war with my father?"

"Your father is here and he gave me strict orders to return home when I found you."

"Where is everyone? Why are the grounds in such bad shape?"

"You are a woman of many questions."

"I am a woman who wants to know what has happened to my home. Either I've forgotten how bad our estate had become, or the May rains have done us in. I was only gone a month."

"Your father needed reinforcement, so he ordered every able-bodied male to the front line to fight. That left only the women and children here and a couple of guards to keep the gate secure."

I shook my head. After experiencing the pleasant courtyards of an interested king, one who took pride in his people and their well-kept lands for the way this reflected his honor, I couldn't believe my own disinterested father would allow things to deteriorate this way. My mother, wherever she was, would be aghast. I remembered her always meticulous instructions regarding the way the gardens were to be trimmed, planted, and maintained. For a moment I had the sense that my mother was nearby. I hadn't felt that way in a long time, not since I was twelve. At that time, I hadn't really missed my mother, not nearly as much as I had missed the idea of having a mother. Never mind that. If my mother were here, she would make sure my father would take charge the way a king needed to.

"If my father is returned home, then why have not all the inhabitants returned with him?"

"He left the men at the scene of the battle. He came all the way back for you, Princess Wren." Aleric had not called me that in several years. He was obviously trying to maintain this new distance between us.

"I've been instructed to take you to your father, now. You'll need to come with me."

"If that is how it must be, we will all go to see King Belodawn." Travin had been silent until now.

"Yes, we will all go with you," Lorenda said.

I was relieved. I wasn't looking forward to facing my father alone.

"Very well."

I was surprised to see Aleric give in without a fight. That wasn't like him. I was also surprised to catch him staring at Lorenda with a strange expression as she turned to remove the saddle from her horse. "Let me," he said, removing the saddle for her. I wondered what he was thinking.

Aleric caught me studying him. He fixed his gaze on me once again. "We need to see your father now. Word will have reached him, and he will be expecting you."

"Let us go," Lorenda said, leaving the stall to stand next to me. The three of us followed Aleric out the stable door and made our way to the front door of the castle.

"The king is seated in the great dining hall." Mrs. Pendelin greeted us at the scullery door. I reached out to embrace the only caregiver I'd ever really known. How I'd missed her sweet smell! "It's so good to see you, Princess." Aleric's mother stepped forward and took me in her stout arms.

I wanted to cry. I didn't think I would ever again see this woman who was like a second mother to me. "It's good to see you too, Mrs. Pendelin," I said emotionally into the crisp clean apron the cook wore.

"Your father will be so glad you're home!" She held me away from her and then drew my face in with both hands to plant a kiss on both cheeks.

Aleric grunted. "Mother, we must be on our way."

"Yes, yes, of course. Welcome home, Princess Wren." She turned and walked through a door a little way down the hall which led into the kitchen.

We continued past the door and went to the end of the hall and through an archway that led into a massive room brightly lit by ten candelabras that hung from the ceiling at regular intervals. Giant red curtains covered huge windows on one side of the room. Long tables sat in two rows below the candelabras.

At the far end of the room, beyond the tables, sat King Belodawn on the throne-like chair made of thick, dark oak wood which he usually sat on when dining. The head of a fierce lion was carved into the end of each of the arms of the chair. The king looked nearly as fierce as the carved lions, staring at each one of us with cool, calculating eyes.

Dressed in black from head to foot except for the crimson robe that hung from his broad shoulders, the king waved his hand, motioning for us to approach the throne.

I could feel my entire body tremble as I and the others walked past the tables to the chair where my father was seated. Stopping at a step in front of him, I curtsied along with Lorenda, while Aleric and Travin bowed before him.

I could see fine lines that had begun to form beneath the king's intense eyes. He looked much older than what I remembered, and his thick blond hair had taken on a silver sheen in the three years since I'd last seen him.

"My king, I present to you Princess Wren." Aleric bowed and gestured toward where I stood. I curtsied once again.

"My Lord," I said, my voice quiet and timid as a deer. How different I felt standing before my father as opposed to wielding a sword on a stage. I was unnerved by how his presence could make me feel like a small child once again.

"Where have you been Princess Wren, and why did you disobey my orders to stay within the castle walls?"

I was unhinged, not certain of what to say. I could face down a dragon but not my own father. "I'm sorry, father. I was lonely and felt trapped." My voice quaked.

"Have I not given you everything you need to live? Yet, my daughter repays my generosity with disobedience."

I looked at the floor, too ashamed to lift my head and face this beast of a king. I was nothing standing before him.

"Answer me!"

I jumped at the crack of his voice.

"I'm sorry, Father. I did not mean to disobey you." The trembling stopped and I became aware of a silent spark growing into a flame inside me. Fear quickly evaporated before the fire of my fury.

I slowly looked up at the king, then aimed my courage into his eyes and spoke again. This time my tongue was a sword pointed at my father.

"I left because there was nothing here for me. Since my mother's disappearance you have acted as if you wished it was me who had disappeared. You haven't spoken even one word to me in years! I've lived completely alone, and what did it concern you?!" Sweat broke out across my forehead and upper lip. My body begin to tremble once again, this time with the force of anger.

"How dare you speak to your king in such a manner? I do what I wish!" King Belodawn cried. "You will leave my presence and take your people with you. If you aren't gone by this time tomorrow I will have the guards use force to remove you!"

I continued to stare, unwilling to let his words affect me. I felt nothing and did not care if he wanted me. He had died to me many years ago when he refused to be part of my life.

"My Lord," Aleric said, bowing low before the king. Travin bowed, and Lorenda did the same. I passed through the company of my friends and led them from the room, refusing to bow.

"That was heartbreaking," I could hear Lorenda say as she stopped beside Aleric. When Travin and I approached them, Lorenda stood shaking as was I from the scene between me and my father. Aleric continued to stare at Lorenda, oblivious to our own fragile state of relationship. I watched as his face grew pink then red. He stared at Lorenda, hardly noticing that Travin and I had come to a halt before him. Obviously, he was smitten with Lorenda.

I felt a small jab in the center of my chest. It was difficult to watch Aleric's interest in someone other than me. I had hoped that one day I would marry him. Then, I would never have believed that things could turn corners in such a short period of time. It seemed only a few days ago that Aleric and I had been ' sneaking away from the castle grounds as cohorts. The sadness that stung was evidence of the way time changes things.

"The evening meal will be served in a short while," Aleric spoke, his voice sputtering and cracking. "I suggest we retire to the kitchen and wait for my mother's delicious cooking, unless you have another plan, Princess."

I frowned. I had never seen Aleric so nervous. He never acted that way around me. This was all so strange.

Aleric offered his arm to Lorenda, rather than me, as a lord of high esteem might offer to escort a visiting princess into the kitchen. She smiled brightly and took his arm, leaving me easily.

Travin nudged me, finally drawing my attention away from Aleric and Lorenda. I smiled, feeling embarrassed for being caught in my attentiveness to the others rather than to the loyal confidant he had become. Taking his arm, I kept my eyes straight ahead and tried to ignore Travin's gaze, which rarely lifted from my face. I felt layers of confusion. I didn't want him to see the bewilderment in my eyes.

The four of us sat at the table in the kitchen saying absolutely nothing for several moments. How I wished I could evaporate. Perhaps I could excuse myself as not being hungry, go to my room, and sleep away my troubles! I hadn't slept in my own bed in such a long time.

"You look tired, Wren. I don't know how to address what happened in the king's hall. Perhaps you should rest a while before we face the foe," Travin said.

I fingered the jade pendant hanging around my neck. My gaze drifted out the high windows that ran along one wall of the kitchen and into the fading light of evening. I could see the glow of the sun starting to set just beyond an outcropping of pine trees that bordered the elaborate garden I used to visit so often as a young girl. Once darkness overtook the light, it wouldn't be long before the dragon would summon me. All my strength faded, along with my willpower, and I sank into the bench that was my seat. I shivered in anticipation of facing the dragon once again.

The silence of our group was broken by angry voices at the front door of the castle. I could hear Mrs. Pendelin arguing with someone.

"You are not permitted here, sir. The king has warned us not to let you in if you show up at this door." Mrs. Pendelin's voice was shrill and filled with fear.

"You, a mere servant, are not permitted to tell me, a king, where I am allowed to go."

Lorenda jumped up from the table and stared at me. "Is there any other way out of here besides through that door?" Lorenda pointed in the direction of the angry voices.

I pointed her to a door next to the windows. "Follow me."

21 |

By the time King Olerion made his way into the kitchen, each of us had escaped through the side door. We went around the outside of the dark stone castle to the front door, passing it on our way to the castle garden. The garden began at the end of a well-worn path from the castle to the garden entrance. The entrance could be seen from the dining hall.

I led the hungry group through Mrs. Pendelin's neatly kept herb garden, passed her vegetable garden, and through the row of pine trees that bordered the entire length of one side of the garden's perimeter. Breaking through the trees, I was reminded of the sad state of my mother's garden. What had once been so lush and lovely in my youth now looked far worse than a manicured graveyard. Since I had been banned from the garden, weeds had grown tall and prickly where irises and tulips had once been. The pond located in the middle of the juniper mazes was covered in thick green sludge. A stone path that led through the grounds was barely visible, it was so overgrown with weeds. Lilac bushes and weeping willow trees were dry and gangly with few leaves. I was certain I had entered a garden that belonged to another castle. This could not be the place that had been such a pleasurable escape when I was young.

The others stood by in silence, looking this way and that as if trying to visualize what it had once looked like.

"I used to spend hours here when I was a child. There were fragrant roses, tall, ornamental grasses, irises, and tulips. I built birdhouses with the grasses and chased after butterflies. It was wonderful."

Lorenda put her hand on my forearm and squeezed it. "It sounds exquisite. I would love to have seen it in all its glory."

I smiled and nodded. Walking around the pond, I found the bench I used to sit on when weaving birdhouses. I sat down and Lorenda joined me, while Travin and Aleric continued to explore around the pond. They investigated here and there, making certain there were no signs of King Olerion or his men. Perhaps, we had successfully evaded them.

My sword rode beside me, an ever-ready layer of protection. If it wasn't Lorenda's enraged father, it was the dragon, which might attack at any moment. If I could survive to tomorrow morning, my own father had banished me. I was a princess without walls of safety, honor or love.

I stared into the pond covered in the thick layer of green slime and wished I could go back in time; all the way back to when my mother had disappeared. If only I had remembered her birthday, perhaps everything would be different today. Maybe I would still be in my father's good graces and have a mother who was at least there to talk to once in a while. Even when I was a little girl, my mother had been distant, but we would have grown closer with time.

If my mother had not disappeared, I probably would never have met Aleric or started sword fighting or entered a contest intended only for men. None of the people with me now would be in my life. That seemed such a cruel trade. I quickly focused on Lorenda sitting nearby, an overwhelming sense of gratitude sweeping over me.

The shadows grew long in the garden as the sun began to set. I gazed with worry in the direction of the castle. I wondered where King Olerion could be at this moment. I looked down at the jade pendant dangling at the center of my chest and, once again, had the urge to rip the chain off of my neck. The pendant began to vibrate. I shut my eyes, hoping I hadn't really felt the necklace move. This had to be a mistake.

"Hello, Princess Wren." The icy voice bellowed from the necklace, causing everyone to stop and stare. When I didn't answer, the voice became insistent. "Princess Wren!"

"Yes? Yes?" Where had my strength gone? It was as if I was about to have my head lopped off and I was merely waiting for the inevitable with my head on the block.

"You will meet me in the arena at your father's castle when the sun disappears, and the evening star is in the sky."

"I will do as you wish." I looked at Lorenda, who remained next to me on the bench, true to her word. She nodded, holding my gaze as if to transfer her own confidence into my soul, and she reached out to pat my arm.

The necklace lay still against my chest. The dragon was gone for the next few moments before it became dark. "What was that, Wren?" The young men were beside us. "I have never heard such a horrible voice. It sounded like the voice of a demon." Travin turned to examine the chain about my neck.

"That is - because - it belongs - to a demon. It's the voice of the dragon that torments me."

Travin grasped my hand and pulled me to my feet, then into his arms. I began to cry, not caring that Aleric or Lorenda saw me. I couldn't hold the emotion inside.

"We need a plan!" I heard Lorenda say with an incredulous gasp.

Aleric answered. "You are right, of course, my lady. What did you hear the dragon order? We'll start there."

I pulled away from Travin and looked at all three of them. "I suggest you all leave. I will deal with the dragon. I got myself into this predicament and it's up to me to get out of it."

"We aren't leaving, Wren." Travin's face hardened and then grew soft once again as he stared at me. "You wouldn't abandon me if I was the one facing this monster. You must realize that we all care for you."

I shook my head. "I couldn't bear it if something happened to any one of you. I can't be responsible for your injury or death."

"We are each responsible for ourselves." Aleric nodded at Travin. "He's right, Wren. You can't force us to leave you now. Alas, you've forgotten that you and I are the champions of two kingdoms!"

"Princess Wren!" The horrible voice sounded from my pendant once again. "I am hungry now. You must come to the arena now with my meal, or I will destroy the castle and set the village on fire."

I looked down one of the paths leading away from the pond. I began to run in the direction I was so familiar with, hoping the others would not be able to catch up. Crashing through the tall trees that surrounded the garden, I made my way to the familiar arena where I had learned to ride a horse.

Stopping, I viewed the dragon standing in the middle of the oval centered in the structure where jousting matches and sword fights also took place. The head of the scaly beast rose nearly as tall as the step at the top of the arena on the main floor. Its giant wings spanned the width of the arena floor and its red-orange, reptilian eyes followed me as I walked through one of the side doors.

"Ah, there you are, Princess Wren. I was worried you wouldn't show up and I didn't fancy having to hunt for my own meal for the evening among the villagers. Speaking of my meal, where is my food?" The demon's giant mouth dripped in anticipation.

Then I noticed the eyes of the dragon focusing on something behind me. I turned around and saw Travin, Aleric and Lorenda enter the arena.

"And who are these with you?" There was irritation in the dark, eerie voice and I began to shake. I felt for the sword hanging by my side.

"These are my friends who insisted on coming with me to meet you." Dread crept up my legs.

"Is that so? Congratulations. They will make a very pleasing meal, Princess Wren."

I turned my back on my companions to face the beast once and for all, fury coursing through my veins. "They are not your food!"

Flames shot from the dragon's mouth only a few feet from where I stood. I could feel the heat of the fire searing my face.

"Don't forget who holds the power here, Princess! I will make a meal with whatever is presented to me."

I drew my sword. "I've had enough of you! You will no longer control me!" Something inside snapped to attention, and I forgot my fear. All I knew was that I had to be free from this horrific obligation.

The dragon began to laugh, a screeching sound that grated on the ears. Travin, Lorenda and Aleric came to stand beside me as the demon eerily laughed some more.

"Spread out!" Aleric shouted.

I saw my friends sprint to separate posts.

The head of the dragon swayed and twisted to see where each of its claws would aim next. "Child, you are starting a battle that won't end well for you. I can do as I please to you and your friends. Make no mistake."

"Lorenda, get away from that creature!" It was King Olerion, crying out to his daughter from the doorway directly behind the dragon. He and the guards with him had approached in full armor while we assumed our naive stance to confront the beast. For the first time, I felt envious to see their steely armor. Why was I not better prepared? The king ran toward his daughter.

"What is going on here?" The roar of the dragon spewed fire and ashes over us. Another stream of fire shot from the beast's mouth, encapsulating one of the three men who came with King Olerion.

Ignoring the screams of the soldier, King Olerion screamed at me. "How dare you put my daughter in danger!" The father rushed to cover his beloved daughter with his robe. The dragon heaved another stream of fire at Lorenda. I hadn't noticed any other movement until Aleric reached the one we all treasured and grabbed her. Aleric pulled her away from the bolt of fire. Placing Lorenda behind him, he unsheathed his sword from his side and began swinging it in front of him as he advanced toward the dragon.

King Olerion also jumped away from the searing stream of fire and ventured into the arena. He aimed his sword in the direction of the dragon. Quickly, I leapt to the side of the king, wielding my own powerful, sharp sword.

Keeping his eye on the beast, King Olerion yelled at me, "I knew I should never have trusted you. You said everything was taken care of and yet, here stands the beast!"

The dragon's enormous tail swung around on the ground and knocked us both off our feet.

"Wren!" Travin rushed to my side and held my head in his hands. I pushed myself through the dizzying effect to my feet and doubled over at a new pain in my backside.

Brushing Travin aside, I pointed my sword and ran at the dragon with wild abandon.

The beast did not see me coming. It spewed a stream of fiery lava at another one of King Olerion's men, who became another sacrifice. As the dragon outstretched its claw to grasp the burning appetizer, I ran toward it holding the hilt of my sword close to my chest with both hands. I readied myself to plunge the blade up and into its mark. When I found my place beneath it, the dragon turned its head, dropping its jaw to snag me, but I reached for its neck as it closed in. Then, I plunged my sword into the center of its chest. Instinctively, I continued to run, not knowing where the heft of neck, tail, and limbs would fall.

The dragon roared and twisted. Trying to locate the aggressor that pierced it, the mighty beast fell to the ground, writhing in pain. Only the guard, grip, and pommel of my sword could be seen protruding from the creature's chest. I realized my sword had found its mark, and had sunk deep into the flesh, as I watched the tail lash wildly in the dragon's death throes.

I took a few steps back and stared at the hideous beast as it squirmed. I turned around and realized that all eyes were on me and the dying thing thumping the ground beyond me. King Olerion stood in soot, next to Lorenda and Aleric. Travin, untrained for battle, was the one who crouched right behind me. Three armored men stood near the side exits as if ready to escape.

I turned back around and saw the strangest thing. The dragon's scales were falling to the ground at a rapid rate. The black scales grew into a large pile on the floor of the stadium, so high that the pile became taller than me. My companions and I backed up the arena stairs, removing ourselves from harm's way.

There was a strange sound as well. The scales were heavy and shattered into a myriad of pieces as they fell. The sound was like the roar of an entire marketplace of plates toppling and crashing to the ground and the tinkling sound of many goblets being tapped with knives in announcement of a cheer. Combined, the noise resembled a giant mirror breaking into a thousand shards.

The cacophony stopped.

I held my sword out in front of me as I circled the pile of scales, trying to find the downed head of the dragon. Travin, who stood sooty and shaking to my right, began to point at something in the center of the pile.

Running to stand beside him, I looked in the direction his finger indicated and saw something that knocked the air out of my chest. Jumping over piles of fallen scales up to my knees, I raked my hands over the shards to unveil someone I hadn't seen in more than eight years. I fell to my knees.

22

My mother lay in a heap, blood oozing from her chest in the same spot that I had pierced the dragon with my sword. The blood stained the light blue dress she wore, the same dress she was wearing the day she disappeared from the garden.

I knelt beside my mother, putting her head in my lap. Her icy gray eyes looked up at me and she struggled to speak.

"My precious daughter," she said, gasping for breath after each word. "I never thought I would see you again."

I stroked my mother's mat of oily honey strands now streaked with grays. I gasped. "Mother! I didn't know it was you. Mother, I didn't know!" I sobbed.

"Shhh. It's not your fault, Wren. It's my own fault. I'm the one who made the bargain."

I wiped my face and eyes. "What do you mean?"

"You...such a lovely young woman."

"Mother, what do you mean *bargain*?"

I stared down into my mother's eyes and felt an old anger that had hunkered down there since I was a little girl. A terrible stench filled my nostrils. Memories of mother telling me that I would never grow into a graceful, young lady came to mind. Now, after all this time living as a scaly reptile herself, she could finally find no fault in me.

"The day I left the garden." she coughed and moaned. "A witch with red hair lured me away. I had no idea..."

I frowned. "How did she lure you away?"

My mother looked away from me, distracted for a moment by her many pains.

"Mother, how did the witch lure you away?" My impatience was turning to anger once again.

My mother looked up at me. "I'm ashamed... You must not think badly. I was young and naive... lonely... your father gave me very little..." My mother winced and sputtered. "...to enjoy...finer things."

In my mind's eye, my mother twirled before her bedroom mirror in lavish, expensive gowns. In my memory it didn't appear that my mother wanted for anything.

"Go on, mother."

She coughed once again. "Witch appeared... startled me. She asked me if I wanted more out of life than what... I said 'yes,' of course."

"Of course," I wondered why our family and position, the life my mother had been given was not enough.

"I followed her... out... of the garden. Long, red hair... a beacon, so easy... to follow."

I wanted to tell my mother that I knew about the witch, that I had seen her myself, but time was running short. My mother was now gasping for each breath.

I looked away from her. My chest heaved with emotion. Lorenda stood nearby.

"She saw the witch too, Lorenda." I raised my eyebrows as if to say, "See, I'm not insane."

Lorenda nodded stiffly.

I shifted my focus back to my mother, but tears clouded my vision.

Her eyes were fluttering and closing.

"Wait, mother, don't go! Please, you must..." I gasped, "Tell me what happened!"

My mother opened her eyes and began to speak once again. "By the waterfall by the crystal pool...witch..."

"I've been there many times." I stroked my mother's dirty forehead and cheek.

"She asked if I wanted untold riches for a...small sacrifice."

A tear fell from her eye and ran down the side of her dirty, fair-skinned cheek. The gray in her eyes grew darker, like a storm brewing in the heavens above. "I told her 'Yes'. She seemed to know I would say yes. She muttered something and waved her hands in front of me."

I watched as my mother moaned and writhed in pain. The blood continued to spread across the bodice of the silk dress that was no longer light blue.

My mother began to pant. "I felt a heaviness that forced me to lie down on the ground and go to sleep. I dreamt of fire and blood...ahh, ahh." My mother swallowed slowly and continued.

"I craved the taste of blood and felt a burning sensation in my stomach and up through my throat. I somehow knew the only thing that would cool the fire burning inside me was blood. When I awoke, I was the beast you've been feeding. I was the demon that everyone has come to fear."

All of a sudden there was silence. I stared at my mother's pale face and saw that her lips were still moving. She was whispering. I put my ear close to her lips.

"When I awoke," she said in a tone I could barely hear. "witch...smiled...told me I could take any treasure I desired. I was no longer...frail, timid queen, living on the scraps my husband chose to give me. I was all powerful."

I heard a wail. It came from my friend standing above us. "You're the one who killed my mother." Lorenda stared down at both me and my mother. "Your mother killed my mother." I had never seen a look of such anger on Lorenda's face. "The dragon is your mother," she directed toward me, "and the dragon killed my mother."

Tears streamed down my face as I stared up at her and watched pain etch across her grief-stricken face. I was at a loss for words. What can one say to respond to such a horrible truth? "I'm sorry" seemed woefully inadequate.

Lorenda shook her head, turned and ran.

"Lorenda! Lorenda!" I called out to her, but it was of no use. She kept running.

I looked back down at my mother. Her eyes were closed, and her breathing was becoming shallow. She began to whisper something once again. With tears wetting my cheeks and hers, I lowered my head toward her lips.

"You must forgive me...daughter. Forgive me for choosing...riches over you...your father. I know... I made...very bad...decision."

I ran my trembling hand over my mother's hair, pushing it away from her face. I thought of my lonely childhood and wondered what it would have been like if my mother had not disappeared. Something told me it would have been a different kind of misery. My mother always seemed so displeased with me. She was either displeased or she didn't see me at all. I knew now nothing would have made my mother happy. Growing up without her was not the worst thing.

"I forgive you, mother," I whispered back in my mother's ear.

Gulping for air, the beast-turned-mother managed to force forth a few more words. "I love you, Wren. I have not known how to show you my love, but I have loved you."

I was silent. Had there ever been another time when my mother had told me she loved me? I wasn't sure what to think or feel. I wanted to believe her.

"I am proud to call...you my daughter. You...released me...this terrible bondage. At last,...I am free." My mother's head fell to the side as she breathed her last.

I laid my hand over my mother's eyes, pushing the eyelids closed. I began to sob. Just when I heard the words I had always longed to hear from her, I had to let her go. I gently laid her head on the ground.

"Wren!" Travin pulled me to my feet, taking me into his arms. I buried my face in his chest and wailed.

After what seemed like a long while, I pulled away from him, wondering where I might find Lorenda. I saw that she had found comfort in the arms of Aleric and her father. Her father was holding her to himself awkwardly. I could hear her crying. Aleric stood nearby, his strong hand caressing her hair.

"I can't face them, Travin," I said, wiping tears from my face. "I'm so ashamed. It was my mother who made Lorenda motherless. How will I ever be friends with her again?"

"Give things time, Wren. You did nothing wrong. You are not to blame for Lorenda's pain. The two of you have faced life without your mothers. This is a strong bond which cannot be easily broken."

"King Olerion will never forgive me for what I have done to his daughter."

"Your mother drew Lorenda into this story, Wren."

I watched as King Olerion put his hand on Aleric's shoulder and brought him close. I wondered what was being said. The king seemed to like Aleric.

"Wren! What is going on here?" King Belodawn rushed into the arena. He wore his armor and wielded a sword in front of him.

When he saw my mother lying on the ground at my feet, he dropped his sword and fell to his knees.

"Catherine," I heard my father whisper, pulling his wife's shoulders onto his lap and rocking back and forth in woe. "It has been eight long years since I last saw you and now you lay here as lifeless as the grave."

He looked up at me, glaring with an unquenchable anger. "You did this. You made her disappear and now you have killed her! Get out! Get out of here, all of you!"

"But, father!" I panted in despair. How could I begin to explain all of the events leading to this moment?

Travin grabbed my hand. He pulled and tugged me toward the exit. Aleric, Lorenda and King Olerion were already ahead of us. With my father shouting obscenities after me, I began to run. I ran as hard and as fast as I could go. Intentionally, I took a different route than the way I had led the others here to lose them. Travin managed to follow me through the garden into the barn where we gathered our horses. He and I rode away without looking back.

I wore no hood this time when we approached my father's castle gate. I could let my short, wavy hair be tousled by the wind. For the first time I was truly free, and it felt wonderfully surreal in the midst of the sadness surrounding me.

We rode into the woods with the moon lighting our way along the forest path. I was quiet for a time. I wasn't sure how to put what I felt into words. There were too many emotions coursing through me--deep sadness, relief, elation, and fear. I wasn't sure what the next step would be.

Finally, I pulled up my steed and spoke. "I'm afraid, Travin. Where am I to live? My father has disowned me, and I don't think Lorenda will ever speak to me again, much less her father. He won't allow me to be around her."

Travin coaxed his mount closer to mine. "We will find a plan that works. Don't worry, my love. I am right here with you." Then, this extraordinary friend leaned toward me in his saddle and smiled through shining eyes. "I will never leave you."

I smiled back through confused tears. "God has blessed me with your loyalty, Travin. I would be so lost without you."

We rode on until we reached the waterfall. The moonlight on the pool of water was intoxicating. A warm breeze caressed my skin. I wanted so badly to disrobe and wade into the pool. My skin was sooty with ash and there was blood on the dress I wore from kneeling with my dying mother.

Reading my thoughts, Travin said "If you wish to bathe, I will wait in the woods nearby."

He trotted with the horse back to the edge of the woods. I slid down from my horse and wasted no time pulling my dress over my head. I walked slowly into the cool water. The pool was shallow, and the blazing sun had warmed the brisk, mountain water. It hadn't yet cooled off in the night air.

Leaning forward, I dove beneath the water and slowly swam to the far side of the pool. I sat on a smooth rock that was lodged between two other rocks. This was the perfect seat. The water covered me, but only up to my shoulders. I settled on the rock and looked out over the water. Bright moonlight swayed and sloped with the rippling of the water. I could feel every muscle in my body begin to relax. I began to pray.

"Heavenly Father, are You there? I believe You are, and I ask with all humility for Your help. I have nowhere to go."

I listened but heard only the evening breeze whispering over the water. It's not that I expected to hear God's voice, but it would have been a welcome ending to a tragic day.

A thought floated by like a gentle lapping at my ear. "I know the number of hairs on your head. I clothe the lilies of the field in splendor. I know what you need." After these thoughts, I no longer felt afraid. I knew God was with me. He would provide.

Swimming back across the pool of water, I climbed out and pulled my dress over my cool, damp body. Running my hands through my hair, I climbed into Flynn's saddle and rode toward the spot where I had seen Travin disappear into the woods.

I found him sitting on the ground, leaning against a tree beside his horse.

"That was a short swim." His voice startled me.

"I want to keep riding. I believe the Heavenly Father will show us what we should do to find shelter."

Travin frowned. "How do you know?"

"He told me He knows the number of hairs on my head and that He clothes the lilies of the field with splendor."

Travin's eyes grew wide. "I thought the same thing not long ago. I was speaking to the Heavenly Father while you were bathing and the very thing you just said threaded its way through my mind."

I slid off my horse and stood next to Travin. We both heard the sound of horses' hooves on the trail at the same instant. Lorenda and her father bypassed us, unconscious of our nearness, in their hurry to ride home.

He reached out and grabbed my hand, pulling me against his warm body.

"You are so cold." He whispered as Lorenda and her father passed by us.

I nodded and shivered. "The night air is so...that...I got chilled putting...on my dress." I shuddered more violently and Travin pulled me close. We stood that way for some time until I stopped shaking.

I looked up at him as he held me, his lips pressed against my own. His lips were gentle. He broke away and released his hold on me. "I think we had better ride on now."

Travin hoisted himself up into the saddle. "I have an idea."

I climbed into my saddle, covering my bare legs with the cloak Lorenda had given me when we arrived at my father's castle. It was no longer my home, so I refused to think of it in that manner.

Lorenda wanted me to have the cloak that I now had wrapped around my knees to remember our friendship, as if I could have ever forgotten such a thing. It bothered me that the gift was given before Lorenda discovered that my mother had killed her mother. There was no way to overcome something like that. We would never be friends again.

We rode in the direction of King Olerion's castle. I said nothing at first. We rode around a bend in the trail where the houses of the townspeople began to appear on the side of the road.

I could stand it no longer. "Travin, we can't go to King Olerion's castle. They don't want to see me after what has transpired."

"We aren't going to the castle. We're going to the house of a friend. Trust the guidance of the Heavenly Father, Wren."

A guard stood at the castle gate. It was the same guard who had stood there when I snuck into the sword fighting contest. I quickly covered my head with the cloak to keep him from recognizing me.

"State your business, Travin," the guard sneered. Apparently, the guard knew Travin well and did not favor him.

"We wish to visit a friend in the village." I wondered if King Olerion had given the guard special instructions if he encountered Travin. He treated Travin like a common peasant, not a king's courtier.

"You may not enter the castle. The king has given strict orders that no one enters the castle but those who are family members of the king."

I knew that this order was meant to keep me away from Lorenda. Our friendship was over.

"We will only visit my friend in the village," Travin assured him. "You have my word, my friend."

The guard grunted and turned a wheel to open the gate. I wanted to cry. I didn't want to keep repeating the past, being in a place that did not welcome me.

Travin led through the village, down the cobblestone street lit up by the moon, and stopped at a cozy-looking cottage at the end of the street.

"Wait here, Wren. I will return shortly."

I watched as Travin tied his horse to the tree that stood to the side of the cottage and then made his way to the door.

"Travin!" I heard a familiar voice exclaim. It was Mrs. Craddenbrook. She had a voice like a bubbling brook, merry and dancing with sound.

"Of course you can stay here. You are always welcome."

Travin walked back to where I waited and led my horse to be tethered next to his near a tree. Helping me out of the saddle, he led me inside the cottage.

Mrs. Craddenbrook beamed up at me from her petite frame, which only reached my shoulder. Her dark eyes were as merry as her voice. "Such a delight to see you again, child."

"And you as well, Mrs. Craddenbrook."

"Please, call me Nora."

I blushed. The woman was so kind and friendly to me that it made me blush with discomfort; especially after what had recently occurred with Lorenda and my mother. I didn't feel I deserved such kindness.

Mrs. Craddenbrook grabbed my hand and led me through the main living area, where a blazing fire crackled in the hearth. She pulled me into the kitchen toward a small wooden table next to a side window. A clean, lace tablecloth covered the top of the table. Mrs. Craddenbrook nodded toward one of the chairs, indicating that I should sit down.

Grabbing a tea kettle, she ladled water from the water bucket into it and then placed it on the hearth.

Travin sat down next to me at the table, and Mrs. Craddenbrook took a third chair.

"Thank you for giving us shelter for the evening, Mrs. Craddenbrook -- I mean Nora," I said, trying to smile. Instead, unexpected tears welled to the surface, and I shivered without control. Mrs. Craddenbrook was so motherly. She reminded me of Mrs. Pendelin, who reminded me of the mother I never had, which caused me to regret the extraordinary loss of my own mother and the loss of what might have been. In one evening, I had lost not only my mother but two of my dearest friends. Who knew if I would ever be allowed to visit Mrs. Pendelin again! There were no more tears to cry.

Mrs. Craddenbrook held one of my hands in both of hers and patted the top of it. "There, there child. You've had a difficult day. Travin explained that you have just learned that your mother passed and that Princess Lorenda is angry with you at the same time."

I pulled away from the kind lady's grasp, put my face in my hands and wailed. It was kind of Travin to explain my difficulties only briefly.

"Grief is a strange thing, Lady Wren. It often comes in unexpected waves. The waves will wash over you and then subside." Nora handed me a handkerchief.

I blotted my face and eyes with the cloth. Numb, I felt, somehow, cleansed.

"No matter. Whatever it is you will face, the Heavenly Father will walk with you through it. He will make a way to tomorrow." Mrs. Craddenbrook gazed at me with a confident, peaceful look in her eyes. I knew she was speaking the truth.

A high-pitched whistle came from the hearth. Mrs. Craddenbrook rose carefully from her chair and walked stiff-legged to retrieve the tea kettle.

Travin grasped my hand in his own and whispered, "It will all be fine. We are safe here."

I looked into his eyes and could tell he believed what he said. Now if only I could believe. It was startling to have my faith waiver when I most needed it. Only a short time ago I was at the waterfall where I felt the Heavenly Father speak to me, telling me He would provide. He knew every hair on my head. Now I felt lost and afraid again. Staying with Mrs. Craddenbrook was not the answer I was looking for. This fall from grace felt so disquieting.

Mrs. Craddenbrook brought the kettle to the table and poured hot water into each of the three mugs sitting there. She offered sugar and cream and then sat back down, a mug centered between her hands. "You can stay here as long as you need, Lady Wren and Travin. These things take time to work out."

"I appreciate that, Mrs. Craddenbrook...uh...Nora," I stammered, seeing her raised her eyebrows at me when I started to call her by her last name. "I would never want to burden you for more than one evening."

"Lady Wren," Nora said, laying a plump hand across my hand. "You are not a burden. You are a friend who is welcome in my home."

I felt the tears return but willed them back as I focused on my anger from the anguish my mother had caused. This kept the tears at bay. I yawned, suddenly feeling the mental fatigue and physical exhaustion of the day.

"To bed with you both. Lady Wren, you will sleep in John Christopher's bedroom. Travin, I have made a pallet of blankets and hay near the hearth for you." Nora took a tentative sip of her tea, stood and called to me as she walked into another room off the kitchen. Without energy to refuse, I followed her as told.

Nora lit a lantern beside the bed, illuminating the room. It was tiny with barely enough space for a bed and storage trunk. The walls were plain, but two painted images of horses hung on opposite walls.

"My son, John Christopher, loved to paint and was particularly fond of painting horses."

"If this is his bedroom, I should not be sleeping here."

"Oh, he doesn't live here any longer. He is a grown man with a wife and children of his own."

I nodded, offering her a weak smile.

"Goodnight, Princess," Nora said as she embraced me for the second time before leaving the room. "Your sleeping gown is laying on the bed."

Nora shut the door behind her, and I collapsed on the bed. Forcing myself to sit up, I removed my dress and shoes and slipped the sleeping gown over my slender body. Crawling under the covers, I laid my head on the feather pillow and fell asleep.

23 |

The sunrays streamed thick and bright through the window when an urgent knock on my bedroom door woke me. "Princess Wren? Lady Wren?"

"Yes, just one moment." Mrs. Craddenbrook called from the other side of the door. I leapt from the bed, pulled off my sleeping gown and struggled into my soiled dress from yesterday. I had nothing else to wear.

When I opened the door, there stood Mrs. Craddenbrook holding a fresh dress across her outstretched arms. I recognized the dress almost immediately. It was one of Lorenda's, a dark blue satin skirt with a velvet bodice. It was one of my favorites.

"A castle messenger brought this by the house this morning along with a letter for you."

I took the garment from her and the letter even more eagerly.

"As soon as you're dressed, come have some lunch child. It's high noon."

Pink crimson spread across my fair cheeks. I couldn't believe I slept away the morning. Nora walked back toward the kitchen and I shut the door.

Laying the dress on the bed, I untied the ribbon holding the letter closed and rolled open the small piece of parchment. "Meet me in the garden today at twilight. Lorenda"

My hands trembled. I was both excited and terrified. Did this mean there was a chance that she could somehow forgive what lay between us, or would I be given an ultimatum to leave the village or face her father's dungeon?

I laid the letter on the bed and put on the dress Lorenda had sent me. Surely this was some sort of peace offering.

I opened the door and joined Nora in the kitchen.

"You look lovely, Princess Wren." I looked down at the dark blue dress, my thin white arms extending from the sleeves that stopped at my elbow. I suddenly remembered that I hadn't attended to my hair. Running my hands through my hair, I hoped I looked as presentable as Nora saw me.

"Your hair lies in soft, golden waves, Princess. It looks as lovely as your dress."

It was true. The dress made my blue eyes appear as a storm's dark blue hue. My eyes, pink cheeks, and lips stood in stark contrast to my pale skin and, according to Nora, I looked beautiful.

"It appears that Princess Lorenda is not holding a grudge after all."

I nodded. "I hope what you say is true. She may tell me to leave or face the dungeon."

"Life has been difficult for you, hasn't it, Lady Wren?"

"I suppose. I'm sure life has been harder for others."

"Life is especially hard if you don't know you are loved."

I looked down at my hands resting on top of the kitchen table. I didn't know what to say and even if I did, I wouldn't be able to speak because of the large lump in the middle of my throat. What Nora said was true. I had never known for certain that I was loved.

Nora poured me some tea.

"Thank you." I warmed my cold hands on the cup.

"It's true that no person will love you perfectly. People will let you down. However, the Heavenly Father will always show you perfect love. He will never leave or forsake you."

I heard the words echo from last evening when I thought I heard God talking to me. A warm feeling ran through me and I suddenly felt like everything was going to be fine.

"I know that what you are saying is true. I believe the Heavenly Father is with us right now."

"Oh, He certainly is." Nora smiled with warmth. "Are you hungry, Lady Wren?"

I felt my stomach rumble and realized I was indeed quite ravenous. Yesterday had been a long day and I had eaten very little.

"I have some porridge and a loaf of rye bread. I'll bring them to the table." Nora rose and took a loaf of bread from the larder, sitting it on the table with a bowl of fresh butter. She walked to the hearth and retrieved a warm pot.

I watched as Nora filled a small bowl with the porridge and then cut a thick slice of rye bread, placing it on a small plate. She handed me a knife and spoon. I laid the knife on the plate and dug the spoon into the steaming porridge. Blowing several times across the spoon, I took a bite. It was smooth and creamy with a hint of cinnamon. Delicious! I took another bite and then another and finished the bowl in little time.

"Would you like more, Princess?"

I felt my cheeks flush with color. "Yes, please. It's delicious."

Nora smiled again and held her hand out for me to give her the bowl. After finishing my second bowl, I took several sips of the mint tea in my cup and spread a thick layer of butter on the piece of bread in front of me.

The butter melted against my tongue as I chewed the dark, moist bread. It was as if I had never enjoyed food before today.

With my belly full, I felt a little drowsy and wanted to return to bed. I would not allow myself to think of leaving the kitchen without cleaning the dishes. I rose and began clearing the dishes from the table.

"Princess Wren, you are most gracious to help me with the task of the dishes," Nora said, rising to her feet. "However, you are still a princess and I will not allow someone of royal blood to fulfill the duties that are mine alone to do. Please set the dishes down and rest for a time." Nora gently pulled the dishes from my hands. "You need a rest. Grief is very exhausting."

I could see that Nora was not going to allow me to help. I felt a little embarrassed that I had forgotten how villagers saw me, and wished to uphold my status. Being without a home and disowned by my father, I no longer saw myself as a princess. I wished I could just forget about where I came from. It only made me miserable.

Nora shuffled away from the table, shooing me out of the room. I found myself in John Christopher's bedroom once again. A heavy sadness overcame me and I decided to take Nora's advice and lie down.

I awoke gradually to voices outside my door being spoken in hushed whispers. My room was bathed in darkness. I could make out Travin and Nora talking in the kitchen. Oh, no! Lorenda! I sat up straight, and ran out the door into the kitchen.

Nora and Travin sat at the small table and looked up at me as if they were expecting me. Travin stood as I exclaimed, "I was supposed to meet Lorenda in the garden at twilight!"

"The sun just went down. I will escort you to the garden. Surely Lady Lorenda is still there," he said.

"Oh, yes, please, Travin. I must hurry."

"When you return, we shall have the soup I prepared," Nora called to us as we rushed out the front door.

Travin took my hand and began to run. "Follow me. I know a secret path to the garden."

I ran beside Travin, the cool, moist earth cushioning my slippered feet. I was cold, but the urgency I felt about meeting with Lorenda brought on waves of heat. I couldn't let my friend down again. I could hardly bear the guilt I felt over my mother being the cause of Lorenda's mother's death.

Travin stopped at the edge of the castle and unlocked a narrow door with a key that was hidden beneath a rock positioned next to the door. He pulled me forward into a dark hall that connected with another dark hall. "I know the way. Don't be afraid," he whispered.

I entered the dark hall and began walking forward without sight. At times I could see slats of light coming from above.

"This is a tunnel under the castle. It leads to the back of the castle by the garden." Travin squeezed my hand a little tighter and continued to move straight ahead. We came to another door, which he opened very carefully in order to make certain there were no guards in the garden.

I could already smell the lilac bushes that surrounded the field beyond the castle. I shuddered. How could such a beautiful, delicate scent bring forth memories of terror and horror? It was this fragrance that painted the air on the evenings I had offered my sacrifice to the dragon, my mother. I still could not believe this was true. My mind could scarcely grasp it.

"Wren!" Lorenda's voice came from within the bushes. "Over here."

I left Travin standing on the path beside the trees and darted into the grove. Lorenda stood a few feet in front of me. I could not make out her facial features, but I knew it was her from the petite shape that was silhouetted against the moonlight-covered bushes.

"Let's walk through the field," Lorenda said, without looking into my eyes. She moved through the lilacs toward the open space.

"Yes, all right. Just a moment." I ducked out of the bushes to speak to Travin. "I'm going to walk with Lorenda through the field. I will return to this same spot as soon as we are finished with our conversation."

Travin nodded and agreed to wait.

Lorenda was at the edge of the field when I returned. When she saw me, she turned and started walking. I fell in beside her and we walked through the moist grass in silence for a time. Finally, Lorenda began to speak.

"Wren, I want you to know that I do not blame you for my mother's death. It was not your fault that my mother died at the hands of the dragon. Your mother did not have control over her hunger when she became the beast. I do not hold a grudge against her, either."

I felt a sob of relief escape from my throat. I stopped in my place. How I desperately wanted Lorenda's forgiveness and acceptance. I couldn't bear to lose her friendship.

Lorenda stopped and turned toward me. She opened her arms and embraced me. "I'm sorry I couldn't reassure you when I stood there beside your mother. I was brought back to my own mother's death and I could scarcely bear the feelings that erupted."

"I thought you hated me," I whispered.

"Oh, Wren. You still do not trust our friendship. Perhaps someday you will."

I was so relieved to know my friend did not hate me that I did not hear Travin run up behind us.

24

"**P**rincess Wren and Princess Lorenda! You must hide. One of the king's men has started a revolt and has taken King Olerion captive. He is threatening to kill you, Wren. He believes you are the reason the king has grown weak in his judgement. The man heard a rumor that the dragon was your mother. The dragon burned his family home, killing both of his parents. He's had years to feed the anger that grows in him even now."

"Where shall we go?" I cried.

"We will go down by the river and hope he...."

There was a crashing sound by the bushes. Suddenly, a large group of armed soldiers spilled through a space in the lilacs. The man leading the revolt shouted and waved his sword in front of them as he dragged King Olerion by a chain behind him.

He stopped a stone's throw away from where I stood with Travin and Lorenda.

"Hand over Princess Wren or the king will die!"

He dragged the king around in front of him and positioned his sword at the king's neck.

"Father!" Lorenda began to run toward King Olerion. I ran after her.

"No, Lorenda!" I stepped in front of her just as an arrow flew through the air.

I screamed as the cold, metal tip of the arrow entered my left shoulder. In an instant I fell to the ground.

"Wren!" I heard Travin yell from behind me. Warm blood spilled down my left arm, forming a large red pool on the ground. I could see Travin's face while he stood over me. My body grew unbearably cold and darkness overtook my sight.

I awoke in Nora's son's old bedroom. Warm sunlight streamed through the window. I had no idea what time it was or even what day it was. The last thing I remembered was Travin standing above me as the icy hot tip of the arrow shot pain through the left side of my body.

"Travin? Nora?" I tried to rise from the bed but felt too weak to move.

The bedroom door opened and Travin ran to me, scooping me up in his arms.

"Ouch!" My shoulder was very tender and could not withstand the force of Travin's embrace. He gently laid me back on the pillow beneath my head and brushed my lips with his own as soft as a butterfly.

"What happened?"

"You've been asleep for two days. Lorenda and King Olerion have both been by to see you. We were all afraid we had lost you."

"King Olerion came here to see me?" I frowned, almost unable to comprehend what Travin said.

"Yes, Wren. He's indebted to you. You saved his daughter's life."

I reached up and touched my shoulder, remembering the agonizing pain I had felt when the arrow entered my body. The arrow was gone and there were layers of cloth soaked in some sort of salve held against my shoulder with a white cloth.

"What happened to the uprising?" It was all coming back to me now.

"King Olerion's loyal soldiers came from behind and captured the men who were revolting against the king. The leader was struck down with a sword. I grabbed you and carried you toward the passageway under the castle. I was able to get you to Mrs. Craddenbrook's in no time at all, but even then, you had lost a lot of blood."

I looked at Travin, reaching out to touch his cheek. "Thank you for saving me. You've kept me safe and I am grateful."

"I didn't keep the arrow from finding you, but you are here and that's all that matters."

"Is Lorenda well?"

Travin smiled. "You amaze me, always thinking of others. She is well and is waiting outside the room to see you."

My eyes popped wide open. "Bring her in!"

Lorenda tip-toed into the room and sat beside me on the bed. Taking one of my hands, she kissed it.

"Thank you, Wren."

"For what?" I had no idea what she was talking about.

"For saving my life. I am forever indebted to you."

"Let's just say that debts are canceled out." I winced and lay back against the pillow. "I wish I could bring your mother back, Lorenda. I feel terrible about that."

"It's not your fault, Wren. You are a blessing to me. You must know that."

My eyes grew moist.

A knock came at the bedroom door.

"Come in," I called.

Aleric walked through the door, strolling past Travin while nodding at him. Lorenda stepped away from the bed and Aleric squeezed her shoulder with his hand, smiling at her before turning his attention toward me.

I looked from Aleric to Lorenda and then back to Aleric.

"It's so good to see you awake."

"Besides the searing pain in my shoulder, it's good to be awake." I winced again and then tried to smile at Aleric.

"I'm sorry you're in pain. It will take some time to heal."

I nodded, wishing he had not reminded me.

"What are you doing here, Aleric?" I wondered why he was not at my father's castle, assisting King Belodawn. He wasn't really my father any longer. He had banished me from his kingdom and disowned me as his daughter.

"King Olerion asked me to be one of his personal guards." Aleric looked at me and then at Lorenda, who was smiling at us both from the end of the bed.

I could tell there was something going on between the two of them. I was anxious to talk to Lorenda alone.

"Aleric, Travin, I have some womanly matters to discuss with Lorenda. Would you two please excuse us?"

"Certainly, Princess." Aleric turned around and walked out of the room. Travin followed, stating, "I'll be back in a short while to check on you. You must not push yourself too hard, Wren. You are injured."

I nodded at Travin as he disappeared out the door.

"He really loves you, Wren," Lorenda said, sitting down on the side of the bed.

"And Aleric loves you."

Lorenda smiled and shrugged. I could tell I spoke the truth. A patch of red eased its way up Lorenda's neck and spread across her face. I had never seen her blush like that.

"Do you love him?"

Lorenda nodded, her eyes downcast.

"It's not a problem for me if you do. I love Travin and he loves me. Whatever was between me and Aleric is only friendship."

"Are you certain?" Lorenda's eyes were pleading.

"Yes. It's truly fine." I felt the sting of something dying. It made me a little sad to think of the way things had changed. And yet, there was Travin, someone I had not expected to meet. He turned the entire story upside down.

"I can see sadness in your eyes, Wren."

I looked at Lorenda and knew, by the look of longing desperation in her eyes, that she was supposed to be with Aleric.

"You have my blessing." I smiled and yawned, letting go of what was "supposed to be."

"I will leave now so you can sleep."

I looked at my friend, my eyes growing heavy. "You are a good, true friend, Lorenda."

"As are you, Wren."

These were the last words I heard before I fell into deep sleep once again.

I awoke to find Travin sitting beside my bed, staring down at me. A candle flickered on the table beside the bed, casting a warm glow on his face. He smiled.

"You are so peaceful when you sleep, Princess."

Another knock came at the door and Travin answered a bit tersely, "Yes?!"

Nora opened the door and peeked inside, holding out a clay jar that contained the salve she was putting on my shoulder. It had a minty scent and made the air seem cleaner.

"I am here to apply more salve."

Travin stepped away from my bed to make room for Nora.

"How are you, child?"

"It hurts, but I'm okay."

Nora reached out and patted my cheek. "You are a brave soul." Without another word, she removed my bandages and opened the jar. Dipping her fingers into the pot, she retrieved the ointment. Gently, she applied salve to my shoulder.

I winced again and then relaxed as I felt the searing pain in my shoulder start to fade. The healing salve Nora put on my wound was doing its work.

"I will leave you two alone." Nora nodded at both of us and left as quietly as she had come.

Travin walked back over to the bed and sat down next to me. He took my right hand in both of his and kissed the tips of my fingers. "You are the bravest woman I have ever met, Lady Wren."

I shook my head. "I'm not brave. I wasn't brave enough to tell King Olerion the truth that I was unable to slay the dragon. I wasn't brave enough to tell you the truth. It seems I'm always hiding."

Travin brushed his lips against the back of my hand. "You don't have to hide anymore, Wren. You have nothing to fear as long as I am beside you."

I felt a tear slide down the side of my face. I had never felt love like this. I had never had anyone be so protective.

"And you are brave. You faced the beast. You jumped in front of Lorenda and saved her life. You endured the scrutiny of the staged contests time and time again and fought valiantly. You are anything but a coward."

A soft knock came at the door. Travin opened it to find Nora with a tray laden with soup, bread and a glass of wine.

"I hope I gave you two enough time alone before I forced my way in with dinner. Wren, you really must try and take a few bites." She walked to the edge of the bed and laid the tray in front of me.

Travin walked over to the other side of the bed in order to help me into a sitting position. Nora lifted the tray once again while Travin gently lifted my back at the rib cage and pushed me into a sitting position so that I could eat.

I tried not to wince, but I let out a small yelp from the shooting pain in my shoulder.

"I'm sorry, sweet love," Travin said, a grimace appearing on his face. "I hate to cause you pain."

"It's okay," I said, breathless from the throbbing in my shoulder. "I know I need to move a bit."

"And eat a bit," Nora said, placing a spoon in my hand.

"I must leave and attend to some orders King Olerion gave me. I will return shortly." Travin kissed my forehead and left the room.

Nora sat down in the chair near my bed and watched me as I took my first sip of soup. I felt a little uncomfortable because she just stared at me for a moment.

"Lady Wren, I must tell you something. I have been thinking about what happened to you a few days ago and I believe the Heavenly Father wants me to tell you this."

I set my spoon down on the tray that lay across my lap.

"You nearly died in that fight but you were spared. The Heavenly Father has a purpose for you. You are meant to be here."

I wondered what that purpose was. I felt so lost. My mother was dead and my father had disowned me. I had no home. It would be easy to see myself as a burden.

Nora spoke once again. "I believe part of that calling has something to do with being a companion for Travin."

I had never considered what it would mean to Travin to have me in his life as his wife. I had always thought of our relationship as him being a blessing to me. Perhaps it would bring him great joy as well for me to be his wife.

Confessing this to Nora, I told her that I had never considered Travin might need me.

"You have more influence than you realize, Lady Wren." Nora smiled. "Now eat your soup!

25

After several weeks I was able to move about Nora's cottage. Travin visited me there daily after he was reinstated as King Olerion's courtier. After the revolt, the king seemed to have a change of heart not only toward me but also toward Travin. The days grew shorter as the silver blue of winter overshadowed the reds and golds of autumn.

It was mid-day when Travin arrived. He carried a fur cloak as he walked through the front door of Nora's cottage.

He came over to where I sat in a chair by the hearth and sat down next to me in another chair. Scooting the chair close to mine, he took my hands in his and looked me in the eye.

"Wren," he said solemnly, "I was hoping we could take a short walk in the garden. I brought this cloak from Lorenda for you to wear as we walk."

I nodded. "I will walk with you." I felt much less certain about a walk in the garden than I let on, but I didn't want to disappoint Travin. I still felt very weak and I tired easily.

I hadn't been out of the cottage since being injured. I held on tightly to the arm Travin offered me and walked slowly, taking in the crisp fall-to-winter air. It felt wonderful against my warm skin and the cold quickly turned my fair cheeks a rosy pink. My blonde hair had grown long and touched my shoulder, falling loose along the back of my neck in gentle waves. Travin kept glancing sideways at me. I wondered if I looked strange to him because he continued to glance at me.

Finally, Travin spoke. "I apologize for staring, but you look so beautiful that I can't help it."

I smiled and squeezed his arm. "Thank you."

We walked to the garden behind the castle. The red and gold trees glowed against the dark gray October sky. Travin stopped near the lilac bushes and turned to face me.

I looked up into his dark eyes and felt myself grow heady. Travin seemed to have this effect on me often. He got down on one knee and looked up at me, a secret smile spreading across his face.

"Travin?" I frowned, confused by his posture.

"Lady Wren, from the moment I saw you, I knew I wanted to make you my wife. Your courage and determination make you even more beautiful to me than when I first laid eyes on you. You are free to choose, and I hope I'm not mistaken in asking if you would be my wife. Will you marry me, my love?" Travin's eyes were undemanding, yet full of hope.

I felt tears rise to the surface of my eyes. I smiled, and as the tears fell down my cheeks, I whispered "Yes."

Travin stood and embraced me gently, carefully placing his right arm underneath my left arm to avoid touching my shoulder. "I love you, Wren," he said quietly and firmly.

"And I love you, Travin."

I lifted my head away from his chest so I could see his face. I kissed him with an intensity that I did not know existed inside me.

We stood that way for what seemed like an eternity. I grew weak and my knees began to shake.

"I've kept you out too long. You need to rest now, my sweet wife to be." Travin smiled and then put his left hand and arm under my knees, lifting me from the ground, cradling me like a baby.

"I can walk. I'm just a little weak."

"I will carry you for a time as we make our way back to Nora's."

Travin held me in his arms as he walked back through the garden and through the castle. When we arrived at the entrance hall, I could see Lorenda sitting next to Aleric in front of the blazing fire in the great room.

"Lorenda!" Travin gently placed me on the ground. I nearly ran to where the two were sitting.

Lorenda stood and embraced me and then Travin, who walked up behind me. Aleric hugged me and shook Travin's hand.

"We have something to tell you both." I know my eyes were sparkling, and I grinned from ear to ear.

"And we have something to tell you," Lorenda said, nodding at Aleric. "You go first, Wren."

I grabbed Travin's hand and squeezed it. "Travin and I are getting married."

Lorenda's mouth dropped open. "I can't believe this!"

I frowned, fearing that Lorenda was less than pleased with the news.

"Aleric just asked me to marry him," Lorenda cried.

I embraced her as we both laughed and cried. Taking a step back while holding Lorenda's hands, I looked at her and smiled. "You know what this means?"

Lorenda shook her head back and forth.

"We can have our weddings on the same day. We can get married together!"

Lorenda's eyes grew large. "That's a fantastic idea. This will be so much fun. Who will post the notice on the church door?"

I looked around the great room, at the majestic fireplace on one wall, the fine art covering the walls and the marble floor.

"We should have the wedding right here in this room."

"Another brilliant idea. I love it!" Lorenda kept smiling as she looked from me to Aleric and then Travin.

Travin and Aleric shrugged and then Travin spoke. "It is my pleasure to do what brings you joy, Wren." He walked over to stand next to me and took my hand, raising it to his lips to kiss it.

I blushed and felt the weakness once again spread its way through my body. I still wasn't at my full strength and needed to rest.

Travin frowned as he studied my pale cheeks. "We need to get you back to your bed and resting once again. We can make wedding plans later."

Without another word, Travin scooped me into his arms and began walking toward the front door.

"Rest, Wren. We will have plenty of time to plan."

Lorenda waved good-bye as Travin walked out the door and into the chilled air outside.

I told Travin I could walk several times, but he insisted on carrying me. When we arrived at Nora's cottage, Nora bustled about making me some hot tea and serving me a bowl of stew. In no time I had eaten and was back in bed about to fall asleep.

"Rest now sweet, Wren. We will be husband and wife soon enough and will celebrate our union before the Heavenly Father."

"Yes," I whispered as I began to drift effortlessly into sleep. "We will be husband and wife."

Two months had passed since that day in the garden. My wedding day had finally arrived. Lorenda and I sat in her bedchambers in our wedding gowns, both of us feeling butterflies swirling about in our stomachs.

I wore a deep blue satin gown that hugged tight to my waist and hips with silver rope edges. Lorenda donned a new blue lace bodice cascading over a full forest green embroidered skirt. She wore her auburn hair in a simple plait, long and red running down the center of her back. My own hair had grown long enough to wear in soft curls framing my face. We decorated our hair with tiny daisies and rose buds.

A knock at the door made us jump at the same time. Lorenda giggled. "We really must relax." I chuckled softly, wishing I could make my hands stop trembling.

Lorenda opened the door. A castle messenger stood at attention. "Lady Wren and Lady Lorenda, the grooms await you downstairs."

Lorenda thanked the steward, shut the door and then ran across the room grabbing my hands. "Here we go!"

We walked slowly down the hall to the stairs. I could hear the mandolin chorus with wooden flutes, our cue that it was time to make an appearance.

Lorenda practically floated down the stairs and into the great room first. I quickly followed, trying to hold back my thrill-pumped athletic steps. We marveled at the beauty of the scene before us. Snow fell softly and lightly through the cold twilight air outside. Inside, candles flickered and glowed in every corner of the wood-paneled room hung with enormous banners and tall vases of Autumn flowers in the center. The villagers sat in chairs facing the fireplace.

I watched Lorenda walked down the center aisle, and took my cues from her. To the left of the fireplace was a stone pulpit where the priest stood waiting to perform the ceremony.

Travin stood to the right of the pulpit. His eyes never left my face as I walked toward him. Aleric waited to the left. He and Lorenda kept smiling at one another.

Travin took my hand and stood beside me now, facing the priest. Lorenda and Aleric faced the priest as well. Lorenda bent her head forward to see if she could catch my eye. I sensed Lorenda's eyes on me and looked around Travin at her. We both smiled and then straightened, looking at the priest once again.

The priest spoke family blessings over us and led in the sacred marriage vows. Then, he offered the wedding sacraments. Travin squeezed my hand several times. I knew he was just as excited as I was to become husband and wife.

The ceremony seemed to end just as it had begun with merry woodwinds and mandolins. I knew a great deal of time had passed by the appearance of the velvet darkness outside. It created a dramatic backdrop to the glittering snow that shone in the moonlight.

The wedding party and guests made their way into the dance hall where meats and cheeses of every kind were displayed on long tables along the opposite walls. Musicians played the harp and lyre and people began to dance.

Travin left my side for a moment to say hello to a friend. I watched as Lorenda and her father, King Olerion, danced together. A small pinprick of pain rose in my chest as I thought about my own father. Of course, we had sent him a personal invitation, but he had not made it to the wedding. We had heard nothing by way of response. I had hoped he would set aside his pride and come, but that was not to be.

When there was a break in the music, Lorenda walked over to me. "My father would like to have the next dance with you, Wren."

I frowned, not certain what to make of this. The king and I were now friends, but I didn't expect him to dance with me.

"Better not keep the king waiting," Lorenda whispered as she bent close to my ear.

I walked over to where King Olerion stood. Without a word, he took my hand and led me to the line of dancers in the center of the room. The music started, and I began to mirror his steps as was called for by this particular dance.

"Lady Wren, you look absolutely beautiful."

"Thank you, my King."

As we danced, I thought of my mother and father. I tried to smile, but my lips quivered and wouldn't respond. The gravity of my mother's death and my father's abandonment weighed heavily on my heart. Half of my heart was dancing for joy at the thought that I had just married Travin. The other half lay dying in a barren land. I had no family.

"Lady Wren, you seem forlorn. What troubles you on this most joyous occasion?"

Tears welled and fell, in spite of how I held my breath trying to stop them. Finally, I spoke. "I am sorry for showing my sadness at this wonderful event. I am only sorrowful because I have no family, no mother or father."

The king gently grasped my hand and twirled me around as the musicians played a cherry, celebratory tune on the flute and lyre.

Having completed the turn, I looked back at the king, whose eyes beheld me with tenderness.

"Families are not always about blood ties. If there is a bond of the heart, there is family."

I smiled, trying to believe what he said.

"The Heavenly Father has given you a new family, Lady Wren. We are your family now."

The song ended and the king stepped toward me and embraced me. He whispered, "You are a daughter to me. I will be a father to you."

"Thank you," I whispered back.

Travin came to me from where he'd been standing with Lorenda while I danced with the king. He held out his arm. "Come, my lady," he said, winking. "Your future awaits."

I smiled, this time feeling the smile in my heart. I marveled at how my life had changed in such a short time. I was filled with wonder over what the king had said. The Heavenly Father truly loved me and I was no longer alone. God had given me a family and I had a place where I belonged.

Acknowledgements

This book would not exist if it were not for my writers' group. Being more specific, when the women of my writers' group banded together to put on a writing conference, I was asked to facilitate a workshop called *The Discipline of Creativity*. As I practiced what I preached, this book was formed in the process. My thanks goes to Laura Bartnick, Tonya Blessing, Diane Andrews and M.B. Wentz for your dedication and hard work in making the first Golden Writer's Conference happen and, in turn, helping me to realize this book.

Thank you, Ian Groff, for the amazing illustrations to enliven this book. Thank you, Sue Carter, for handling the first copy edit of my book and the final edit. I have learned so much from your excellent editing skills. Beatrice Bruno, your proofreading was a wonderful addition and gift for which I am deeply grateful. Thank you to Laura Bartnick and Victoria Pless for their careful attention to line editing my book. I so appreciate my fellow author, Kathy Joy Hoffner, for finding "fresh-eye" issues in the last go around of the book. I couldn't be more thrilled by the final product of our collaborative efforts. Your skills turned Wren's story into my personal treasure.

I am grateful to my husband for supporting me day-in-and-day-out as I crawled into Wren's world and disappeared to write. Thank you for understanding my focus and determination.

Above all, I thank God for the ability to craft stories that matter.

CHARMAYNE HAFEN, AUTHOR

The best compliment you can give an author is to share your review with a book club, or on the Nook, Goodreads, or Amazon.

CAPTURE BOOKS

ABOUT THE AUTHOR

In Colorado, Lady Charmayne and Lord John Hafen live with two castle guards, their Chihuahuas, Pepe and Frida near a beautiful lake. Lady Charmayne spends her days overseeing a their kingdom which includes two small, private business. She can also be found writing, skiing, painting, collaging, or frolicking about with her kind-hearted niece. She finds inspiration from lands she ventures to when the occasion arises as well as from some wonderful relationships.

Charmayne holds a masters degree in community counseling and is available to facilitate workshops related to using the imagination, writing, and the arts in grief counseling.

Charmayne invites you to follow her on her writing journey on Facebook, Instagram or Twitter.
